Deadly Crossings

To Dolores
With very best wishes
Gemma Bloom

Deadly Crossings

A Mystery

Gemma Bloom

iUniverse, Inc.
New York Lincoln Shanghai

Deadly Crossings

A Mystery

iUniverse books may be ordered through booksellers or by contacting:

iUniverse
2021 Pine Lake Road, Suite 100
Lincoln, NE 68512
www.iuniverse.com
1-800-Authors (1-800-288-4677)

ISBN: 978-0-595-44737-4 (pbk)
ISBN: 978-0-595-69082-4 (cloth)

Printed in the United States of America

CHAPTER 1

Sophie Skala stepped out onto the little balcony and leaned her forearms on the wood railing. Beyond the shadowed lawn and across the faded blacktop road, the lake kicked up in mounds of muddy pewter meringue that made her shiver, as the crisp October air had not, and shrug further down into the collar of her fleece jacket.

It had been a rough crossing. The waves had converged from different directions at the mouth of the bay, sending the big catamaran alternately slamming against them and momentarily airborne, so that she had had to clutch at the edges of the metal table and jam her legs back against the few boxes shoved under the seat to remain in it. And that was pretty much how it would be for the final few weeks before the ferry stopped running altogether until spring, whenever that came. And that, in turn, was why she was making these last harrowing trips between the mainland and the island, anxiously going through her belongings on the one side and her supplies on the other and attempting to get enough of each to the right side.

There was a dull thud below, and she turned away from the ragged landscape and scampered down the narrow stairs, as Carl Jacobsen's tanned face appeared over the banister, his shout drifting up to meet her.

"Well, that's the last of them!"

"Yes, thank you," she said breathlessly, pulling herself to a halt on the other side of the railing.

"Sorry. Didn't mean to bellow, only I thought you were still up there," he mumbled.

"I was." She glanced at the small—too small, she was sure—stack of cartons on the floor of the front hall. "Thanks for your help. I really appreciate it. Can I offer you a cup of coffee? It'll only take a few minutes to brew, as soon as I find the coffeemaker," she gestured vaguely.

"No, thanks." His own gaze travelled to the cardboard boxes and back to somewhere around Sophie's middle, then up to her face. "So, you really gonna spend the winter here, huh?"

"Yes. Why not? People *do* live here year round."

"Some people," he answered stiffly. "Mostly people who have grown up here, people whose families have owned land here for generations. Not people who come out from the city to party in the summer. Well," he shrugged before Sophie could protest, "none of my business. But if I were you, I'd be laying in anything available in a can, bottle, jar or package. Powdered milk, powdered eggs, that sort of thing. Should've gotten a bigger freezer too. Meat."

She gave a dismissive little snort. "You make it sound primitive, if not downright third world. There is an airport, after all. Planes *do* fly things in from the mainland, don't they?"

"Yeah, when the weather allows. Most of the time you should be able to get the necessaries at the grocery across from the dock. But I wouldn't expect to find a large selection of fresh meat and produce. No tenderloin and truffles," he smiled dryly, and she stiffened. "And whatever you do get, you'll pay through the nose for. Costs money to fly the stuff over," he added, shoving his hands in his coat pockets and turning to leave. "Powdered milk. Nobody likes it, but …"

"Yes, thanks again. I will be making a careful inventory of what I have and what I'll need."

"All right then," he said, pulling open the front door. "If the lake is no worse than today, we'll be making a couple runs tomorrow, if you're interested. Arrive about eleven."

"I'll probably see you tomorrow then."

"Must be costing you a baby fortune to ride back and forth all the time like that," he muttered his way down the front steps.

It was Sophie's turn to shrug. "What can I do? Tomorrow," she nodded and pushed the door closed. "Cheery sort," she said, eyeing the boxes glumly, then hefting one and transporting it to the kitchen counter. Well, she could see his point, she thought, tearing off the packing tape and pulling out cans of creamed corn and boxed macaroni and cheese dinners. She had certainly asked herself repeatedly over the last couple months what she thought she'd been thinking when she had rented the old cottage with its tuffa stone facing and humpy little front wall. Getting away from it all. That was the idea. But Carl was right. It was one thing to fantasize in the heat and the sun of a clear summer day about isolating oneself cozily in an island cottage for the winter, but another thing entirely to consider whether one had enough firewood to keep from freezing to death in the dark should a particularly wicked storm blow down from Canada and disrupt electrical service. In fairness, it was herself and not Carl Jacobsen with whom she was annoyed.

She yanked open all the cupboard doors and stared, absently raking a thumbnail across the edge of her front teeth before pushing the contents into neat little rows to make room for more. Canned vegetables in one, canned fruit in another, cereals and dry mixes in a third. She must try to get more bread mixes. She expected to be making most of her own bread, so the automatic bread machine had come over in one of the first carloads, along with the bulk of her winter clothing, a basic toolbox, a small TV, matches and candles, and two boxes of books that she sincerely hoped would occupy her until spring.

There was the small library on the outskirts of town near the school, and while she had not yet taken the opportunity to investigate, she supposed it might supplement her meager stash in a pinch. And Dickie's Lighthouse Inn down on the square had published an ad proclaiming the arrival to the island of Internet service in the form of an Internet cafe that promised them the lion's share of the winter business. Assuming they'd meant now and not the beginning of the summer tourist season, she could always avail herself of the services of Amazon.com—assuming the mail could be delivered.

She sighed and bit the corner of her lower lip as she shoved at a can of garbanzos. What had she wanted with garbanzos anyway? What had she wanted with any of this? No, this was no romantic illusion of seclusion and renewal, and it had been hard to hold her tongue and not tell Carl Jacobsen that she was not the foolish and spoiled tourist playing at camping out that he took her for. She'd *had* to do something, go somewhere after that whole unfortunate business with Peter …

Eighteen ounces of peaches hurtled to the floor and rolled beneath the table as Sophie spun quavering toward the back door. The determined thump was repeated, and she gulped for air and fumbled at the doorknob. The screen door had already creaked open on its hinges, so that Sophie found herself prematurely face to face with a blocky little woman in a mud brown corduroy barn jacket that served only to augment the impression of dull angularity.

"Thought you'd be here. In the kitchen," the woman nodded toward the area behind Sophie. "Unpacking. Food," she continued resolutely, as Sophie gave no sign of comprehension.

"I'm sorry. I ..." She motioned the woman in and offered her hand, pulling it back awkwardly as she realized her visitor clutched an object in each arm. "I mean, you surprised me. Please, come in," she added unnecessarily, as the other woman had already sidled up to the counter, where she relieved herself of a low pot.

"Casserole," she said, turning back to Sophie and wiping a stubby hand along her pant leg before clasping Sophie's hand and pumping it. "Bea Baskin. Oh, and there's this." She held up a metal pyramid that swayed and clattered heavily on its chain. "Housewarming."

"That's very kind," smiled Sophie, recovering her public presence. She took the hanging chain in one hand and the clanger in the other so as to still the thick reverberation and placed it respectfully on the table.

"Maine buoy bell windchime. I've got one. Always found something comforting about the sound. Tell you something about what the wind's doing too, though. Functional, as you might say."

"It's beautiful. Thank you. And," Sophie indicated the pot, "for the casserole too. It smells wonderful."

"Venison. Course, Patch McKay wanted me to tell you it was possum," snorted Bea Baskin. "But don't pay him any mind if he ribs you about it. Been here forever and then some, and he's kinda cynical about newcomers, but he's okay really. Be the first one over here with a plow if you get snowed in."

"Well, that's good to know," replied Sophie, flashing a self-conscious smile and shifting uncomfortably. Bea Baskin stared at her in apparent anticipation, but of what Sophie had no idea. "Would you like some coffee?"

"That'd be nice. But first, who *are* you?"

"I beg your pardon?"

"What's your *name*?"

"Oh," she flushed foolishly. "I'm sorry. Sophie." She hesitated. Then, "Sophie Westenra," she smiled broadly. "I'll just get the coffeemaker. It's in the dining room. Please, sit down. I won't be a minute."

She darted down the narrow hall and into the tiny dining room that shared a wall with the kitchen, rummaging nervously through the cardboard cartons that sprawled on the polished wood floor until she found what she wanted. She stood for a moment hugging the coffeemaker to her absently. Well, it was done now. She'd made the only choice she could, the choice she had known she would make when she'd opened the new bank and credit card accounts and signed the lease on the cottage. But it hadn't seemed real or final until she'd tossed it out there in the kitchen. She pressed her lips together hard, took a deep breath and returned to the kitchen where her new neighbor reposed.

Or perhaps "reposed" was not the right word. Bea Baskin stared into one of the cupboards, balancing next to her shoulder like a dumbbell the can of peaches she had retrieved from beneath the table.

"Oh, next one over," pointed Sophie, as she plugged in the coffeemaker and slid her special Gevalia canister off the little shelf above the stove. "Thank you. I forgot I'd dropped that, I'm afraid." She felt the heat suffuse her face again as she realized how mindless she must sound, as though it was a common thing for her to drop canned food on the floor and forget about it. "What do you take in your coffee?" she asked, pouring the water through the screen and flipping the switch.

"A little cream would be nice," said Bea Baskin, closing the cupboard door and settling into one of the vinyl-clad chairs at the kitchen table.

Sophie pulled two cups out of another cupboard where she had already stacked the single set of dishes she would be keeping. She would give away the others in the spring, but for now, they would sit on the sideboard in the silent dining room far away where the grandfather clock stood mute in the corner. It was odd to think of them there, collecting dust, unseen and unused, where they had been set so often to grace the elegant mahogany table at so many dinner parties. "I only have non-dairy creamer. I hope that's all right," she said, closing the refrigerator door and holding up the carton.

"Course. That's all anybody's got here. It keeps. That and the powdered stuff."

Sophie poured the coffee, set a cup and the creamer in front of her guest and sank down into the chair opposite her. "So …"

"Bea."

"Bea. How did you know I was here? Carl Jacobsen? I wouldn't have thought he would—"

"Carl?" She made a gurgling sound that Sophie surmised was a laugh, but which served nonetheless to reinforce Sophie's image of her as a small brown troll. "Nah. He's mainland. Knows everybody on the island, naturally. Even stays here sometimes. Built himself a cabin toward the middle of the island. But he's not permanent, as you'd say, so I think he figures island gossip is for islanders. Well, you've met him. Man of few words anyway," she gurgled again. "No, I knew you were here because there are a hundred and sixty-three permanent residents on the island. So when a hundred and sixty-fourth shows up, everybody knows. Small island, small community. No secrets here," she said, gazing over the top of her cup at Sophie, who wriggled unconsciously in her chair. "Least nothing that stays secret for long."

"That sounds ominous," Sophie observed with a forced giggle.

"Oh, I didn't mean it to sound like that. Just with so few people thrown together in so small an area, well, folks get to know each other. And there doesn't seem much point in hiding things. And that being the case, there's probably less *to* hide, if you see what I mean."

"Do you mean," Sophie asked stiffly, as she pressed her back against the chair, "that the fear of discovery keeps people honest?"

"Well, I hadn't quite worked it out like that, but yeah, I suppose it does."

"I will bear that in mind," smiled Sophie.

"Oh, now, I didn't mean you. Nah, folks are just curious about you. Natural enough."

"I see," Sophie said truthfully, as it became suddenly clear to her. Bea Baskin had been appointed the official gatherer of information. She inhaled deeply, her fingers drifting absently across her lips, and leaned forward to rest her elbows on the table. "Well, let's see. I'm a freelance writer. Magazine and newspaper articles mostly."

"That a fact? I won't deny folks always wonder what people do for a living. I mean, if they don't have jobs on the island. A writer. That makes sense. Because naturally, if somebody doesn't work on the island, and they don't work on the mainland, then folks wonder."

"I guess that's to be expected. They probably also wonder why a person, particularly a middle-aged woman, would choose to move here. Besides the obvious charm of the place," she hastened to add.

"That too."

"I guess the general answer is that I felt I needed a change." A significant change. A change that would distance her from the shock and the horror and the fearful accusations of those months, and most of all, from the hurtful whispers and sidelong glances afterwards. "And," she said with another deep breath, "I'd always enjoyed my visits here, so I thought it would be a good place to settle."

"Yeah, it is that, and I expect more people would do it if they could. Course then we'd be overrun," shrugged Bea. "But then most people wouldn't be able to, because of family or jobs. Be harder for a married couple, say."

"I'm sure it would." It was clear enough to Sophie what Bea Baskin was after. But rather than being annoyed with the woman's transparent attempt to coax the information out of her, she was relieved that she'd been given the opportunity to impart the facts she wanted to impart in such a way as to satisfy the curiosity of the community that there was no more to learn. "Fortunately for me, that wasn't a consideration," she smiled.

Bea Baskin's mouth slid to one side and she sniffed indifferently. "You're not married then."

"Not any more." She leaned back in the chair instinctively to signal an end to the "interview." "More coffee?"

"No, but thanks," answered Bea Baskin, as she extricated herself from the tubular steel and vinyl chair that had become "retro" in the city, but was here, in Dorothy Hardesty's kitchen, just part of Dorothy Hardesty's old dinette set. "Time for me to be moseying along. I hope you don't mind me asking"—she rested one hand on the back of the chair and cocked her head away from Sophie, who thought the hope belated and smiled inwardly—"but it was my understanding that Dorothy's—that'd be Dorothy Hardesty, this was her house, you know—that her son was looking to sell the place. He change his mind, or you weren't buying?"

In fact, Sophie had had no difficulty convincing George Hardesty, comfortably ensconced in his suburban home across the bay and some sixty miles east, to lease her the house he had grown up in and now wanted no part of. He had been frankly relieved to have someone occupying the place, and even happier with the prospect of generating some income from it. "No, he still wants to sell it. But since it's such a big decision for me, such a major change, he was kind enough to allow me to lease it for awhile, to see whether it will work out before I buy it."

"Hm! Probably just glad to have somebody in the place," Bea Baskin noted cannily. "Well," she stuck out her hand in gesture of farewell, "time for me to get, Sophie. Say, how did you pronounce your last name again?"

Sophie took the extended hand and said deliberately, "West-en-ra." As she renewed her thanks and saw Bea Baskin out the back door, she smiled. Not at Bea Baskin, but because she had really done it. She *was* Sophie Westenra now. Sophie Skala had been left back on the mainland with Peter. In the grave.

CHAPTER 2

Sophie stood puffing, her heart pounding, cheeks red and cold in the brisk morning air, and grabbed at the railing to steady herself as the catamaran lurched away from the dock. She'd just made it. Whether because the concentrated effort that had gone into securing the cottage and implementing the move had caught up with her, or because the mattress on her new bed was so comfortable, or because she was no longer fearful, she had overslept. It had meant scrambling to get dressed and scribbling off a list of things she wanted not to forget over a quick cup of coffee, but it had been worth it. She had not slept so well in a long time or greeted the morning more heartened.

"Baby fortune."

She gulped in mid-puff and swung around to find Carl Jacobsen shaking his head at her. "Well," she said, turning back toward the waves that flung up dense and gray around them, "what am I supposed to do? I need things."

"You could have made fewer trips if you'd a brought your car once in awhile."

"I was going to do that today, but I didn't know if the other ferry would be running, and you said—"

"It's running."

"Well, I didn't know that."

"You shoulda called."

"Yes, I suppose I should have, but there wasn't time. I overslept," she added defiantly.

Carl said nothing, but stood watching her, shifting his weight effortlessly to compensate for the movement of the boat, the lines that fanned out from the corners of his eyes giving him the suggestion of a permanent squint. She frowned at what she perceived to be his rude indifference and pressed her back up against the railing for stability. "Better to do something than nothing, no?"

She hadn't really expected a response, but as he continued to stare at her indolently, she shivered and hugged herself, rubbing absently at her coat sleeves. "Cold."

"The water." His casual gaze panned the deck and the lake and the pallid sky. "It's the wet cold that goes right through your clothes and crawls inside your bones. Winter is always colder on the water. And on the island," he nodded significantly.

Sophie stole a surprised glance in his direction at the tender of even this small contribution to conversation. Not wanting to be the one to let it lapse now, she offered a general observation by way of acknowledgement. "It sounds as though you've spent a lot of time near the water. Have you?" she asked gingerly.

"Near? Yeah, I guess. Near, on. In," he replied vaguely.

"You must like it though." It was one of those neutral things one said in the interest of maintaining polite communication, and he called her on it.

"Oh, I must, huh?"

She flushed and stammered, "Sorry. I only meant ... well, you make your living from it. And somebody told me you have a cabin on the island, so I just thought—"

"Somebody," he smiled cynically. "Yeah, there's always *somebody* eager to tell you something. Usually everything they know and some things they don't. Gossips," he spat.

"Then why would you want a house there?"

"Well, I don't know, *Sophie*," he said deliberately. "Why do *you*? You'll be the hot topic for some time now, ya know. Yeah, they'll be wanting to know everything about you," he smirked. "Especially any little whiff of scandal, even if they have to invent it."

She shrank back against the rail and glanced over at him unhappily, wondering at the same time about his apparent disdain for the islanders. She considered the wisdom of saying anything that might be interpreted as critical of them, but somehow Carl Jacobsen did not strike her as the type to set a trap for her on their behalf. He was rough around the edges certainly. But as she looked at him now, careful not to let her gaze linger too long, she saw nothing in his eyes betokening malice or manipulation.

She took a breath and a chance. "I guess I understand what you're getting at. Bea Baskin paid me a welcoming call yesterday. And I had the distinct impression that she'd been delegated to find out all she could about me and why I'm here," she said with a wry smile.

"Yep. Most outsiders who think they're gonna stay there permanent don't. And that's why."

"What about you, though? I get the impression that if you're an outsider, it's by choice."

He chuffed and looked at her as though she was hopelessly stupid. "You've got a lot of impressions for somebody that's just arrived and doesn't know squat."

She clucked impatiently. "All I meant was that you don't seem to have a very high opinion of them as a community, so why do you want to have a place on the island at all?"

"Why do *you*?" She shrugged him off in disgust. "Everybody's got something they want to keep to themselves or for themselves, you know?" His gaze penetrated her like the wet cold of which he spoke, and she felt a momentary rush of fear, as though he knew something about her. About Peter. But his shoulders relaxed almost imperceptibly, and his voice modulated. "All I'm saying is they don't make it easy. Doesn't mean you can't have a good life there. Just be careful is all." Her frown registered incomprehension. "I don't say don't get along with folks. But just don't be too quick to get too cozy or share too much. It won't make you one of 'em, you know?"

She nodded slowly. "Why are you telling me all this? I mean," she stumbled, "why would you care one way or another about helping me?"

He stared at her for a moment, before one corner of his mouth crept up into a wicked grin. "You got a nice ass for a woman your age."

She gasped and pitched forward in mute protest, but Carl Jacobsen only chuckled and shook his head pityingly. Her mouth swelled out into a pout, then subsided into an injured grimace, as he showed no sign of remorse.

"Come on, you asked for it," he said simply. "I was just trying to give you a heads-up. That should be enough."

She heaved a cognizant sigh. "I know," she said. "And I appreciate it." A helpless shiver rattled up and down her, and she clutched at the railing again as a particularly vicious gust blew across the deck and sent the boat airborne.

Carl Jacobsen nodded toward the metal steps in the interior. "Why don't you go inside. Still cold, but at least you'll be out of the wind." She hesitated, then nodded and turned toward the stairs. "Oh," he called after her, "and if you don't have a thick down parka, some sturdy boots and flannel-lined jeans, I'd forget about the canned garbanzos and get some."

She froze, then rolled her eyes and clattered up the stairs, sinking down onto an upholstered bench as far from the windows as she could get and snuggling down into her woefully inadequate jacket. She glanced around the cabin, hard and monochromatic but for the red vinyl seats. The low ceiling and the rows of benches gave it a cramped feeling despite its size, and contributed to a general sense of dimness that the pale October sun could not dispel.

A motion in her peripheral vision drew her attention to the seats across the cabin, from which two other passengers studied her with furtive interest. She nodded toward them genially: a round-faced woman in her thirties, her dull brown hair hanging lank around the shoulders of her green parka, and a pale red-head, whose most noticeable characteristic, apart from her broad thighs, was a generous spattering of freckles that appeared to have been applied through a layer of baby Swiss. She supposed they would assume from her tardy arrival that she had been talking to Carl Jacobsen, and the fingers of one hand fanned across her mouth apprehensively. She would have to be more careful. She'd been careless back there. He had warned her against being too open with her new neighbors too quickly. But whether out of a sense of isolation and loneliness, or something else, she had probably shared more with Carl Jacobsen than she should have. She mustn't become too friendly with anyone. Not yet. It was all too soon, too new, and if she were to fumble it now, before she had been accepted into the community, the whole plan would fall apart, and starting over again would be that much harder.

She rose when she felt the engines slow and saw the dock rise off to one side, and made her way to the stairs, fishing in her pocket somewhat foolishly for the car keys in order to give the impression of purpose.

"We pull out at three," called Carl, tossing a rope over a pylon. "And that means three and not five after. Nobody wants to risk being caught out there after dark."

"I'll be here," she answered a little sourly. "I won't be oversleeping again." His mouth curled up into a smug smile, and she flushed with self-conscious annoyance. The two other passengers waited nearby, and she could feel their scrutiny, as well as the mild curiosity of another member of the tiny crew who had arrived to help Carl with the gangplank.

He was callous and intrusive, and she guessed that would teach her to be more careful. She clutched her shoulderbag to her side and scampered past him and down onto the pier without even a glance in his direction. Then pushing at a sleeve to check her watch, she plunged up the steep incline to the street above, Carl Jacobsen, the islanders and the island receding in her consciousness.

Anxious to see Reney, she hurried unnecessarily the few blocks to the cafe, where she huddled on the sidewalk and tried to peer into the interior without appearing conspicuous. She was saved the decision of whether to wait inside as an elegant brunette rounded the corner, spotting her and hastening her own step.

"Reney," she cried, hugging her sister to her, "it's so good to see you. God, I've missed you."

"Oh, Sophie, I've missed you too! But let's get in out of this wind and get warm." She pulled open the door and nudged her older sister through it and toward an empty booth near the back. Once they had ordered, she wriggled forward in her seat and leaned on the table. "I like your hair that color," she smiled. Sophie huffed and jerked her head to one side forlornly. "No, I do. And let's face it, sister, it's closer to your natural color anyway. And that's not a bad thing."

"I suppose," Sophie answered dully. "Oh, but how are you, Reney?"

"I'm fine. Muddling along the same as always with the job and the kids."

"How are the kids? They ... you ... well, you don't have any *trouble*, do you?" Her voice dropped to a whisper.

"Of course not. And believe me, if anybody said anything to me, I'd put them in their place quick enough. You know that. Because," she insisted, leaning forward and placing a hand over her sister's, "there is no reason for anyone to say anything. The Grand Jury made their decision, and it was the right one. Which brings me—" She stopped abruptly, and both she and Sophie sat back in their seats as the waitress placed sandwiches and coffee before them, then smiled and retreated toward the kitchen. "Which brings me," Reney resumed, "to the question of whether this is the right thing for you to be doing now, Sophie. You don't have to, you know. I mean, you're still working. Nobody's cut you off."

"Reney." Sophie shook her head and leaned her mouth on her knuckles.

"Sophie," implored her sister, "damn it, we *miss* you! There's no *need*."

"No, Reney, what there isn't is somebody *else*," hissed Sophie.

"No, they just haven't *found* somebody else. There's a difference."

Sophie looked up directly into Reney's large brown eyes. "Come on, Reney," she said gently, "haven't you ever—"

"No, I have not ever!" Reney interrupted hotly. "I know we're not supposed to speak ill of the dead—"

Sophie gave an admonishing shake of the head.

"No, Sophie. We all thought Peter was a great guy, too, at first. And don't look at me like that. What he was was a mean, amoral, two-timing bastard who maybe got what he deserved. And *that's* where somebody ought to be looking."

"That's where they figured they *were* looking," Sophie said sullenly.

"Sophie, it's over. It's *over.* Come back to your life."

"Oh, Reney, don't you understand? It will never be over for me as long as there's no one else for people to point a finger at. Maybe not even then." She stared down at the sandwich with the little waves of bacon and the frill of lettuce sticking out over the edges of the bread, but what she saw again was Peter lying pale and contorted, the congealed blood pooled dark and shiny like a grotesque halo around his head. *She had had to lean over him to see clearly …*

"Nobody thinks—"

"Reney, don't be naive. Of course, somebody thinks," she said bitterly. "And one of the things they think is that I would have been justified."

"*I* think that," Reney answered obstinately.

"And that's the problem, little sister. Innocence and justifiable homicide are two different things. But as long as it doesn't matter one way or the other to my own family …" Her voice trailed off sadly.

Reney sighed and made a savage poke at her sandwich. "I wish you'd change your mind."

"Reney, you know I love you, don't you? Then please accept that I can't right now. Right now, this is where I need to be, what I need to do, for myself. To *heal* myself," she pleaded. "Look, I'll be fine. As you've said, I'm still employable, so that's all right. But a lot has happened. A lot of people know more about my private affairs than I'd like them to, and I need a change from that, you see?"

"All right. All *right.* But what about the holidays? You'll come and stay with us then, won't you?"

"I don't know. I'll have to see how things look to me. But I'll be okay."

"Sophie, I don't like to think of you alone, stranded maybe, on that stupid island in the dead of winter. What if you got sick?"

Sophie chuckled and squeezed her sister's hand. "It's not Devil's Island, you know. Planes fly in and out all winter. And it's not uninhabited. There are people there, people who seem normal enough. And nice enough." The smile froze on her face as she thought of the women on the boat and prying Bea Baskin—and Carl Jacobsen. But she pushed aside her misgivings for Reney's sake and changed tack. "I'll be *fine.* It's you I'm concerned about."

"*Me*?"

"Are you very sure you don't mind looking after the house for now? Just until spring, by which time I hope something else will have displaced all of this in the public's imagination, and I can put it on the market with some hope of success."

"Don't be an idiot, Sophie. Of course I don't mind. But that's one thing on which I agree with you completely—you need to get rid of that damned house. I never liked it anyway," she frowned. "*Peter's* house. That's what it was, *is*," she continued over Sophie's protests. "I just hope the darling neighbors won't stick their noses in and try to screw up a sale."

"Are you kidding? And risk lowering their own property values?" smiled Sophie. The smile turned grim, and she looked past Reney vacantly. "Still, perhaps murder sells houses."

"Sophie," cautioned her sister.

Sophie turned back to her and relaxed into a warm smile. "Dear Reney. Let's pay the check and get out of here. You can help me do some shopping. It seems I need an Eskimo parka and some mukluks," she laughed irreverently.

"God, Sophie," said Reney with a heavenward glance.

The sisters spent the next couple hours making their way from store to store, alternately admiring and laughing at one another as they tried on clothing, their difficulties temporarily forgotten. The downtown shopping area was small, but adequate, and by the time they had finished, Sophie found herself awkwardly jostling her purchases down toward the dock just as the ferry arrived. She and Reney hugged each other hard, with a promise to meet again soon, and Sophie fumbled her packages aboard, turning and waving to her sister as the boat pulled away. She watched until Reney had disappeared back up to the street, then turned back toward the deck, feeling suddenly bereft. A clangor echoed from the metal stairs, and she saw that her former companions were making the return journey with her.

After the happy afternoon she had spent with Reney, she hadn't the heart to sit for their renewed examination and steeled herself to put up with Carl Jacobsen's company instead. At least there was only one of him, she thought gloomily. But to her chagrin, Carl Jacobsen did not appear, and she made the crossing shivering alone in the bitter wind of late afternoon.

Chapter 3

Leaves skittered dull and raspy around Sophie's feet as she stepped down onto the sidewalk outside Island Market and Cheese World. A large wooden bin full of pumpkins stood against the wall next to the door. She wanted one or two good-sized ones to carve into jack-o-lanterns, but she would have to drive down later to pick them up. She could not possibly juggle even one home on foot along with her groceries.

She took a deep breath and looked around her. Since she'd become accustomed to the nearly constant chill, it seemed to her a very pleasant day. The sky was the blue of a good topaz, and the sun, while not warm, was strong and illuminated leaves the colors of polished agate and carnelian that still clung to their parent trees. But it was the quiet of human inactivity, almost like a feature of the landscape, that most struck her. So very different from what it had been when she and Peter had come in the summer. The heavy bicycle traffic and the throngs of people entering and exiting shops and restaurants had given way to the occasional car going in one direction or the other on the road that ran along the perimeter of the island, and to small clumps of people bringing their custom to the grocery or the single bar and restaurant that stayed open all winter as a watering hole for the locals.

Still, the grocery had had a fairly steady stream of shoppers, and she supposed that people came there and to the few other stores along the waterfront as much for company as for graham crackers and laundry detergent. In fact, she suspected that Island Market and Cheese World was at the center of island life.

She had been puzzled at first by the wine section, consisting largely of products from the local DeKalb winery across the island less than two miles distant.

But the proprietor, a loquacious woman by the name of Nila Celestine, was quick to introduce herself to Sophie as a DeKalb by birth. Her brother Reg oversaw the operation of the winery, while she provided the largest outlet for the wine, which was, however (she assured Sophie), justifiably famous on the mainland as well. Sophie had smiled and selected a three year-old Merlot.

She had also bought some smoked cheddar and what was, just by its presence, a lovely chunk of Stilton. While "Cheese World" might have been something of an exaggeration, the Celestines did stock a larger variety of cheeses than Sophie would have thought advisable for so small a population. But Bob Celestine was fond of cheese, and among his other strategies for putting the island on the map as more than a summer tourist attraction was a series of wine and cheese tasting parties. In fact, he had already hosted one. But since it had been the end of September, and too late to attract the tourists, only a dozen or so people had attended, and most of those with Celestine and DeKalb family connections.

But Nila Celestine had seemed genuinely warm and outgoing, hanging politely on Sophie's every word, no matter how few they were in relation to her own, and had insisted on introducing her to everyone who came in, for frozen pot pies or a pack of cigarettes. Sophie had greeted them amiably, not least because it was in the intervals during which Nila was required to wait on her other customers that Sophie had managed to do her own shopping.

And she had done rather well, she reflected, as she stood on the sidewalk and gazed across the street to the little park that stood in for a town square. Whatever shortages there might be later, there was more than enough now of fresh things to give her a sense of peace and plenty and the illusion at least of genteel living. Most of the canned and boxed items could remain tucked away in cupboards for the time being. Besides the wine and cheese, there were brown eggs and fresh milk, crispy leaf lettuce and rosy apples just harvested from a small orchard on the island. There had not been too much to choose from in the way of fresh meat, but she could understand that. The prices reflected the cost of bringing it from the mainland. But the beef stew had looked nice, and she would get several meals out of it. One of the advantages, she supposed, of living alone. *She had had to lean over to see him clearly because of the swelling above one cheek ...*

"Now, that's something you could do."

She turned a startled look on Bea Baskin. "I'm sorry. I didn't see you," she smiled, recouping her cordial exterior. "What's something I could do?"

"Eggs." Bea Baskin nodded toward the basket that Sophie found easier than plastic bags to carry the little distance to the cottage. "One thing you can pretty much count on getting fresh and reasonable around here is eggs. Bob Haskell's

Rhode Island Reds," she added, as Sophie resumed her expression of incomprehension.

"Oh, the brown eggs. Yes, I was happy to get them. I thought they'd be pricier."

"That's my point. They're not as pricey as they would be coming from the mainland, but they're still pricier than they could be if Bob Haskell had a little competition."

"Oh, you're not suggesting," said Sophie with a bemused smile, "that I raise *chickens*?"

"Well, sure. Why not? Be perfect for you. Pull in a little extra money too."

"In the first place, I don't know the first thing about chickens—"

"Bob Haskell be more than happy to help get you started."

"Bob *Haskell*? Wouldn't he mind the competition?"

"Nah! Those eggs get snapped up as fast as the hens can lay them. And when the summer people come, a lot of times the rest of us have to get mainland eggs. Naw, you'd do well, and if nothing else, you wouldn't have to pay for eggs any more."

"No," laughed Sophie, "just chicken feed."

"Well," Bea gave a grudging chuckle, "it's not much. And you'd actually be doing Bob a favor, seeing as he owns the docks on the east side, and that keeps him pretty busy most of the year."

"I should have known he'd wear more than one hat."

"Yep, most folks on the island do. How we manage to get along and hold on to what we've got, I guess. Not everyone wants to rent out their house."

"I suppose I hadn't looked at it that way," said Sophie with a conciliatory nod.

"So," puffed Bea by way of a segue, "you going home to write a magazine article? You oughta write about the island."

"I may do that. But for right now, I thought I'd put my groceries away and then go to the library. I haven't been there yet."

"The library." Bea Baskin perked up suddenly. "Crystal Holliday—sounds like a porno star, dunnit?" she laughed. "Anyhow, she's the librarian. Now, there's an interesting story." She halted on the brink of what promised to be a scandal and stared as a black pickup truck turned the corner. "And there's another one, kind of," she nodded ambiguously.

Carl Jacobsen caught Sophie's gaze for a moment as he drove by, and she thought she saw him acknowledge her briefly, but she could have been wrong. "Why?" asked Sophie, turning back to Bea and trying to give an impression of neutral curiosity.

Bea's eyes narrowed, and she tilted her head slightly to one side, as if sizing up Sophie. "Oh, lots of reasons," she mumbled vaguely, her assessment made. "But the word is Carl's spending the winter on the island, and that'd be a first." She looked directly into Sophie's eyes. "People are curious about that, I can tell you."

Sophie tried to shrug off a flush of embarrassment she had no reason to feel. "Maybe he wants to get away from it all," she said with deliberate indifference.

"Not from *all* of it, I'm thinking," Bea smiled shrewdly. Sophie stiffened next to her, but she gave Sophie's arm a quick tap to announce her departure. "Well, I'm off home. Things to do. But never too busy for company, so you just come on over any time you have a mind to. Little blue house with the picket fence about half a mile down that way," she nodded in the direction Carl had gone.

"Thank you," smiled Sophie, and stepped out into the road that ran past the cottage. A number of thoughts occupied her as she walked the quarter mile or so. First, if not chief among them was the incongruous picture of her raising chickens. It was startling enough to realize she had gone from being the well-heeled wife of a doctor, with a marginally successful, if unnecessary, career of her own, to becoming a widow living on an island in the middle of the lake, without the addition of chickens. It was not that she missed the loss of position and privilege, for which she had paid too steep a price. *She had had to lean over Peter's prone body to see clearly because of the swelling above her cheek. She had confronted him about his latest affair, which he hadn't bothered to deny, and he'd hit her. Hit her hard and sent her toppling over the sofa table.*

She stepped around the dry remains of a dead bird in the road and sighed unhappily. She had planned to meet with Auggie Dussault that Monday to have him draw up the divorce papers. But by Monday, Peter was dead, and there was no need to divorce him. Still, she would rather have divorced him. People were fools who speculated that it was sometimes easier for a spouse to die than to go through a sticky public divorce. She knew better. Particularly if the spouse didn't simply die quietly of natural causes.

And if it was speculation one wanted to talk about, there was Bea Baskin, suggesting—perhaps innocently, perhaps not—that she might need the extra income from *eggs*. She blew out the chuckle of incredulity she had had to suppress when she'd heard that. Despite the protests of some people who thought they had a claim to Peter's fortune, and others who didn't, but were prompted by jealousy or mean-spiritedness, she had been granted the bulk of Peter's estate. And while it didn't purge the nightmare that her marriage had been, at least she had that.

Of course, that wasn't all Bea Baskin had hinted at. The suggestion of intrigue—about the librarian, about Carl Jacobsen—hovered around her almost like tangible particles that made Sophie more uneasy than curious. Uneasy, and when it came to it, annoyed. The big story on the librarian was probably that she had been the bubbly homecoming queen somewhere or other back in 1972 and, having squandered the promise of youth, had ended up the faded and bitter librarian in an equally faded and musty library in the middle of nowhere.

And if Carl Jacobsen chose to spend the winter in what was, after all, his house, she guessed that was his business too, and no one need impute to it anything either sinister or mysterious. She set her mouth angrily and shifted the basket to her other arm as the low stone wall before the cottage came into view. But before she could work up a really healthy ire, she jerked to a halt at the edge of the front yard, and her brow furrowed. A black pickup had pulled to the far end of the driveway, only its back quarter visible from the road. She swallowed and hurried up the drive. There was no point in going in the front door when she clearly had company at the back one.

Carl had been leaning against the truck and straightened up as Sophie crept around the corner of the house. She looked one question, but asked another. "How long have you been here?"

"Not long. Figured you'd get here sooner or later, depending on how long Bea Baskin bent your ear."

Sophie gave him an involuntary smile. "Not long. I think she was disappointed that I didn't seem to warm to the idea of keeping chickens."

"Jeee-sus," he laughed.

"Mm. So, would you like some coffee this time?"

"Maybe."

"Well," she said, pushing open the back door, "while you're deciding, why don't you come in? I want to put my groceries away."

He followed her into the house, but not before he'd opened the door of the truck and retrieved a foil-wrapped package from the passenger seat. He slid it across the dinette table and sprawled in one of the chairs.

"What's that?" she asked, setting the egg carton on the counter and nodding toward the foil lump.

"Fresh walleye."

"You're kidding!" she grinned. "Oh, I don't believe it. I was so hoping to find some at the market. You can't imagine ... well, I thought *surely* they'd have some. Or some perch. But—nothing."

"They'll have some soon as I take it down there. But they'll charge you an arm and a leg for it, because there aren't as many to be had as there used to be. Now, that's okay for those of us who catch 'em. Make a tidy little sum, especially in the summer, since all the restaurat*eurs*," he snickered, "pride themselves on having fresh lake fish on the menu. Part of the *ambience*, I guess you could say. Anyway," he sniffed with apparent nonchalance, "I thought you might like some."

"I'd love some, but ..." She hesitated and bit her lip as she wondered how best to broach the subject of payment. He had seemed gruff, if not downright insulted, when she had offered to pay him for carrying in the scads of boxes from the ferry.

"Well, I don't want to get laid in exchange for a pile of dead fish, if that's what you're worried about. I'm not that hard up."

Her mouth dropped open in astonishment. "Well, I'm very glad to hear that! Since," she spluttered, too stunned to come up with anything more cutting on such short notice, "I wouldn't sleep with you if you were the last man on the island!"

He leaned back in the chair and laughed. "Sophie, I hate to be the one to tell you this, but where you're concerned, honey, I *am* the last man on the island."

"I can't believe you'd say that! Do we even *know* each other?"

He smirked up at the magenta cashmere sweater with the u-neck that hovered just above provocative. "Not my fault if we don't. But that could be remedied."

"Look, I don't know *why* you think you can—"

"Aw, cut the self-righteous indignation." It was an effortless jab, and he watched her wrath deflate and dissipate. "It's a present, okay?"

She felt both chastened and foolish. "Why?" she pouted over at him.

She shrank away from what was becoming the familiar expression of insolence. "Told ya. You got a nice ass for a woman your age."

"Oh, for heaven's sake," she whined, and snatched up the package. "Are you at least going to tell me the best way to cook it?"

"Well, now, I was kinda hoping you'd know that. See, I had you figured for one of those women with pots and pans that cost as much as a used truck. Kitchen with copper things hanging from the ceiling. Twelve-burner brushed stainless steel stove so's you could make, I don't know," he waved, "dog doodle in aspic to impress people with season tickets to the symphony or some shit."

Fighting the urge to fling the packet of fish at him, she thumped it back down on the table instead and leaned over to confront him. "You obviously have a very low opinion of me. So why do you keep doing things like—I don't know—helping me, bringing me *fish*, for God's sake? And don't you *dare*—"

He smiled and ran an idle tongue across his upper lip. "You do, though. Not that I've seen it as close as I might like."

"Shall I tell you," she howled, "what you can do with your fish?"

"Well, my mama told me never to play with my food. And anyway, that fishy smell ..." He shook his head and grinned up at her.

Nearly in tears now, Sophie sank into the chair opposite him and reached out to shove the fish across the table at him. But his hand came down suddenly to cover hers, and leaning forward, he said earnestly, "You gotta lighten up."

"I have to *what*?" she said, trying to pull her hand from his grasp.

"Woman, if you wanna last the winter here, you damn well better lighten up. I would think you would already have figured that out."

She pressed her lips together to keep them from quivering as she felt the fiction she had adopted shudder beneath her. "I have no idea what you're talking about."

"I'll tell ya then," he said so quietly that she found herself straining to listen. "People who take themselves too seriously get in trouble."

"Voice of experience?" she said coldly.

"Maybe."

Now she heard not insolence, but something like vulnerability, and her anger and humiliation gave way to grudging sympathy. "We're back to maybe?" she sighed. "Have we at least managed to arrive at a yes or a no to coffee?"

"Yes," he said simply.

"And now we're back to the taciturn man of few words, huh? Okay," she said, getting up to make the coffee, "what about the fish?"

"What about it? Do I know how to cook it, you mean?"

"I guess," she said, setting a mug in front of him and resuming her own seat, "I'm asking if you want to stay for dinner."

"Depends."

"On?"

"Couple of things. First of all, was I right? *Are* you one of those women who'd starve to death before they'd eat anything fried?"

"Very funny."

"All right. I suppose you know what'll happen if people see my truck here."

"Oh, that." The fingers of one hand fanned out in dismissal. "I expect somebody already has, don't you? And weren't you the one who told me I should lighten up?"

"Yeah, lighten up, not be careless."

"Well, I hardly think that even the islanders are so benighted as to be scandalized by my having a dinner guest. I mean, it's not," she added archly, "as though you're spending the night."

His lip curled up into a wry smile. "Now, that's just the point, Sophie. I might as well."

Chapter 4

The fragrance of green tea drifted up from the mug Sophie cradled against her thick terry robe and made her feel comfortable and unhurried. Brushing the embroidered curtain to one side, she gazed out the bedroom window at the waves that churned and crashed against the rock-lined shore, and considered how she would spend the day.

First on the list was the library. She really didn't mind that Carl's arrival had prevented her going the day before. In fact, once she had come to understand that his crude humor and generally brusque demeanor were his way of not taking himself or anyone else too seriously, she had enjoyed the company. The few hours spent with him had alleviated the loneliness she hadn't realized she'd felt. Still, she wondered, as she always did of people who were simultaneously blunt and indirect in their expression, just what his bluntness was meant to forestall, and why.

Well. She let the curtain drop back into place, took a sip of tea and set about getting dressed. She would stop by the market and pick up some pumpkins on the way. Halloween was only a few days away, and she hadn't done anything yet about decorating. And she must remember to ask in town whether the island children trick-or-treated. She had no idea even how many children there were among the permanent residents, although clearly there were some, since there was a school. She remembered passing it in the summer, the marquee in front congratulating the single member of the graduating class. When she had pointed it out, Peter had been disinterested, as he had been about most things.

Well. She spent the next few minutes running a comb through her hair and applying a minimum of makeup, then pulled on a pair of boots and a thick wool sweater from Ecuador, flung her purse over her shoulder and tugged the door closed behind her. It was a drive of only two or three minutes to the center of the town, and she had no problem finding a parking place directly in front of the market door.

She turned one after another pumpkin in the bin to examine their suitability for carving, returning the polite smiles of those few people who passed her, before hefting her selections, one in each arm, with the intention of going inside to pay for them. She stared at the door handle, and was just about to set one of the pumpkins down to open the door when a suede arm reached around and saved her the trouble.

"You're out and about early," said Carl Jacobsen.

She responded with a resigned smile. "Not that early. But here you are once again just in time to rescue me."

He relieved her of the pumpkins and motioned her inside. "More like rescuing the pumpkins before you drop them," he muttered, carrying them in and depositing them on the long wooden counter.

"Morning to you, Carl," chirped Nila Celestine. "Planning to make a pumpkin pie? Oh, good morning, Ms. Westenra!"

"Good morning. And please, it's Sophie, and those are my pumpkins. I was having a little problem with the door, and Carl—Mr. Jacobsen—came along just in the nick of time to help me out."

"Well, that was a lucky coincidence, wasn't it?" she gushed, smiling at one and then the other.

"Yes, it was," Sophie replied casually. "But I was wondering, Mrs. Celestine—Nila—whether I should get some candy for trick-or-treaters. I mean, I wasn't sure, with the houses spread out and all ..."

"Oh, no, hon, they don't trick-or-treat, for just that reason. No, instead we have a community Halloween potluck party. Down at the community center, in the same building as the library," she added, with a glance in Carl's direction. "Bobbing for apples and pumpkin carving for the kids, and everybody brings something. Well, you'll *come*, won't you? Be a wonderful opportunity for you to meet everybody."

"That sounds like great fun," Sophie replied, and paid for the pumpkins. "I'll have to think about what to bring. I have a very good recipe for barbecued beans and sausage," she smiled, sliding a pumpkin across the counter and into her arms. Carl took it from her, and grabbing up the other, nodded to Nila and sauntered out the door after Sophie.

As he leaned into her car and placed them on the floor, he said quietly, "Told ya, didn't I? The rumor mill is already hard at work on the news that I'm staying the winter, and you can bet Nila will toss this little tidbit into the mix."

Sophie sighed. "I know, Carl. And if it's a problem—"

"It's not a problem for me, Sophie. I don't much give a good goddamn what they think of me. I was thinking of you."

"Oh, the whole thing's just silly," she said in disgust. "Tempest in a teapot." She gazed off toward the dock and saw the approach of the ferry. "Ferry's running," she said redundantly.

"I know. I'm working the run over and back."

"Oh. I wondered how you happened to be here just now."

"Yeah, I should get going, I guess. But I'm glad I ran into you. I wanted to thank you for supper anyway."

"You brought the main course," she laughed.

"Yeah, well ..." He turned to go, but hesitated. "Look, Sophie, maybe I could return the favor, have you over to my place."

She nodded slowly and smiled. "All right. I'd like that. And I'll bring something. When?"

"Tonight? I should be back about four," he said, hurrying off toward the dock.

"But, how will I—"

"Don't worry," he called back over his shoulder.

She watched him leap up the gangplank and disappear into the interior of the catamaran. "Talk about blind dates," she murmured. "I don't even know where he lives, let alone what time I'm supposed to be there." Her eyes drifted upward, and she slid into her car. As she pulled away from the curb, she caught a glimpse of Nila Celestine's face peering over the Budweiser sign in the market window and thought of frogs.

As the gift shops and bars and ice cream parlor were left behind, the spaces between the houses, situated at increasingly greater intervals, seemed suddenly vast and empty, and a feeling of melancholy began to creep over her. Leaves, dead or dying, drifted down from backlit trees, glancing off the car and scattering in little flocks around the tires, as she remembered other leaves in other autumns.

Things had not always been bad between her and Peter. In the early years, they had walked together along wooded paths carpeted with leaves pale and sodden, or trudged through brittle and skeletal mounds that rustled over the tops of their feet or crackled beneath them. Peter had seemed to notice things then, to notice her. But that had changed gradually, as he'd acquired more baggage to supply his burgeoning position. She had never really wanted the position. She'd only wanted Peter. And now Peter was dead, and that made her sad, because death eradicated all hope of rapprochement. There could be no happy ending to their story now.

Just as she spotted the sign for the library ahead, her eye was drawn to her immediate right, where a man perhaps twenty years or so her senior, with a flat cap and a polished walking stick, ambled along next to a large Labrador Retriever. He waved and smiled as he caught her eye, then cut across the lawn to the library, so that he arrived at the entrance just as she pulled into the lot and got out of the car.

"Well," he said, turning toward her, the dog taking the opportunity to sit down next to him and pant quietly. "So you're our new arrival."

She liked him instantly. His eyes were kind, and there was no hint about him of calculation or deception. She was glad he had waited for her. "Yes, I am. Sophie," she smiled, offering her hand, then hesitating before she added, "Sophie Westenra."

"That right. Well, Sophie, I'm Joe Wisdom, and this," he smiled down at the Lab, "is Crow. We're happy to make your acquaintance. I've been hoping to meet you, and I thought you just might show up at the library at some point. Shall we go in?" he smiled, placing a hand on her elbow and shepherding her through the door.

Sophie nodded down at Crow with some surprise. "Don't they mind?"

"Nooo," he answered emphatically. "This is the island, Sophie. People are pretty laid back about things like that, and anyway, Crow's managed to insinuate himself into most aspects of island life," he laughed, and Crow wagged his tail and grinned.

"Well, I like your Crow," smiled Sophie, reaching over to stroke the big, shiny head and looking around her.

The interior was neither dark nor musty. It was relatively small, but what space there was was used efficiently to give a sense of light and comfort. It was two stories, but the second level consisted of a wraparound loft filled with stacks, dotted here or there with a brightly colored couch or a desk, while the center was open from first floor to ceiling to impart a sense of spaciousness. It was more than adequate for the small population and struck Sophie as a very pleasant place to pass a chill or gloomy afternoon.

"I'm sorry. Why did you think I'd show up at the library?" she asked with a bemused smile.

"Writer, aren't you? Library would be someplace you'd naturally gravitate to, I would think."

"Well, I guess you're right," she laughed. "Here I am."

"Come on. I'll introduce you to our very able librarian. And then, Miss Sophie, I hope to extract from you a promise to join me for a jaw over coffee. Talk a little shop maybe." His eyes crinkled up as he smiled now.

"Are you a writer?" she asked in wonder.

"Aw, I'm researching a book on shipwrecks in the island area. Interest of mine from my youth, I guess. I used to work the lake freighters."

"I'm intrigued. I'd love to hear more. And I will certainly take you up on your invitation."

"I was hoping that would be your reaction," he winked. "And you'd be welcome. Little gray house with the stone chimney right up the road. You come along any time," he said, patting her hand. "Now, Miss Crystal," he said, turning toward the large checkout desk in the center of the room, "here's someone I want you to meet. This is our new neighbor, Miss Sophie Westenra. Miss Sophie, this efficient young lady is Miss Crystal Holliday, without whom we bookworms would be lost."

"Oh, Joe, stop it," giggled the woman behind the desk. She appeared to be in her late thirties, trim and graceful, her silky blonde hair twisted up behind her head in a haphazard fashion that suggested casual unconcern, but worked for her. She really was very attractive and clearly not the 1972 homecoming queen of anywhere.

"Hello," Sophie said pleasantly. "It's nice to meet you. What a lovely library. You must enjoy working here."

The corners of Crystal Holliday's mouth dipped infinitesimally, and something like mild distaste flashed across her eyes as she blinked over at Sophie. "Yes, I guess I was lucky to come along looking for a job just when the position opened up. Miss Evinrude had finally retired. She'd been the librarian here since 1946, I think."

"Yes, indeed," Joe Wisdom interjected. "Of course, the place didn't look like this then. In fact, there are some good old photographs of it over there." He jerked his chin toward an area on the far wall where a number of pictures hung next to a low table and a couple of plush blue chairs. "Make sure you have a look at them. I think you'll enjoy them. And on that note, I'll take my leave of you ladies and get on with my own piddling pursuits," he laughed.

"I hardly think they're that," replied Sophie. "And you have to promise to tell me all about your project."

"I will hold you to that, my dear," he grinned and turned toward the steps, Crow following patiently at his heels.

"Guess he told you about the new book he's working on, huh?" asked Crystal Holliday, as Sophie turned back toward her a little awkwardly.

"Yes. He seems very knowledgeable about the area."

"Oh, Joe's a local legend. Knows pretty much everything there is to know about the island and its history. Well, his other books are over there." She pointed at a small rack near the stairs. "Those are all books about the island."

"I had no idea," said Sophie, walking over and lifting a handsome hardcover book from the rack. She turned it over and gave a little gasp of delight as she recognized Joe Wisdom's photo on the jacket.

"Yep, he's got three of them. They sell them in some of the gift shops. He's sold quite a few. Tourists wanting something a little more highbrow, I guess, than the usual sweatshirts."

"Huh," puffed Sophie, "he didn't tell me."

"No, he doesn't like to brag. But he's tickled when someone else brings it up," she shrugged.

"Well, I'll take this one out, if I may."

"That's what they're here for. It's a library," said Crystal Holliday with a restrained smile. "Of course, you'll have to fill out the form so I can issue you a card."

"Of course," agreed Sophie, bringing the book with her to the counter and leaning over to fill out the little slip of paper the younger woman pushed across at her. She scribbled her first name, then caught herself and hesitated before turning the second S into a misshapen W. She looked up uncomfortably to find Crystal studying her through narrow green eyes.

"Wes-ten-ra," said Crystal, sliding the paper around so she could read it. "Unusual name."

"Yes," Sophie agreed with forced good humor. "Smith or Jones certainly would have been easier to spell."

"Guess you could have kept your maiden name."

"I suppose it never occurred to me at the time."

"No," Crystal Holliday said a little wistfully, "it wouldn't occur to me either. Well, anyway." She inhaled and pulled herself upright. "It didn't work out, huh? A lot of them don't, I guess."

"I'm sorry?"

"You're here by yourself. Everybody pretty much knows that. So I just figured ..."

Sophie took a deep breath to push down the anger that had begun to well up, no longer the least bit curious about the source of Carl Jacobsen's irritability toward the islanders. But at the same time, it occurred to her that the only way she would get any relief from the continual prying into her private life was to give some account of it. She had no doubt that Crystal Holliday would see it got around to everyone else. "I'm a widow," she said simply. "My husband died in an accident."

"Sorry," replied the other woman. "I understand what that's like, because the man I was going to marry died too. In an accident," she said quietly.

A chill stole up Sophie's spine, and she glanced unthinking toward the door for the source of a draft. "I'm sorry."

"So," said Crystal, a thin brow arching and falling in an expression of apparent ennui, "I guess we have something in common. Probably more than one thing." As this speculation elicited no response from Sophie, she flashed a quick, embarrassed smile. "Anyway, how are you finding life on our little island? Have you met everybody?"

"No, not everyone. Maybe a dozen or so, but I've only really talked with a handful—Bea Baskin, Nila Celestine, Joe," she nodded toward the stairs, "Carl Jacobsen. And you, of course," she added with a gracious smile.

"Carl Jacobsen." Crystal Holliday forgot for a moment to smile. "I can't imagine how you managed to engage him in a conversation," she said coolly. "He keeps pretty much to himself," she tittered in afterthought.

But she'd tipped her hand, and Sophie was quick to grasp the advantage to deflect what would, after all, have been a groundless suspicion. "Oh, he was kind enough to help me get some of my things from the ferry to my house, so we had no choice but to exchange a few words."

"I suppose he didn't tell you much about himself then."

Before she could respond, Sophie felt a hand on her arm and turned to find Joe Wisdom at her elbow. "Well," he beamed, "I see the two of you have been getting to know each other, and Miss Sophie, you've found something to interest you."

"You might have told me," she teased, grateful for his intrusion into what had clearly become an uneasy conversation. "But now you really do have to tell me everything." She hooked her arm through his and picked his book up off the counter. "So nice to meet you, Crystal," she said, pivoting toward the door with Joe Wisdom in tow.

Once outside, she turned toward him, her gaze fixed on the thick plaid muffler around his throat. "Forgive me. I don't even know whether you were ready to leave. I don't know what I was thinking."

"Now, Miss Sophie," he said kindly, "don't give it another thought. Anyway, I *was* on my way out."

"Can I at least give you and Crow a ride home?"

"Well, thank you kindly, but Crow is pretty particular about his afternoon walk," he laughed, pulling open the car door for her. "But I will be expecting a visit from you, and soon." She smiled up at him with a vigorous bob of her head. "Oh, and Miss Sophie, I wouldn't take anything Crystal might say too much to heart. She's a nice girl. Just had some bad breaks. That business with Carl Jacobsen," he said sadly. "Unfortunate all around. She left the island after that. And then didn't things get worse for her instead of better."

She looked up in embarrassment as she realized that Joe Wisdom had stopped talking. She had been preoccupied in congratulating herself on having correctly surmised a relationship between Carl and Crystal, although why she should have derived satisfaction from that fact escaped her for the moment. But that meant that the lie about the fiancé who had died was clearly a face-saving measure. The death of a lover was preferable to being dumped, she thought sardonically. "No, I won't," she smiled, then waved as he and Crow meandered off across the lawn. Just before she pulled the car door closed, she caught a glimpse of Crystal Holliday framed in the long glass door.

Chapter 5

"Sophie?"

"Carl?" she choked, shifting the phone to her other ear.

"What's wrong?"

"Nothing," she answered, trying too hard to keep any disappointment out of her voice. Silly. And unreasonable, to suppose people their age ought not to have pasts. God knew *she* did. "No, I just walked in the door. I was out. At the library." Not hard enough. "It's ... lovely."

There was no immediate response from the other end. Then, "I wouldn't know. Haven't been there in a long time. Something happen, Sophie?"

"No. No, of course not. What would make you think something happened?"

"Okay," replied Carl. His voice was flat and lacked conviction. "Then are we still on for supper?"

"Oh, Carl, I don't know. I wanted to bring some stroganoff, but I got sidetracked and didn't get back in time to make it."

"I'll scrounge up something. What the hell's that matter?" There was an exasperated sigh on the other end of the line. "Sophie, I need to talk to you."

Here it came. He would assume Crystal Holliday had spilled the beans and shared with her all the titillating details of their affair, so there would follow the inevitable attempt to minimize the damage. She had two choices. She could broach the subject first, right here, right now, and assure him that it was no business of hers. Or she could join him for dinner as planned and let him tell her in his own way. *And* she would have company for dinner.

Crystal Holliday was younger. A little. And prettier. She pressed her lips together and her brows went flat. But it was *her* company he sought now. "All right, Carl," she smiled, brows sliding upward in sign of capitulation. "Where am I going?"

He gave her directions—nothing on the island was hard to find—with the injunction that she should head east and avoid the center of town. She wondered if he wasn't being a little paranoid, but she dragged on her coat and headed out the door. In a moment of inspiration, she snatched up the bottle of Merlot, and the lettuce and tomatoes with the intention of making a salad.

It was already dark, and her headlights afforded the only illumination on the uninhabited stretches of road. It made her drowsy to watch the pavement blur away beneath them and the trees dissolve into her peripheral vision, so she was glad to turn up the long gravel driveway he had described, and shook herself awake.

Grabbing bag and bottle off the seat, she slammed the car door and looked around her. It was a surprisingly large and secluded lot, considering how small the island was, with a modest log cabin set well back from the road. She remembered it. They had passed it on a bike ride across the island on one of the rare occasions she had been able to persuade Peter to accompany her, before things between them had deteriorated irreparably. She had wondered then, as she often did of houses she passed, what the interior was like and what it would be like to live there. But it felt strange to be here now, almost as though she was intruding on someone else's life.

She climbed the steps slowly, but before she had reached the door, it swung open to flood the covered porch with a warm glow. Carl ushered her in with a sweep of his arm. "Well, this is it. Have a seat. I'm still looking for food."

"Well, while you're looking, could you open this?" she asked sweetly, and handed him the bottle.

He made for the kitchen area and jerked open drawers, jumbling their contents, before finally lifting a corkscrew and shaking it loose of its companion utensils. "I meant to get something. But I don't do a lot of cooking, and I didn't get around to food shopping."

"So, you built this?" It was small, but open, with no room divisions in the living area. An open stair along one wall led to the loft bedroom above. But the centerpiece of the place was a charming island stone hearth on the wall opposite the entrance, in which a fire already crackled.

"Not single-handed, but yeah."

"Still, I'm impressed. It's lovely, very cozy. I like it," she smiled.

"I'm glad," he said abruptly, and handed her a glass. The wine rocked gently, clinging to the sides of the glass, dense and rich as garnet as it passed before the flames. "So," he groused, rattling and slamming around the kitchen, "I'm sure Crystal Holliday had plenty to say."

"Carl," she said gently. She saw no need for the guilty confession that looked like coming, much less for toga tearing.

But he seemed intent on unburdening himself. "Look, I'd have told you, Sophie. I just didn't see the point in doing it right off." He flung open a cupboard.

"Carl," she repeated. "Why don't I help you look for dinner?"

"I found it," he said, his tone somewhere between sour and embarrassed, and held up a can. "Soup." Yanking open the refrigerator, he pulled out a limp package. "And there's some bacon." He peeled back the wrapper and sniffed it. "Yeah, it's still good."

She lowered her face into her knuckles to keep from laughing. Then emptying the bag of lettuce and tomatoes onto the counter, she asked, "Do you have bread?"

"Yeah."

"How about mayonnaise?"

He began to rattle jars in the racks in the refrigerator door. "Yeah."

"Perfect. We'll have soup and BLTs."

"I'm not making any excuses or apologies, but it was a long time ago. It's just something that happened, but it's in the past, it's over." He flung slices of unoffending bacon onto a rack and chucked it into the microwave.

"I know. Now why don't you heat up the soup and give me the toaster."

"I should have told you, because I should've known Crystal wouldn't waste any time," he said bitterly.

"Carl, Crystal didn't tell me anything. Not really. Of course, it wasn't hard to figure out from the way she acted. And then Joe Wisdom more or less corroborated what I already knew. He said she'd even left the island—"

"Joe *Wisdom*!" He squeezed his temples between the fingers and thumb of one hand and shook his head. "There. That's what I meant, Sophie, what I tried to warn you about. Everybody sticking their noses into everybody else's business. They just won't let the past alone!" He set his jaw and glared over at her in challenge. "All right, now you know. So what I want to know is why you're here."

"Because you invited me?" Her brows rose to perplexed points.

"And you don't care."

"Should I?" she replied lamely.

He eyed her narrowly, as if trying to decide whether to believe her, before subsiding into a grudging nod. "Sophie, it was over a long time ago, and I've paid for my mistake. I need you to know that."

She was both puzzled and impressed with the apparent depth of his feelings. Carl Jacobsen was just about the last man she'd have pegged as a gushing romantic. Right behind Peter. *Peter lying there on the hearth, the hair behind his ear stuck together in dark clumps* ... "Carl, it doesn't matter."

"Doesn't it, Sophie?"

"If things like that mattered, there would be an awful lot of people keeping themselves to themselves."

"There are, though. It's what I've done," he said ruefully.

"I imagine we've all done that from time to time." She stared down at her hands, a knife in the one, a tomato in the other, and recalled a lunch cancelled or a visit missed, because she hadn't had the heart to listen to another angry lecture from Reney on the subject of the latest row or the latest bruise.

Carl transferred the bacon strips carefully to a paper towel and glanced over at her. "I guess I should have known you'd understand. In fact, I suppose that's one of the reasons ..." He appeared to reconsider, sniffed nonchalantly and shoved his shoulders back. "Well, that and," he grinned, as the bread sprang up out of the toaster to land on the counter, "because you got a nice ass for a woman your age."

She had just scooped up a spoonful of mayonnaise, which she now calmly dragged down the front of his shirt in a single unhurried motion, before resuming assembly of the sandwiches.

"Woman, you're all right," he laughed, picking up the soup bowls and conveying them to the coffee table in front of the fireplace. "Do you mind if we eat here?"

"No," she said, tossing a towel at him and bringing out the sandwiches. "But you might want to wipe your shirt. You have mayonnaise all over it."

They sat on the floor, he cross-legged, she with legs tucked neatly off to one side. Refilling the glasses, he leaned forward. "Cheers. Look, I'm sorry about dinner. I wanted—"

"Oh, stop. In the first place, I like tomato soup and BLTs. And in the second place, this is *fun*," she smiled like a guilty child, "sitting here on the floor having a casual meal with you. Ever since I arrived, I've been either relatively comfortable in the cottage with my things or relatively *un*comfortable outside it under public scrutiny. Do you mind my asking," she said, setting down her spoon and scooting forward, "whether that's why you don't live on the island."

"Of course it is." He glanced around the room. "I like it here. And do you know what 'home' is for me on the mainland? An efficiency apartment."

"That seems like an extreme position. But you've obviously changed your mind. Why?" she asked over the rim of her glass.

One corner of his mouth slid up, and once again he trained on her that look that pierced the outer layers and got down inside her like the icy wind off the lake. "Don't fish. I'm here because of you. And not just for the reasons you think."

What do you mean?" she asked warily.

"I mean, I knew what you'd be in for. You're too good a story."

"*Why?*"

"Because a woman like you doesn't just get a bug up her butt to spend a brutal winter on some godforsaken friggin' island in the middle of nowhere for a change of scenery."

"People have done stranger things," she said cautiously.

"Now, Sophie, you know I'm not judging. I'm just saying that's how people are."

She drooped resignedly and picked at the sandwich on her plate. "So you decided to protect me," she smiled at the crumbs.

"I'm a sucker for a woman who'll smear mayonnaise all over me."

"Oh," she snorted and tossed a crust at him.

He lunged around the table to grab her, and she scrambled aside giggling. A little shriek escaped her as he clutched at her and bore her backward onto the rug before the fireplace. Her breath caught, resuming in shallow little puffs through parted lips as she stared up into his eyes. They were—like hers, she knew—frank and eager, and she heard a rush of blood whoosh through her ears as he leaned down and covered her mouth with his.

"Am I outta line, Sophie?" he whispered.

"Yes," she replied, pulling him down and returning his kiss. "You haven't shown me the upstairs."

"I'll get to it," he smiled, peeling off his shirt and snatching at a quilt that lay draped over the back of the sofa. "Right now, you look too pretty in the firelight."

She emitted a poignant little sigh and grasped his hand to pull him back down. As she began to tug her sweater over her head, he said, "Let me do that. Please." Setting the sweater aside, he reached around behind her to unhook her bra, his lips brushing along her neck and shoulder, as she tilted her head to nuzzle against his hair and breathe in his scent.

"Listen to the wind howling," she gasped, as a violent blast collided with the cabin.

"That's not the wind," he murmured, settling her back and leaning down for another kiss before he unzipped her jeans and began to slide them down her legs. She wriggled out and kicked free of her panties, then dragged him down on top of her, working his belt buckle loose and looking up in silent plea. It was a language he understood, and a moment later, he was tucking her into the blanket and his embrace, his clothing in a pile on the floor, her leg sliding dizzyingly along his.

He was of two minds about abandoning her heady kisses, but as he slid his hands down along her sides and over her hips and then up between her thighs, she rolled up toward him, and he began to inch his way slowly downward. But her legs tightened around him and pressed into his back to let him know the nature of her desire. And he understood that too, since it was also what he most wanted, this desperate shedding of passion.

It was swift and reckless, and over soon, this first slaking act, and they lay for a long moment afterward languid and silent. Then tracing his finger gently along the curve of her shoulder, "All right?" he asked.

"No." He looked crestfallen, and she laughed quietly and rose up on her elbow to kiss his mouth. "You still haven't shown me the upstairs."

He wagged his head and laughed. "Now, that's a cold thing to do to a man. Hussy."

"It was wonderful," she murmured coquettishly, her fingertips trailing over his cheek so that he leaned toward her and closed his eyes. "You?"

"No," he drawled. "I wanted you to smear mayonnaise all over me."

"Oh, you!" she laughed, as he hugged her to him. "Oh, my God, look, it's snowing," she motioned toward a window.

"Hell, it's starting early. Looks like it's really coming down too."

"Do you think the roads will be bad?"

"Sophie, you're not thinking about leaving."

"Not if you want me to stay," she said shyly.

He cupped her chin in his hand and kissed her again. "You know I do. I still have to show you the upstairs. How about we take a hot bath?"

"Oh, yes, please! I'd love that."

"Good." He zipped his jeans and, bundling her into the quilt, swept her up the stairs. "The master suite," he smiled and settled her onto the big bed.

"It's perfect," she beamed, eyeing the large corner tub.

"Now, you stay wrapped up while I run the water and grab the wine."

"You're spoiling me. First, tomato soup and BLTs, and now this," she laughed, as he bounded down the stairs, then returned a moment later with the bottle and glasses.

He helped her into the tub, and she leaned back against him, her expression one of blissful abandon. "How did this happen?" she asked, turning her head to look up into his face.

"Fate, coincidence, dumb luck? I don't much give a damn, angel." He pushed her hair up off her neck and began to press his fingers into the muscles. "All I care is that you're here with me now. The rest doesn't matter."

She twisted around to kiss him. "You're right. We have right now, and the rest *doesn't* matter." *Peter slapping her, Peter lying on the bricks with his head bashed in, Peter in his coffin, his face waxy and expressionless ...*

"Do you miss him?"

"*What?*"

"Your husband. Come on, Sophie. I'm not such a fool that I don't know you had a husband."

She slumped into a sigh. Sooner or later, she supposed she'd have to tell him everything. But not now. She couldn't bear to spoil it now. "We weren't very happy. But why would you ask me that now?"

"Because I don't want you to miss him." He lifted her hand and put it to his lips.

"You know, I think what I missed was being close to someone, feeling what I feel now."

He stepped out of the tub and dried off, then helped her up and into a towel. As he pulled her close, he said, "Come climb into bed with me, and this time we won't be in any hurry."

The snow had stopped, and the moon had risen high and white by the time they fell away exhausted and then crept together again to nestle snug under the thick blankets in each other's arms.

CHAPTER 6

She put her hand on his shoulder and stretched up on her toes to kiss his cheek, then strolled over to the kitchen window. "Huh. There's hardly anything on the ground."

"It's early in the season for it, and the ground's not frozen yet. That'll change soon enough now, though."

"Well, at least I won't having any trouble getting back."

"You wouldn't anyway. There's just one advantage to living in a little place like this in the winter. Even if nothing can get over from the mainland, the road crew generally gets the roads cleared pretty quick."

"Road crew, singular?"

"Yep. One dump truck, two, maybe three guys. Matter of fact, since I'm gonna be hanging around here anyway, I signed on as the number two man."

"What?"

"Yep. I'll put a plow on my truck and help Sam Coombs. Figured I might as well make some money. Pay for a few cheap dates."

"I *know* you're not talking about me," she said imperiously.

"I don't know about that, angel. Didn't seem to take much at all," he smirked. "Can of soup and some limp bacon."

"Oh, for heaven's sake!" she flushed. "I was very hungry is all."

"Yeah, you sure as hell *were*," he laughed outright. "Aw, Sophie honey, come on," he said, pulling her over to him. He pushed her hair aside and kissed her throat. "You didn't want me half as bad as I wanted you. Speaking of which, do you have to leave this morning?"

"I should, yes. For one thing, I need fresh underwear," she blushed.

"That mean you're leaving me the panties you wore yesterday?" He flashed a wicked grin and squeezed her bottom.

"Oh! You are disgusting!"

"You love it. Come on, you do," he cajoled. She giggled helplessly as he grabbed hold and tickled her.

"Stop it," she smiled foolishly. "What's for breakfast?"

"Toast?" He turned and opened a cupboard, shook a dilapidated cereal box, then picked out a flake and tasted it. "Nope, stale. No milk anyway."

"Oh? What about powdered milk? You were so insistent that I should get some."

"Can't stand the stuff. And I wasn't planning to need it, ya know?"

"One more reason I need to go back to the cottage. Otherwise, we'll both starve." One eyebrow rose in emphasis as breakfast shot up out of the toaster. He gathered it off the counter and slapped it on a plate before her.

"Eh, maybe just as well," he said glumly. "No sense feeding the piranhas. The more time we spend together, the more fodder we give them."

"Oh, Carl," she moaned. "What does it matter? You said it was a long time ago. And I was counting on your going to the Halloween party with me."

"Aw, Jesus, Sophie! No," he said, shaking his head and turning away from her.

"But I said I'd go, mostly because I thought you'd insist on it, if, as you put it, I'm going to survive the winter here."

"You, honey. Not me. And especially not me with you. Don't you know what kinda heat you'd come under?"

She set her jaw and considered. What was the worst that could happen if the islanders *did* start delving into things and found out who she really was? The Grand Jury had failed to indict. "I don't care," she said obstinately. "Please?"

He slumped forward against the counter and sighed. "All right, Sophie. All right. But I'll expect your sweet ass back here afterwards with a full jar of Miracle Whip."

"Oh," she chuckled, grasping him in a hug and leaning her head against his chest. "So, what will you do today?"

"Well, since you won't stay and play, I guess I'll work the middle run."

"Oh, I could come with you!" she said excitedly. "We could have lunch, do a little shopping. Oh, please!"

"No. Absolutely not."

"But why?"

"You see those clouds?" he asked, hustling her over to the window. "Just because we're not buried doesn't mean there isn't more coming. And do you know what that water is going to be like today? Of course you don't. Nope, too dangerous. You're staying here."

"If it's too dangerous for *me*—"

"No, Sophie."

"—then why isn't it too dangerous for you? Or for other passengers?"

"It's my job, and I'm used to it. And there generally *aren't* any passengers."

"But if it's dangerous and nobody goes anyway, why do they run the thing at all?"

"Cargo runs, honey. Picking up orders, mostly for the market and the bars. Anyway, don't you have to worry about making something for that damn party?"

"Not till tomorrow. But," she pouted, "I suppose I should go to the market and get what I need. When will you be back?"

"With any luck, we'll get it done a little early. No later than four. Course, then I have to meet Sam Coombs at Dickie's, sort out this road crew thing."

"Oh," she deflated. "I thought I'd make that stroganoff."

"Meeting with Sam won't last long if I cut the beers short. How about if I stop by on my way home?"

"All right," she smiled. "I'd better get going then. But," she added soberly, "you *will* be careful, won't you?"

"You know I will. You can find your way back okay, right?" he asked, as she wriggled into her coat and grabbed her purse. She nodded and smiled and kissed him goodbye.

In the daylight, she was surprised to find that it was a drive of less than ten minutes from Carl's house to the cottage, and she arrived home with the pleasant feeling that she had gotten a head start on the day. She let herself in the front door and jogged up the stairs. She would take a quick bath and change her clothes, set the beef out to thaw and go to the market for sour cream and sausage, the one for tonight's dinner, the other for tomorrow's potluck dish.

As the water was running in the bath, she went to the bedroom to get some fresh underthings and noticed the light blinking red on the answering machine. The first message was from Reney, and she felt a moment's guilt that she had not been here to talk to her. Reney would be at work now in the publicity department of the theater foundation, so she would have to take a break from Carl that evening long enough to call her back, she thought with an impish smile.

The other message was from Joe Wisdom, a renewal of his invitation, and that one she would return right after her bath. She would have her shopping done and the stroganoff made—except for adding the sour cream when she was ready to serve it—easily by noon. That would leave her with a whole afternoon to fill, an hour or so of which she would enjoy passing with Joe. It would work out perfectly, and she was grateful for his call. So forty-five minutes later—one o'clock would be fine, and he would be looking forward to her visit—she was back out the door and on her way to the market.

The lake flung up against the rocks that formed the natural breakwall along which the road ran, throwing spray high into the air to mist well up over the grassy banks above, and as she glanced uneasily out the car window at the gathering clouds, she grew anxious for Carl. Maybe he would change his mind about making the trip, or maybe the ferry captain would decide not to leave the mainland at all. Lord, she thought, pulling into the parking space and putting a nervous hand to her mouth, it was agonizing to care.

She supposed her anxiety was visible in her face, since she had no sooner stepped inside the market than Bea Baskin greeted her with, "Coming early this year all right, and looks like it'll get worse soon." Bea stood in a huddle with Nila Celestine and a third woman Sophie did not know.

"Yes, I was surprised to see it arrive last night and even more surprised this morning to see that it wasn't worse than it was. But those clouds," she said with a glance over her shoulder.

"Musta been noisy as all get out at your place."

Sophie drew a momentary blank before answering, "Oh, the wind. Yes, it was terrible."

"I know that. I meant that buoy bell windchime musta kept you awake most of the night."

"Oh, well, yes," she said evasively, "it certainly left no doubt about the wind."

"You didn't have any trouble though, I guess," to which Sophie responded with a quick shake of the head and a wan smile. "Didn't think so. I stopped by early this morning to check on you, but you weren't home."

Momentarily taken aback, Sophie stammered, "Actually, I took a drive around to the other side of the island to see if there was any damage. The wind sounded so ferocious. But I didn't see any." The three women exchanged a covert glance, and her heart began to pound as it occurred to her that there might have been significant damage across the island, damage that one could not possibly miss if one went looking for it. And her fear made her angry in turn, as though she needed to explain to—piranhas, he'd called them—much less lie to them about having spent the night with Carl. It was none of their business if the two of them wanted to hole up together permanently and remain in bed till spring.

"Well, where are my manners?" Bea broke the silence a little too heartily. "Sophie, this is Mattie Coombs. Lives on the north side of the island. Probably why you two haven't met before. Sounds crazy though, dunnit?" she snorted. "And the whole thing not more than two miles wide and five long."

"How do you do," nodded Sophie with sudden comprehension. The woman who looked out through tiny pale eyes that were all but lost in a large, flaccid face must be the other half of the other half of the road crew.

"Nice to meet you." It fell a little short of sincere, she thought, preparing to excuse herself.

Bea Baskin stopped her. "You're coming to the Halloween party tomorrow, aren't you? Pretty much everybody'll be there."

Sophie turned back to her with a reserved smile. "I had planned to," she said noncommittally. But now she didn't think she would. Carl was right, and she'd rather spend the evening with him, watching horror movies on TV and making love. She hadn't realized how much she'd missed being with a man. "That's why I'm here, in fact. I needed a few things for my potluck dish. Bulk sausage," she said deliberately.

There was a split second's silence before Nila swept around behind the small meat case. "Yep, we have it," she smiled broadly. "Nice, too. Just came in fresh yesterday. How much you need, Sophie?"

"Pound and a half, please. Oh, and some sour cream?"

"Right down there in the dairy case, hon." Nila pointed to the far end of the store with one hand and placed a mound of sausage on the scale with the other.

Sophie nodded and headed toward the back of the store, snatching up a plastic shopping basket as she walked, since she had forgotten to bring her own. She heard behind her manic murmurs, punctuated by a hiss—that would be Bea Baskin attempting to hush the others—and followed by what would scarcely pass for even an abnormally loud whisper. "I don't *care*. It's not *right*." She considered for a moment striding back up the aisle to confront the woman and ask her just what it was that wasn't "right." Instead, she put the sour cream in the basket, along with a box of fresh mushrooms and some decent asparagus that stood up in little bundles in a tray of ice, and plunked the basket down on the counter.

As Nila rang up her purchases on the old National cash register that had probably been there nearly as long as the market itself, Bea Baskin asked whether she would have time for coffee. "We thought we'd pop next door to Dickie's, get warmed up and have a little girl talk."

"That is kind," she replied, softening the slightest bit toward Bea Baskin. After all, she could not very well be the subject of their gossip if she joined them. "But I've promised to pay Joe Wisdom a visit." She allowed a moment for that niblet to sink in. "He was nice enough to ask several times, so I didn't see how I could refuse," she smiled demurely, and paid Nila in exact change. "But I'd love to join you another time if I may."

She felt their eyes boring into her back, and only relaxed when she had pulled away from the curb and turned the corner out of their range. "Tempest in a teapot," she muttered to herself, as she turned into the driveway and followed it to the back of the house. She was still muttering a moment later when, jostling her bags up the steps, she tripped over a large metallic object and looked down to see the buoy bell windchime that had been placed neatly on the top step. She slumped in surrender and stepped around it.

She was glad she had set her visit with Joe Wisdom for one o'clock. Although she bustled around the kitchen with a considerable energy born of anger, she had been too long in the market, and by the time the stroganoff was finished, it was already twelve forty-five. She pulled on her coat and dashed out the door, pausing just long enough to nudge the windchime clattering to the ground with her toe.

"Oh, this is a treat, Sophie," beamed Joe Wisdom, as he pushed open the storm door a few minutes later. He put a hand on her shoulder and guided her to an overstuffed chair near the fireplace in the living room, as Crow trotted out of the kitchen and panted his greeting.

"It is for me," she smiled up graciously. He placed a tray on the table between them and poured her a cup of coffee, before sitting down in the twin chair to her own. "I'm overwhelmed to be in the company of so prolific an author. But I have to confess," she flushed, "that I haven't yet read the book I checked out of the library. I'd planned to start it later this afternoon." And that was the truth, provided she got back before Carl arrived.

"Ah, don't you feel obligated to read that, dear. Boring stuff," he crinkled up his face and chuckled.

"But I want to. I don't think it's boring at all. And besides, I'd like to know more about where I'm living."

"In that case," he said, his face suddenly somber, "you don't want to read that. You see, Sophie," he leaned forward and rested his arms on his knees, "it might be more useful to you to know something of the dynamic of the community."

"I'm sorry," she replied a little awkwardly, "I didn't realize there was a particular dynamic."

"Oh, my yes! Now, they're not bad people. But they do have a sense of community and about looking out for their own."

"And I'm an intruder," she supplied with a wry smile.

"Well, it's not so much a question of your being a newcomer as it is whether or not you want to fit in, if you see the difference."

"You're trying to warn me. Why? Have I done something to violate some unspoken code? Do *you* think I've done something wrong?"

"Wrong?" he repeated thoughtfully. "You know, Sophie, I'm pretty much a fixture here. Crow and I are like a benign background presence, no threat to anyone, and no one gives us much thought. One hears things."

Her lip curled in sour acknowledgement. "A good many, I imagine. But what I can't understand, Joe, is what difference it should make to anyone."

"Let me tell you a little story by way of illustration. Maybe you've heard parts of it, maybe you haven't. Anyway, there was this young woman who grew up on the island, a pretty, vivacious girl who maybe felt confined. It's not an easy thing to live in a place like this and maybe get the feeling of being cut off from the rest of the wide world, you see?

"Anyway, this young woman was a bit of a flirt—nothing wrong in that—and she dated different men—nothing wrong with that either. Now, it didn't so much matter when she dated men on the mainland. But it was a little stickier when she would date men on the island. Well, you know how it is—you can't go anywhere without running into somebody you know. And eventually, as so often happens, there was jealousy, and then tragedy. Lives disrupted. Tragedy," he repeated, catching and holding Sophie's gaze.

"And then this young woman met a man who came to the island, and she fell in love with him. Again, what one might expect. He had a profession and money—and a wife. She saw him when she could, but eventually she wanted a life with him, and she moved to the mainland and took a job near him in the hope that he would leave his wife."

"I guess that sort of thing happens a lot," Sophie said stiffly.

"Oh, yes. One of the regular acts of human drama. But in this instance, the man did not leave his wife. He died, some thought by misadventure, others not. His wife came under suspicion of murder—I believe her name was Sophie too," he said softly.

Sophie sloshed coffee into her saucer in her haste to set the cup down. "You must forgive me. I've kept you much too long." She made as if to rise, but he placed a hand on hers.

"Please," he said gently, and she sank back into the chair, pale and unnerved. "Allow me to finish the story. Although the wife was suspected, there was no evidence whatever, and she was never tried."

"I have to go," she whispered, scrambling into her coat.

"Sophie, I mean you no harm. Believe that," he called after her.

She halted before the door as she felt Crow's big head bump her hand and heard his whimper. "Then why tell me this?"

"Because," he said quietly, "there are those who think some of the responsibility for this young woman's—"

"Crystal!"

"Yes, for Crystal's unhappiness—lies with others. Just be careful," he said earnestly.

She stumbled down the front steps and into the car, her knees shaking so badly that she simultaneously hauled the shifter into Reverse and pressed down hard on the accelerator. The car shot backward, jarring her from side to side and throwing up gravel in its wake. A small sedan approached from the other direction just as she swung out into the road and slammed the car into Drive, and for one eternal second, she saw Crystal Holliday's stony stare through the windshield.

Chapter 7

It was blowing in across the open waters from the northwest in a nearly horizontal stream that pelted the windshield and reduced visibility to almost nothing. Despite the warning clouds, it had seemed to come out of nowhere, and immediately, and by the time she reached home, she could just determine the outline of the driveway, and cranked the steering wheel to skid up into it. As she felt it jab at her like tiny pinpricks in the short interval between the car and the kitchen, she thought how fluid was the interface between the physical and the mental, how easily one could supplant the other. Focus on the physical discomfort, and the most violent emotional distress seemed insignificant. Become immersed in an emotional quagmire, and physical pain had no meaning. She was certain she was cold, but it felt some other way.

She threw her back against the door and tossed her purse and keys onto the table, before turning the burner on under the kettle. She needed a cup of tea. And a fire, she thought, hurrying through the hall to the living room and dropping to her knees on the hearth to start one. She struck a match that didn't catch, and then another and another, before burying her face in her hands and sobbing. She wished Carl would come and prayed that he didn't. It was almost inconceivable, and a monumental joke, that she should have become involved with a man who had been involved with the last woman with whom Peter had had an affair.

She let out a gasp as a furious gust slammed against the window, then sprang up as the teakettle began to shriek, stumbling into the kitchen doorframe when the house went suddenly dark. She fumbled with trembling fingers in a utility cupboard and lit several jar candles, wishing she had bought them by the case and making a senseless mental note to do so at the first opportunity.

She made the tea by candlelight, arranged the candles on a plate and balanced it all back to the living room and onto the coffee table, settling in front of the fireplace again with renewed determination. Her fingers were cold now, and she grasped the mug of tea for a moment to warm them, then struck another match to the fatwood. A tiny flame had just begun to flicker awake when the phone rang, and holding a candle aloft, she picked her way gingerly around furniture to find it.

"Sophie?"

"Carl! Are you all right? Where are you?"

"I'm okay. Had a hell of a time, but we made it. I'm afraid I'm gonna be awhile, though. We've gotta get the main roads cleared, but I'll get there as soon as I can. You're okay, aren't you?"

She hesitated for a moment as she recalled in disjointed snatches the day's events. "Yes, I'm okay. The power went out, but I've managed to get a small fire going."

"What about the backup generator?"

"I don't know anything about any generator."

"All right, Sophie. You stay bundled up by the fire, and I'll get there just as soon as I can."

"Okay. You be careful. I'll hold dinner," she added foolishly, pushing the button to disconnect and feeling suddenly vulnerable and alone. She crossed her arms over her chest and rubbed at them fruitlessly, before taking up the candle and making her way upstairs to drag blankets off the bed and out of cupboards. Then she wrapped herself up and huddled before the fire. And waited.

So, Joe Wisdom knew. And if the others did not, how long would it be before they did? How long before word got back to Carl? She groaned inwardly, wishing she had told him. But what would she have said? *My husband cheated on me and hit me, and then somebody killed him. They think it was me. Do you want fries with that?* And as improbable as that scenario was, the time had passed now when she might have said even that much. Hunkered down into the blankets and her gloom, she had no notion of how long she sat there, and was startled when the phone rang once more.

"Oh, Reney," she moaned, "I'm afraid I've made a mess of things." It tumbled out like a rockslide, chunk by painful chunk.

"Oh lord, Sophie, it's unbelievable. So now we know just what that bastard Peter was up to," she said bitterly. "Look, you have to come home. You have nothing whatever to gain by staying there."

"Reney, didn't you hear me?"

"I heard you. You had a fling. You spent one night with the guy. One night. You'll get over it. *Sophie*," she persisted, over her sister's murmured protest, "do you hear yourself? How long do *you* think it will be before that old character decides to share his secret—if it even *is* one? And darling, think about it: all of a sudden this guy and that little witch are both back on the island and bound to run into each other. Tempting fate," she muttered. "Come home."

Sophie's phone began to beep ominously. "Oh, no, the battery's about to run down. Reney, I couldn't leave right now if I wanted to. I can't get *anywhere* right now. But I'll think about what you've said. I will. And I'll call you just as soon as I can. I love you," she said into empty air. Her shoulders slumped, and she tossed the dead phone onto the sofa. Reney was right. She'd been here less than a month, but already it had become clear that things had not worked out the way she'd thought they would. No anonymity, no blessed escape. Nor was she so naive as to think it would make any life-altering difference to Carl if she left.

She straightened up against the chair seat and cocked her head toward the kitchen, holding her breath as she strained to hear. She *had* heard something, and not a gust against the windows. Pushing the blankets aside, she pulled herself slowly to her feet and crept through the dark hall into the kitchen. The flat of her hand pressed against her chest involuntarily, and she let out a sigh of relief. The back door stood open. Clearly, it had not latched properly when she'd stumbled in and shoved it closed. She pushed it shut now with a shiver and turned the lock, spinning back toward the front of the house as a high beam swept across the windows. That would be—

The thought went unfinished. In a single instant, she heard the dull crack and felt the brain-rattling blow. She clutched at the edge of the counter, but felt only a wrenching pain in her arm as she crashed to the floor.

Sophie! Peter was calling her. "Sophie!" Her eyes fluttered open, and in the dim light, she saw that it was Carl bending over her, his face tight and pale.

"Carl?" she groaned.

"My God, what *happened*?" He scrambled up and jerked open drawers until he found a dish towel, which he ran under warm water before sinking back to his knees next to her and dabbing at her forehead. She flinched and cried out.

"I don't know. Something hit me and I fell."

"Probably this," he said, holding up Joe Wisdom's book, which she had left on the table, and wiping an anxious hand across his mouth. "But I want to know who was on the other end of it."

"What do you mean?"

"Sophie, the damn book didn't jump up off the table and smack you in the head! But who'd wanna hurt you? And why? Why?" he repeated, as though he expected her to confess to having done it herself.

She said nothing, but looked around. "It was dark."

"I know. I got the generator going before I came in and found you."

"Then you must have *seen* someone." He shook his held guiltily. "Prints? In the snow?"

"No, honey, it's coming down hard. Yeah, there were a few faint prints, but I didn't think anything of that. Figured they were yours. And they'll be obliterated by now. But I don't want you to talk. Just lie still while I call the paramedics."

"Carl, no!" she insisted, grabbing his arm to keep him from rising. "I'm all right, and it's cold down here."

He paused and stared into her eyes. "Look at me. How many fingers am I holding up?"

"Oh, for heaven's sake. Three."

"Good," he said, scooping her up and hauling her out to the sofa. He grabbed up a blanket out of the pile on the floor and tucked it around her. "I'm gonna call in a police report. Unfortunately, at this time of year, the police force consists of Mike Hatton, and aside from breaking up the occasional drunken brawl, his experience is pretty much confined to citing people for rolling stops. Not even sure what he can do in this mess," he nodded toward the window.

"You'll have to try the upstairs phone. Charge ran down on this one." She pulled the defective object from between the sofa arm and cushion.

"All right. You stay right here." He jabbed a forefinger at the air in emphasis.

"I'm all right, Carl. Headache."

"Yeah, you're all right headache. Wait till you see the goose egg on your forehead," he called, bounding up the stairs. She reached up and cringed as she touched the lump.

"There's no answer, no voicemail, no nothing," he announced on his return. "I suppose he's up to his eyeballs. I'll try again in few minutes. I just don't get it, any of it." He sank into a chair heavily.

"Don't you?" she asked quietly.

"What's that supposed to mean?"

"Crystal?" she asked glumly.

"*Crystal*? Naw, naw, naw. Sophie, you're way out in left field on this one, okay? What reason would she have to hurt you?"

"I wonder," she whispered into the flames.

"You wonder? Look, that was almost seven years ago, and it's got nothing to do with you and me," he said irritably.

"You're right." There was no object in pursuing her own very different train of thought openly, especially if, as she suspected, he *was* right about that particular point. She caressed his hand instead. "I'm just a little unnerved."

"Aw, honey, of course you are," he said, taking her hand. "I'm sorry. Sorry, angel. You scared the shit outta me is all. Come in here and find you out cold and bleeding."

She shivered. *Peter unconscious on the bricks, she'd thought …* "So, what now?"

"So, now I stay here."

"You going to save me then?" she smiled and squeezed his hand.

"I'm gonna try. Yeah." He looked down and smoothed a hand over her hair. "Who are you, Sophie? Who are you?"

"Who are *you*?"

He looked aside and snorted. "Just a guy with a weakness for a nice ass."

"Oh," she clucked at him. "We might as well eat while we're waiting, don't you think? Are you hungry?"

"Starved."

"Well, there's the stroganoff, but I'm afraid you'll have to warm it up now and add the sour cream."

"Oh, I think I love you," he crooned, bending over to give her a kiss before heading off to the kitchen. He rattled around for ten minutes and returned carrying two plates.

She turned on her side and rose up on one elbow over hers. "Is it getting any better out?"

"No, angel, it isn't. Can't you hear that wind? About as bad as I've seen it for awhile."

"Then how did you get *back*?"

"The worst of it hit after we landed. It comes up so fast sometimes you don't know whether to do something or not. And you think *I'm* crazy? We had a passenger."

"You're kidding. Who?"

"Not sure. Some woman knitting with one needle, I'd say. I was a little too busy to look at her real close, you know?"

"But you knew it was a woman."

"Oh, hell, Sophie, I think I know a woman when I see one. But I couldn't prove it, if that's what you mean. Why you asking?"

She shook her head. "Just curious what could be so important that somebody would take a chance like that." She reached over to set her plate on the coffee table. "I'm so cold. I want a bath," she whined.

"Well, I'll run you a bath and take you up there," he said, gathering up plates and utensils. "Try Mike Hatton again."

"You'll come too, won't you?" she pleaded.

"Don't want much, do you?"

"What do you mean?"

"You want me to lie around in the bathtub with you and then leave you alone."

"Why do you have to leave me alone?"

He huffed in disbelief and touched her forehead. "Because, angel, you got a crack on the head."

She tilted her head and considered. "So, what do I have to think about?"

"Oh, hell," he grumbled and wandered off. She heard the tap running in the kitchen sink and then his footsteps on the stair and water gurgling in the tub overhead, and she was seized by a sudden irrational fear, as though someone was waiting in the shadows to finish what he had started. She was on the verge of calling for Carl when he reappeared and gathered her up off the sofa.

"Mm, the radio," she smiled, as he settled her back against him in the tub. "I'd forgotten I brought it."

"I hope you don't mind. I thought it might help you relax." He reached around and ran his hands over her in soapy circles.

"No, I don't mind. It's nice," she whispered sleepily. "So, you're staying then?"

"I'm staying," he droned.

"Carl?"

"What, angel?" He soaked a wash cloth and squeezed warm water over her.

"Do you think it was an attempted robbery? Because it was dark, and maybe somebody thought there was no one here?"

"Whew. I don't know. Maybe. Makes as much sense as someone deliberately wanting to hurt you."

"But you don't think so, *do* you?"

"Sophie, I don't know what I think. I mean, the idea of somebody trying to—"

"To kill me?"

"Yeah. It's too fantastic. People don't get murdered here," he said shortly. "Now let's get dried off and get you snuggled into some pajamas or whatever you wear."

"Oh, do we have to?" She twisted around and ran her hand over his chest. "Carl, I want to be close to you."

"I know, honey. You're tired and scared and hurt." He reached for a towel and bundled her into it.

"It's not just that."

"I know that," he said, kneading her shoulders. "But I'd be a selfish son of a bitch to do what I really want to. So we'll go sit by the fire and watch some TV, huh? You have a little TV, right? I carried it in for you." She nodded. "That's what we'll do then. And Sophie? We'll get this straightened out. It'll be fine."

"All right," she smiled, and wriggled into a pair of pajamas and her terry robe.

"Let's see if we've got any reception," he said, pulling a blanket over her on the sofa and turning on the TV to a menu of fuzz and static. "Damn. Got some cards? We could play poker." He settled another log on the fire and flopped down on the floor with his back against the sofa.

"I think I have—"

They both froze, staring first at one another for confirmation, then toward the back door. There could be no doubt. Someone was trying to get in. Sophie gasped as Carl leaned across to reach into the pocket of the coat he'd tossed over a chair and pulled out an automatic pistol. He put a finger to his lips in warning and stole into the kitchen, Sophie creeping along behind him. He steadied the pistol and flung open the door.

"Crow!" she screamed. "Carl, it's Crow!" Clumps of ice clung here and there to the thick black fur, and he sank down onto the floor and whimpered. "Oh, lord!" She ran to the living room and snatched up a blanket. "Bring him by the fire."

Carl hefted the big dog and placed him near the hearth. "What the hell do you suppose he's doing out in this? And how did he get *here*? Makes no friggin' sense! Joe would never let him run loose, and especially not in this."

"What's that on his nose?" Both her voice and her hand trembled as she reached down to touch him. "Blood. Carl, it's blood."

But Carl had already begun his examination. "I can't find anything. He doesn't seem to be hurt."

"Nooo," she began to wail, and stumbled backward ashen and quaking against the sofa.

"Calm down," he demanded, grasping her by the shoulders. "Sit here while I call Joe." He turned and sprinted up the steps two at a time, Sophie clambering up awkwardly behind him and clinging to the doorframe. He dialed and held his breath.

Sophie watched. Too long. It was taking too long, and panic rose in her throat.

"No answer." Carl shook his head. "I'll try Mike Hatton again," he said grimly.

"It's too late," she cried, as Crow raised his muzzle toward the ceiling below them and sent up a plaintive howl.

CHAPTER 8

Mike Hatton looked silly and uncomfortable perched precariously, all two hundred twenty pounds of him, on the arm of Sophie's chair, running his fingers along the front edge of the Russian trooper hat in his lap. She wondered why he did not simply sit in the chair.

"What makes you so certain it was an accident?" she mumbled around her knuckles. She sat huddled, feet tucked up beside her, at one end of the sofa and stared into the fire.

"Well, ma'am, there were no signs of forced entry. And from where I found him—bottom of the stairs—it was pretty obvious he'd slipped and fallen down the stairs."

"Was his neck broken?"

"No, ma'am, he hit his head on the bottom step and cracked his skull. But I don't believe I'm really at liberty to be talking to you about this. I'm here in my official capacity to investigate your assault."

"And what about Crow?"

"What about him?"

"How did he get out?"

"Well, now, I don't know, Ms."—he glanced down at his notepad—"West-en-ra. I imagine Joe let him out to do his business and then fell down the stairs before he could let the dog back in. But like I said—"

"What about the blood on his muzzle?"

He shook his head in Carl's direction, the epithet "Women!" understood, and turning back to Sophie, said with exaggerated patience, "Well, I expect he probably hurt himself somehow out in that storm, don't you? Maybe scraped his nose trying to get back in the house."

"Mr. Hatton, don't you find it a startling coincidence that in a single day someone should have broken in and hit me in the back of the head, and that Joe Wisdom should have died in his own home, from blunt force trauma to the back of the head?"

"And just what are you suggesting, ma'am, that there's a crazed killer on the island blundering around in a blizzard and attacking people for no good reason? Now, I'm mighty sorry that you got bumped on the head, and I promise you I will find the culprit responsible. But I have to think that was a botched robbery attempt that was interrupted by Carl's timely arrival."

"An attempted robbery, Mr. Hatton? Do you think it's more likely then for somebody to be, as you put it, 'blundering around in a blizzard' to commit *burglary*? It seems pretty clear to me that somebody tried to kill me and *did* kill Joe Wisdom, *and* used the storm as the perfect cover."

"And I'm telling *you* that whoever it was broke in here—and I'll find them—wasn't trying to kill you. No disrespect, ma'am, but hell, you don't kill somebody by brainin' 'em with a book! And like I said, I can't *discuss* this with you."

"Look, Mike," interjected Carl, "Sophie's had a pretty nasty fall and a pretty bad scare. And she'd just met Joe and all ..."

"Well, I know that, Carl, and I'm real sorry. I'm real sorry," he repeated to Sophie. "And I grant you it seems like a pretty strange coincidence. But that's just what it *is*, a coincidence. I mean, why the hell would anybody wanna murder Joe Wisdom?"

"Why would anybody want to murder me?" she asked stubbornly.

"That's just my point," replied Mike Hatton with growing irritation. "Somebody probably figured, here's a well-to-do woman living alone, probably got money in the house—"

"Does that sort of thing happen often here?"

"Well, of course not!" His face went florid, and his official demeanor hovered on the brink of an unprofessional outburst. "Now, unless you have something to add to your own report, I'll be on my way," he said, springing up off the chair arm and slapping his hat against his thigh. He stopped and turned back to Sophie with a sigh. "Look, Ms. Westenra, I don't blame you for being upset. I'm frankly embarrassed that a thing like this should happen in my jurisdiction, I am. And for what it's worth, there will be an autopsy once we can fly poor old Joe over to the mainland. But they're not gonna find anything suspicious. So I'm gonna get right on this other business, and if you think of anything else, you just call me."

"Thank you, officer," she said quietly, as Carl offered Mike Hatton his hand. "There's just one more thing. What time was Joe killed?"

"Now, there you go again with the 'killed.' Didn't I just tell you—"

"All right, if it's a question of semantics, then what time did he die?"

"You don't quit, do you?" he asked, his neck stretching like a turtle's, before he turned a look on Carl that said "*No* woman is that good in the sack."

"Please, Mr. Hatton. Can you at least tell me whether he died before or after I was attacked? *Please*."

He rested his knuckles on his hips and stared her in the eyes like an alpha dog. "Absolutely not. It would be against policy. Now, good night to you. Carl."

"I'll be here for the time being if you need me, Mike."

Mike Hatton's eyebrow rose as he glanced from Carl to Sophie, but he nodded and headed toward the door. "Oh, and I suppose I'd better take Crow, though lord knows what's gonna happen to him."

"Why can't he stay here, or is there some policy prohibiting that too?" Sophie asked curtly.

"Ya know, ma'am, you don't help your cause any with your attitude."

"What cause would that be, Mr. Hatton? Ever since I arrived here, I've been met with suspicion, not to mention being the object of gossip and now assault."

Mike Hatton opened his mouth to speak, but glanced at Carl and reconsidered. He let out an exasperated sigh instead. "Ma'am, I'm gonna allow as how you've had a bad experience you ought not to have had and leave it at that. If you want to keep Crow here for the time being, I don't expect anybody'd have a problem with that." Just as he was about to tug the door shut securely behind him, he paused with his hand on the knob and shot the sofa a stealthy glance. "Before."

Carl watched as he jammed the hat down onto his head and struggled against the wind to reach the SUV with the official emblem on the doors. "You know, Sophie, Mike's a good guy. He's trying to help."

"I know that," she said impatiently. "But he's not looking at this rationally!"

"Rationally? Look, it's like I told you. People don't get murdered on the island."

"That's exactly what I mean! It's not a logical point of view, it's an *island* point of view, and even *you* have it, Carl!"

"Look, angel, there wouldn't be any reason for anybody to kill Joe Wisdom. He's got no enemies. He's about as harmless—"

"That's exactly what he said."

"*What*?" he scowled in confusion.

"Joe." She gazed up at him, her expression calm and disengaged. "He said that nobody took much notice of him, that he wasn't a threat to anyone."

"*Exactly.*"

"Only *then* he said, 'One hears things.'"

"Aw, come on now, honey. He was probably trying to impress you. You know how some people are—try to make themselves sound important by letting on that they know secrets about other people."

"He didn't strike me as that type at all. And maybe he really *did* know something." She reached down to stroke Crow's big, square head, wishing she could know what *he'd* seen.

"What do you mean, Sophie?"

"He's hungry," she replied, untangling herself and padding off to the kitchen for the remainder of the beef stroganoff. She brought the pan back and placed it in front of the dog, who gulped the food and licked the pan.

"What do you mean?" repeated Carl. "What do you think he knew?" She gave her head a sullen shake and patted Crow's shoulder. "Come on, don't clam up. Tell me what you think Joe Wisdom knew that would get him killed and you attacked."

"I don't know," she moaned wearily. "He warned me."

"*Warned* you? About what?" He sank down next to her on the sofa and grasped her by the arm.

"He told me a story about Crystal—"

"*Crystal* again," he said angrily.

"—about Crystal and a man who died. And then he told me to be careful."

Carl lowered his head to rest on the heel of one hand and closed his eyes. "Jesus, we've been over this, Sophie. And you can't honestly believe I killed Joe Wisdom and tried to kill you. *Can* you, after …"

"*You*? What are you talking about? And what do you mean we've been over this?"

"You told me you understood about Crystal and me—and Gary Coffey." Dread crept over him, drawing the blood away from his face as he saw Sophie's incomprehension. "Sophie, you told me Joe Wisdom told you about it."

"About you and Crystal, about your relationship. But who is Gary Coffey?" she asked in bewilderment.

"Oh, Christ," he groaned.

"Carl?" She placed a hand on his arm, as much to ground herself as to establish a connection to him. She had thought she'd just begun to make some sense of things, that this had all been about Peter and her, and that Crystal Holliday was somehow at the bottom of it.

"You really *don't* know, do you?" He took a deep breath. "Gary Coffey was the man I killed." If he'd thought Sophie would spring away from him in terror, he was surprised when her grip tightened on his arm instead. Her face was pale, her eyes too luminous in the firelight. "It was an accident, Sophie," he choked.

But that meant … something else entirely. She looked around her as though she was suddenly no longer part of the scene. *That* was why he'd been so adamant in asking whether it mattered to her. It wasn't his affair with Crystal that he'd been concerned about, but the fact that he'd killed someone. Her head began to throb, and the skin around her eyes felt tight and dry as tissue. "Tell me, Carl. Please," she begged.

"All right," he said dully, as he saw it all slip away. "I was living on the island then. I'd finished the cabin the previous spring. And," he hesitated, "Crystal and I had been seeing each other. I was stupid, Sophie. I guess I thought it was serious, or at least I thought *she* was serious, and that that somehow obligated me, you know?

"Anyway, come to find out she'd been slipping off to the mainland with Gary Coffey, and eventually, they didn't even bother to do that. I felt like a friggin' idiot. You know what people are like here—the looks, the gossip."

"Why didn't you just—"

"Break it off? That's what I should have done. She told me she was pregnant, and that turned out to be a lie, but by that time, it didn't make much difference." He turned aside and dragged slow fingers along his mouth. "One night I took her to Hoppers—bar on the other side of the island. We'd been arguing, and then Gary walked in. I was loaded and I went after him. Couldn't have been more than three or four punches thrown. Last one, he fell backwards over a stool and hit his head against the edge of the bar."

Tragedy, Joe had said, and that's what Sophie saw in his face now. That, and his horror as he watched, in slow motion, the man crumple to the floor, the ponderous flow, like lava, thick … "It was an accident," she whispered.

"Yeah, I never meant to kill him. But when I saw him lying there, everything changed in a split second, and I saw what a fool I'd been and the things I could've done instead. So then it wasn't an accident, and I *was* responsible. And that's how the law saw it too. I did five years for manslaughter."

"Oh, Carl." Her fingertips brushed along the line of his jaw. "Joe said it had ended in tragedy. I suppose if I thought that was an overly dramatic way to refer to a broken love affair, I didn't think to question it, or him. Now I know what he meant," she said softly and touched her fingers to his lips.

"You're not shocked, or afraid of me?"

"No," she answered, leaning her head against his shoulder. "How many of us make foolish choices and allow ourselves to be hurt and used? What Joe Wisdom would have called one of the regular acts of human drama. Oh, poor you." She turned her head to nuzzle against his neck.

"So that's it," he sighed, reaching over to touch her hair, "a stupid bar fight over the kind of woman who's never worth it. I just wanted to forget all about it and her. One reason why, when I got out last year, I rented an apartment on the mainland, even though I'd heard she left."

"And now she's come back, and so have you."

"I came back because of you. You believe that, don't you?"

"Yes."

"Good. Because there's nothing between Crystal and me, and never could be. She didn't just leave the island, Sophie. She left to be with a man she was having an affair with, a married man."

Sophie turned a weary gaze on him. "I know."

"You *know*?" He pushed aside what his gut was telling him. "Then you can see, can't you, that there's no reason for her to want to hurt you, certainly not on my account."

"On your account?" She smiled bitterly. "Maybe not."

"What are you saying, that she'd have another reason to want to hurt you?" His gut was roiling now like the lake in a normal November, and gave him a feeling of general malaise.

"You asked me about my husband, and I told you we weren't very happy. There were a lot of reasons." *The black eyes, the sprained limbs, the bumps and abrasions—this was not the first goose egg she'd had on her forehead, not the first time she'd been the victim of violence.* "Among those reasons," she continued, as though recounting, like Shaharazad, a fiction, "were his affairs. Oh, Crystal was not the first, but she *was* the last, you see."

"*What*? Sophie, I don't understand."

"Colossal irony, isn't it?" she smiled. "Did you ever hear a better?"

"You knew that and you came here?" He turned a troubled look on her.

"No. Oh, no. Don't you see? That's the irony. When I learned she'd been your lover, I thought I knew all there was to know."

"Then how—"

"Can't you guess, Carl? That's what Joe Wisdom knew, what he told me only today. And what, I'm convinced, cost him his life."

"But that's fantastic, Sophie. It makes no sense. None of this makes any sense."

She sighed. "There's more. Crystal was the last of Peter's conquests only because he died. That's why Crystal came back here. And why I came too," she said quietly. "You see, I was suspected of killing my husband."

Carl pressed his fingers hard into his forehead and peered over at Sophie. "You didn't know anything about … Crystal?"

"No. I came here to escape the very suspicion and gossip that I've—that we've both—come up against anyway."

"That's about the strangest story I've ever heard. I don't know what to say, but I still don't see what this has to do with Joe Wisdom. I still see an accident, just like Mike Hatton. Help me here, Sophie. Who would benefit from keeping Joe quiet about what he knew—besides you?"

"I see," she said coldly. "But I didn't kill Joe Wisdom, Carl. And I certainly didn't hit myself in the back of the head."

"Oh, no, honey, I didn't mean that!" He gathered her into his arms and kissed her face. "But that's just my point. If not you, then who?"

The wind rattled the house from every side at once, as though it wanted to smash and tear and destroy it and all within, and Sophie cowered into the corner of the sofa. She peeked up at the clock on the mantel and announced, "After midnight. It's Halloween, and I never carved my pumpkins." She began to cry, and when Carl pulled her close, sobbed into his chest.

"Listen to me now, angel. It's been a miserable day. I'm gonna bundle up and take Crow out, and then we're gonna bunk down here in front of the fire, all of us. And you and I are gonna hold each other close, and we're all gonna sleep and forget for now, you and me and Crow." Crow thumped a heavy tail against the floor and whimpered.

Chapter 9

Sophie groaned awake and rolled over, reaching blindly for the phone. It wasn't there, but that made no difference, since Carl had already answered it. He knelt next to her in the pile of blankets and handed her a steaming mug.

"How's your head, angel?"

She leaned up on one elbow and smiled drowsily. "Better. A little sore," she demonstrated with a touch and a wince. "How long have you been up?"

"Awhile. Crow's been out, and he was hungry, but since there's no dog food, we had oatmeal and toast. I saved you some, didn't want to wake you."

"Oh, dog food. We have to get some somehow," she said, stroking the big muzzle that appeared suddenly in her face.

"I'll get some. That's why I was just about to wake you when the phone rang."

"Oh, yes. Who was it?"

"Sam Coombs. Snow's stopped and we've gotta get out and clean up this mess so people can get their businesses open. And if you give me a list, I'll stop at the market soon as they get it open. Dog food and whatever else you need."

"Oh, Carl, I don't want to sit here like an invalid while you do everything."

"I don't mind. No sense in us both traipsing around in the cold and snow, and I have to go out anyway. Besides," he smiled, "you *are* kind of an invalid."

She looked up at him uneasily as it all came back to her, the whole previous surreal day. "What happens now?" It had become a familiar refrain.

He rubbed her shoulder. "I guess we take stock. But there's time, and first things first. Power's restored and we'll get things moving again. We can talk when I get back. Shouldn't be more than a few hours, but, Sophie," he said earnestly, "while I'm gone, I want you to keep the doors locked and Crow by you.

Don't open the door for anybody till I get back, unless it would be Mike Hatton. And," he added, reaching toward the lamp table, "you take this." He laid the pistol in her hand.

She blanched. "No, Carl. I don't know anything—"

"You slide the safety off like this—no, you watch, Sophie," he insisted, as she tried to give it back. "If anybody tries to get in here, you slide the safety off, aim and pull the trigger, you understand me? Now, I don't know whether somebody killed Joe Wisdom or not, but I know somebody attacked you, and that's all I'm gonna worry about for right now. Now take it." With a reluctant nod, she placed it within reach on the low coffee table. "Good. Oh, and I'm gonna stop out at my place and pick up some clean clothes and things. You're all right with this, aren't you? Me staying here, I mean."

"Of course," she smiled and caught his hand. "I would have wanted you to anyway."

"Yeah, well, I was hoping to move you out there because it's not so close to the center of things. But that's exactly why I can't now. Too secluded. I wouldn't feel safe leaving you alone there. Not now."

"I wouldn't have believed it, Carl. Wouldn't have believed that things could get worse for me here. Or better. I just thought it would be quiet and uncomplicated. Foolish, I guess, since we drag our baggage around with us."

"Are you sorry you came here?"

She squeezed his hand in response to the unasked question, and recalled his touch and his whispered breath in her ear and the way it felt to be with him. *The walls and the furniture arcing down to disappear beneath her, the stabbing pain at the back of her ribcage, clawing at the back of the sofa to pull her way up. Peter's face, so still and pale ...* "No, I'm not sorry," she smiled. "Now, hadn't you better be going so you can get back? Poor Crow is going to want dinner."

Carl slipped into his coat and pulled his gloves out of the pockets. "Right. Now, remember what I told you." She nodded as he leaned down to kiss her cheek. "And come and bolt the door behind me."

She waved as he backed the truck around and plowed down the drive, then hauled the bread machine out of a cupboard and started a loaf of whole wheat before going upstairs to dress. She could already smell the yeast when she came back down and pulled out the crockpot. She had rooted through the refrigerator and cupboards and assembled the ingredients for her potluck dish before it occurred to her to wonder whether the Halloween party had been or would be cancelled, in deference to either the weather or Joe Wisdom's untimely demise.

She reached across the counter to plug in the crockpot, but the hand holding the plug hovered in mid-air as she heard it: the heavy buoy bell windchime was clanging sonorously in the tree behind the house. She sidled up to the door and peered through the window just as a bundled figure, its face obscured by a fur-trimmed hood, lumbered up the steps. She shrank back in terror, and only then remembered the pistol that sat on a table in the living room. As she turned to flee, the storm door swung open and the intruder began to bang on the inner door.

"Sophie! You in there?"

She let out a gasp, turned the lock and yanked open the door. "Bea!"

"Sophie, you all right? Girl, you look like you seen a ghost or something," said Bea Baskin, stomping the snow off her boots before stepping inside and shutting the door behind her.

"You startled me."

"Aw, you're a little on edge, I expect, aren't you?" She stretched her neck toward the coffeemaker on the counter. "You sit down, and I'll pour the coffee." Sophie got out the creamer and sat down at the table. "Don't suppose anybody would blame you." Bea placed two mugs on the table, threw her hood back and unzipped her parka before flopping down in the chair opposite Sophie. "Understandable, I guess." She took a sip of coffee. "Lord, it's cold out. Way too early for this."

"Yes, it came at rather a bad time," Sophie said quietly.

"Mm," grunted Bea, taking another swig of coffee. "Some kind of bad luck, all right. Never mind what happened to you, and not to mention what happened to poor Joe Wisdom. I'd call it all uncanny, but that's just what life *is* like, innit?"

"I wouldn't like to think so." Nor would she bother to wonder how Bea had found out about the previous day's unfortunate events.

"Oh, I mean in a general sense, you know. Things are always happening. But I grant you so many things don't usually happen at one time here. That's why I'd call it all uncanny."

"And yet you don't really seem surprised. Still, I suppose burglaries occur everywhere, and accidents happen every day."

"Burglaries? Accidents? Pah!" spat Bea, and slurped at the edge of the mug.

"That is Officer Hatton's official take on things."

Yeah, I know it, and he might even believe that. But I doubt it. He may come across as a Barney Fyfe, and I don't think he can get inside the criminal mind, as you'd say, but he can put two and two together and come up with four."

If Bea Baskin had come fishing for information, she appeared in no hurry to arrive at her point, and to Sophie's annoyance, she found herself hoping that Bea might impart to her what she felt certain the other woman knew. "Would you like more coffee?"

"Thanks. But I'll get it while you get that crockpot going. Halloween party, I expect."

"It's still on then?"

"Long as we don't get another white-out. People wouldn't see the point in cancelling and disappointing the kiddies because of an accident and an attempted robbery."

"But I thought you said—"

"Long as that's the official take, that'll be the response. The *public* response, mind you."

"And privately?"

"Privately?" She gave her head a quick shake and set down her mug. "You know, this island's like a beehive is what. And I know, 'cause I've been here most of my life. Married George Baskin in 1960, when I was seventeen years old. Island's been home to me ever since. When he drowned ten years ago, I thought of moving back to the mainland, but nah! this is home now. There. Speaking of accidents, but then, that really *was* one.

"Anyhow, like I was saying, the island is like a beehive, with a rhythm and a routine of its own."

"What about all the tourists who come in the summer?"

"That's part of the rhythm and routine. Been happening as long as anybody can remember. But every year, it ends, and they go away. And then the hive is quiet. Things still go on, but they're routine and under the surface, inside the hive, so to speak. Well, like the Halloween party.

"But sometimes something will come along to stir up the hive, you know? Something that upsets the rhythm and routine." She paused to gulp at the coffee.

"Is that what I am, what I've done? Upset the hive? What, because I haven't lived here all my life?" Sophie asked sulkily, pouring beans into the pot. "You were obviously able to move here and be accepted, and I imagine a lot of others are, as well."

"Not so many as you'd think. 'Sides, I came before recorded history," she gurgled. "But I married an islander, too, and I'd spent quite a bit of time here, visiting my sister, who'd moved here when she got married. How I met George, in fact. All kinds of connections. But naw, it's not that."

"Then what is it?"

"How you choose to relate to folks, I suppose. And what folks in particular you choose to relate *to*," she replied, turning an avian eye on Sophie.

"I see," Sophie said coolly, arranging the last of the ingredients in the ceramic vat. "Joe said something very like that, about whether one wanted to fit in."

"Did he now? When you went to see him, I suppose. Strange, that. Why, it must have happened not more than a few minutes after you left his place."

"I didn't kill Joe Wisdom." She placed the lid on the crockpot and turned the knob to High.

"Well, course you didn't. Who said anything about you killing anybody?" She lifted Joe Wisdom's book and hefted it in one hand. "And you sure couldn't have conked yourself in the back of the head with this, could you?"

"No," answered Sophie, surprised in spite of herself at the extent of the island grapevine, though not by the fact that "official" information should be available to Bea, but not to her. Unwilling to discuss with her the particulars of Joe Wisdom's death, Mike Hatton had apparently had no such reservations about sharing the details of her assault with the community at large.

"Yep, I heard you had Crow over here," nodded Bea, as the dog padded into the kitchen to drink from the mixing bowl Sophie had surrendered as a water bowl for him. "It's like one of those amazing stories you hear about, animals finding their way places they shouldn't be able to and such. Odd how he should have ended up over here, what with all the houses between Joe's and yours."

"We thought so too." Sophie cringed inwardly as she realized she had inadvertently crossed the line between private knowledge and public acknowledgement which Bea had so particularly mentioned, thus making her relationship with Carl a legitimate subject of inquiry.

"Lucky for you Carl happened by when he did, all right."

"I think he was concerned that I might not be aware of how dangerous ... the *weather* can be on the island at this time of year."

Bea Baskin slouched back in her chair and frowned. "Sophie, I wish I knew what to tell you, I really do. But I don't know if this is something you brought with you or something that found you here."

"But you think I'm somehow responsible for Joe Wisdom's death, don't you, you and everyone else?"

"Naw, you're not to blame. But do I think it's some almighty coincidence that he's dead and you're clobbered?" Her head jerked in a kind of troll-tic gesture that dragged one shoulder up with it into a shrug.

"I suppose I should leave then," Sophie said petulantly.

Bea forced a breath through pursed lips. "I wonder if you even could now." She leaned forward and patted Sophie's hand. "Naw, I don't think you should go. But I do think you should be careful."

"Of what, though? Of *whom*?"

But Bea Baskin only shook her head, and hauling herself up out of the chair, placed her mug in the sink and zipped up her parka. "Maybe the strangest thing about all this," she muttered, "is that Carl Jacobsen should be hovering around protecting you like a mother hen. But maybe not."

Before Sophie could press her for an explanation, she was gone, trudging off through the banks of snow, across the backs of neighboring lots toward home.

"Was that Bea Baskin?" scowled Carl, as he climbed down from the truck and bounded up the steps.

"Yes, it was. But you're back early," she smiled.

"Now, Sophie, didn't I tell you not to let anybody in here while I was gone?"

"Oh, Carl, it was Bea—" He set his mouth obstinately. "Yes, you did say that, but—"

"What did she want?"

"I don't really know. See how I was or what she could find out? What's it matter? She's a busybody. But how did you get finished so soon?"

"I'm not." He dropped a large canvas bag on the floor. "I went to get some things from my place like I told you. Somebody broke in there sometime between yesterday and this morning."

"*What*? Did they take anything?"

"Not that I could tell. They broke out a pane of glass in the back door and let themselves in."

Sophie sank heavily against the counter. "But *why*?"

"It looked to me like somebody was just trying to get in out of the storm."

"Oh" she moaned, "what next?"

"I don't know, but that's why I want you to do what I tell you."

"It's her, it's Crystal. It has to be." She crossed her arms and began to pace fretfully.

"Sophie, what is *with* you?"

"Why not? How do you know she didn't break into your house? Maybe she thought you were there. Did you ever think of that?"

"No, I didn't," he said through gritted teeth.

"Well, maybe you should!"

"And maybe *you* oughta get off her," he said angrily.

"Why are you *defending* her?" she turned on him and shouted.

"All right, that's it!" He wrenched open the door. "I have to get to the hardware store and get a piece of glass for the door. I'll be back as soon as I can."

She grasped his arm. "Carl, I'm sorry." He turned back to her. "I'm sorry."

His head dropped to one side, and he eyed her indulgently. "Come here," he said, taking her by the hand and pulling her along to the living room. He flopped down on the sofa and drew her down beside him. "Okay, now tell me calmly why you think Crystal is behind this."

She swallowed. "All right. Joe was killed because of what he knew, I'm convinced of it. Now, what did he know? He knew about you and Crystal and the man you killed."

"Everybody here knows about that."

"I didn't. And he also knew about Crystal and Peter and what happened to Peter. And he knew I was Peter's wife. And I don't expect *that* was common knowledge here."

"So? You don't kill somebody over gossip, Sophie."

"She saw me leaving Joe's place. Suppose she'd found out who I am and that Joe had told me who *she* is. Don't you see that Joe would have to be silenced to keep him from telling anybody else what he knew?"

"Why? Isn't that a little melodramatic?"

"*Is* it? The way Joe told the story, Crystal wanted to marry Peter, but he wouldn't leave me." She wagged her head in frustration. "God, you don't know how much I wish he had! But suppose she'd killed Peter. Crime of passion, who knows? But once she found out who I am, she must have been afraid I would suspect her of having done it and perhaps shared my suspicions with Joe. So she'd have two reasons for wanting me dead, revenge and self-preservation." She hesitated. "And then there's you."

"You're not gonna start that again."

"You asked, so hear me out. Suppose she's never forgiven you for what you did and how it changed her life. What better way to pay you back than to do something similar and kill me? Well, you see, don't you? It's perfect. Talk about killing two birds with one stone!"

"Sophie, it's crazy!"

"Is it? And there's another possibility. Suppose she wants you back," she said quietly.

"Now that's insane! You don't kill somebody—" He shut his mouth abruptly.

"Out of jealousy?" she asked gently.

"Look, Sophie," he sighed, "it's been too long."

"Are you sure? If nothing else, I imagine that from her point of view, you robbed her of Gary Coffey, and I kept her from having Peter. So we owe her, you in one way, me in another."

"It's too far-fetched. But even if it wasn't, why should she break into my house?"

"Because she hoped you'd be there? Because she wanted to be where she'd spent time with you? I don't know. God, Carl, maybe she doesn't know herself! But that's the point, it works any way you look at it."

"Naw, naw," he shook his head obstinately. "She may be a lot of things, but she's not a cold-blooded killer."

"Neither are you."

"How could she have done it? Physically, I mean?"

"Carl," she answered impatiently, "look what happened to me! A blow to the back of the head, certainly not forceful enough to kill me. I got hurt slamming into the floor. But what do you think would have happened if you hadn't arrived? And Joe—well, he wouldn't have been expecting anything. And you mark my words. When the autopsy report comes back, there will be no injuries consistent with a fall down the stairs. He was tripped or pushed backwards to fall against the step."

He sat mute, dragging his fingers back and forth across his forehead as if to work the information in and make sense of it. "Got this all figured out, don't you? But, Sophie honey, it's just too unbelievable. I need to think," he said, rising abruptly and heading for the door. "I'll be back as soon as I get the window fixed."

"Carl, don't forget—"

"The Halloween party? Not likely."

"I meant the dog food."

CHAPTER 10

"You're sure Crow will be all right while we're gone?" Sophie asked anxiously, as Carl helped her up into the truck and settled the pot on her lap.

"I doubt anybody'd wanna kill Crow, since if he knows anything, he can't very well tell us."

"Be serious."

"I am," he said, climbing up into the driver's seat and turning down the drive. "Look, even if somebody wanted to break in to look for something—though God knows what—they wouldn't be likely to do it now. Most of the community will be at this hoe-down," he said distastefully, "and those who aren't will have to be accounted for."

"Carl, you asked me if I was sorry I came here, and I'm not. But are *you*? Sorry I came, I mean."

"Now is not a real good time to ask me that, angel. Talk about running the friggin' gauntlet."

"But wouldn't it have been worse for us not to go, especially now?"

"I doubt it. I imagine they already think one or both of us are guilty. Either I killed Joe and clocked you to make it look good, or you killed Joe, and I clocked you anyway to divert suspicion. Damn," he mumbled, turning into the library parking lot and shutting off the engine.

"Carl," she said, placing a hand over his, "thank you. I know how hard this must be for you."

"Naw," he smiled and touched her cheek, "be a damn sight harder without you. But then, I wouldn't *be* here without you either." He took a deep breath. "Okay, let's go into the arena."

The door to the community center at the back of the library was flanked by bunches of storm-damaged cornstalks that drooped over frostbitten jack-o-lanterns whose toothy grins looked more frozen than usual, and Sophie instinctively huddled closer to Carl as he pulled open the door for her.

"Well, you made it all right." Bea Baskin was upon them. "Pretty good turnout, all things considered," she said heartily. "Nila!" she hollered over her shoulder. "Look who's here!"

"Sophie," smiled Nila Celestine, "I'm glad you felt up to coming. I felt just terrible when I heard what had happened, to you and," she lowered her voice, "to poor Joe, and all in one day. Well, let me take this over for you," she said, relieving Sophie of the pot. "What's in it, hon? Smells wonderful."

"Barbecue beans and sausage."

"Hello, Carl. This *is* a treat. We don't normally get to see you at these functions," she smiled, and whisked the pot off to a table before he'd had a chance to respond with more than a grimace. He shot Sophie a glance that looked like Purgatory.

"Well, come on, come on," resumed Bea Baskin, nudging them toward a table, as a five year-old goblin plowed into Carl. "Come get some food. Look, here's Sam and Mattie." Sam shook Carl's hand around Mattie's mumbled greeting. "And that old fart over there is Patch McKay that I told you about." She settled Sophie into a chair, pulled out another for Carl and plopped down into a third.

"So," Sophie smiled reticently, "how many people do you think are here?"

"Well," replied Bea, scanning the room, "close to a hundred, I'd say. Like I said, good turnout. Course, some of the older folks didn't make it. Too hard for them to get around in the snow and cold, poor souls. But we'll see they get some of the goodies just the same."

"Evening, Carl," nodded Mike Hatton as he sauntered to the table. "Beer?"

"Yeah, thanks, Mike," he said gratefully.

"Ms. Westenra?"

"No, thank you, Mr. Hatton," she smiled tightly.

Mike Hatton returned a moment later, and handing Carl a bottle, turned a chair around and straddled it backward. "Flew Joe Wisdom to the mainland today."

"Aw, Mike," growled Bea Baskin, "now you're not gonna start talking shop. Lord, man, this is supposed to be a party, even if it *is* for Halloween. And I think we all need a breather," she nodded toward the bruise on Sophie's forehead. Sophie looked down at her hands uncomfortably.

"All right, all right, Bea. Just thought I'd mention that is all."

"Well, I'm gonna make up a couple plates for you two," announced Bea, pushing herself out of the chair.

"Oh, Bea—" Sophie began to protest, her gaze following the other woman's broad back. It came to rest a few feet away on Crystal Holliday, who studied them intently from an adjoining table.

"Aw, hell," muttered Carl, as Sophie stiffened beside him. She slipped a hand under the table and squeezed his thigh. It made no discernible difference as Crystal made her resolute way to the table. "Shit."

"Hello, Ms. Westenra."

"Sophie, please. Good evening."

"Carl," she said with a frosty smile.

"Hello, Crystal," he said stonily.

"Sorry to hear what happened to you," she trained a chilly stare on Sophie, "and to poor Joe. Hard to believe he could have died like that, from falling down the stairs. I mean, there aren't even many stairs. But then you'd know that, since you've been to the house."

"*I* didn't really notice," Sophie smiled sweetly, as Carl leaned his forehead on his hand.

"Don't expect it much mattered." A man had edged his way toward the fringe of the group, older than Crystal Holliday, but otherwise so like her that Sophie could surmise at once their shared genes. Clearly another Holliday.

"All right, Mar," said Mike Hatton, extricating himself from the chair and putting out a hand, "we're not gonna talk about this now. Bea chewed my butt for bringing it up, and she was right. So let's just let it go."

"Yeah? Well, if somebody like that's got the gall to show their face among decent people, I guess I have the right to call 'em on it!"

"All right, Mar, I said that's enough!" Mike Hatton moved to grip the other man's arm.

"Somebody like *what,* Mar?" shouted Carl, springing to his feet and pushing back his jacket.

Sophie gasped as she saw the pistol tucked into his waistband. "Carl, let's just go!" she whispered urgently. "Please!"

He looked down into Sophie's desperate face, and glaring around the table, put an arm around her and hustled her toward the door.

Both their spines stiffened as they heard Mar Holliday call out behind them, "Suppose you know you're playing house with a murderer!"

They clambered up into the truck silently. Then, "Damn it!" Carl exploded, pounding the steering wheel.

"I wonder which one of us he meant," sighed Sophie.

"I don't expect *that* much matters!" He started the truck and screeched out of the lot, fishtailing onto the road.

By the time they'd reached the cottage, he had regained enough composure to pat Crow when he trotted out to the kitchen to greet them. Then he flung his coat over a chair and slumped onto the sofa.

Sophie scurried around the kitchen and joined him a few minutes later with two cups of coffee. "Carl?" she pleaded, snuggling against him. He ran a desultory hand along her cheek. "Let's leave."

"What?"

"Let's get out of here, off this stupid, stupid island. We'll take Crow and what few things we need and go. We can come back for the rest later, or not. Who cares? There's no reason we have to stay here. Oh, let's!"

"What would we do?" he asked indulgently, flicking at one of the diamonds that dangled from her ears. "You going to keep me in the fashion to which I'm not accustomed?"

"Oh, stop it. You can work anywhere. So can I. And I've been thinking about maybe starting a business of some kind."

"With your dead husband's money, angel?"

"Why not? I earned every cent of it," she answered coldly.

"Honey." He shook his head.

"Why not?" She put a hand on his shoulder and asked eagerly, "If you could do anything, what would it be? Boat repair business, marina? Pizza franchise?" she laughed. "Oh, please!"

He put his arms around her, and his lips brushed over hers. "All right, if that's what you want."

"What do *you* want?"

He grinned like a man who has dropped his toothbrush into a hotel toilet and found a rare coin in the bottom of the bowl. "Got mayonnaise?"

She fluttered her lashes and smiled. "Six jars."

He pulled her up off the sofa and carried her over his shoulder, laughing and squealing, up the stairs, tossing her onto the bed and climbing in next to her.

"Mmm, why are you over there?" she cooed, pulling him over on top of her.

They made love deliberately, exploring and caressing one another, subtle fingers in velvet places, retreating within each other, each of them intent on banishing from the other's consciousness all vestiges of any world outside themselves.

"They don't matter," she whispered, stroking his hair as he lay panting and depleted across her afterward. "And when we leave, we won't have to think of them again ever."

"Who?" he smiled lazily and snuggled in next to her for what remained of the night.

It was still dark when she shivered awake and found herself alone in the bed, both her nose and the top blanket cold to the touch. She groped for her robe and flung it around her, wincing with shock as her bare feet hit the floor. "Carl?" she called weakly, stumbling toward the top of the stairs.

"Down here, honey," he called up to her, appearing suddenly in the hall, his face vague and eerie in the light of the candle he carried.

She let out a sigh of relief and hurried down the stairs. "What's wrong? I'm so cold."

"Power's out again. I just got a small fire started. Come over here before you catch your death," he urged, pushing her along to the living room.

"Oh, no," she groaned when she saw it blowing in thick clumps against the window and settling into the corners of the frames. It reminded her of an old-fashioned Christmas card with cardinals perched on a branch or a candle burning on the sill.

"Yeah. I'm afraid we're not going to be making any great escape today, angel."

"Oh, Carl, no! This can't happen," she cried. Crow wandered in, tail wagging, and nuzzled next to her, and she put her face in the fur of his shoulder dejectedly. "Everything is ruined."

"Aw, honey, nothing's ruined. It's just postponed," he said, rubbing her shoulders. "Come on now. You sit here and stay warm while I get the damn generator fired up again."

Given little choice, she grabbed a quilt off the sofa, and pulling her knees up, sat huddled before the fire to wait for Carl's return. It was not many minutes before she saw light filtering in from the kitchen. She could smell the coffee brewing and hear the clatter of kibbles dropping into Crow's food dish, and she thought how strangely domestic a scene it was against a background of frost and death.

He placed a mug in her hands and turned on a small table lamp, then settled into the chair behind her as she faced the fire. "I've never seen storms like this so early."

"Honestly, Carl," she said, reaching up to take his hand, "I don't know how much more I can stand. I feel so isolated and claustrophobic. Without you here, or Crow, without any other life in the house but me, I think I'd lose my mind. So you see," she turned to look at him, "you were right to begin with when you pretty much told me I didn't belong here."

"Aw, Sophie honey, I was just trying to get a rise outta you. It's not you. This has been a crazy few days. But don't worry. This weather will clear out, and then so will we. Put this little pile of dirt and rock behind us."

"Do you mean it? You're not just saying it to humor me?"

"No. I mean it. Time to make a fresh start. For both of us. I've heard New Mexico is a nice place, and I thought I might like to go there. Course," he said, looking down at her hand as he held it, "I can't do that just yet. Still got a few months to go on my probation."

"Oh, gawd," she moaned, turning to rest her head on his knee. "It must have been awful for you."

"Huh," he smiled bitterly. "I won't go back." He stared off into the flames. "Time's a funny thing, Sophie. People go about their lives, go to work, drink beer, water their lawns, make love, shovel snow, and the seasons pass one into another without them even noticing, so they can't figure out how they got from the middle of winter to the middle of summer. But prison? In prison, every day has twenty-four hours exactly, all made up of the same number of minutes. And no matter what you're doing, somewhere in the back of your head, you're ticking off the seconds in each of those minutes like a goddamn metronome, each day you make it through bringing you one day closer to freedom."

"I think I understand," she said thoughtfully.

He stirred. "Light out now. Looks like it's let up some."

"Not much at all," she replied, her gaze following his to the window.

"I'll have to go back out."

"Oh, Carl, *no*."

But he wasn't listening, and untangling himself, he jumped up and made for the door, intersecting Crow's similar path. "Mike Hatton," he said, pulling open the door.

Sophie tucked her robe in around her as Officer Hatton stepped in and wiped his feet. "Good morning, Mr. Hatton. Please, sit down." She gestured toward the seat of the chair on whose arm he had perched two days earlier.

He looked uneasily from one to the other and did as he'd been invited, sinking down onto the chair seat this time, but still fiddling with his hat.

"Something wrong, Mike?" asked Carl.

"Afraid so. Seems Crystal Holliday's gone missing," he said to his hat.

"What do you mean 'missing'?" Sophie backed up and tumbled heavily into the chair opposite him.

"Just that. Bea said she never came home after the party."

"Bea Baskin? What's she got to do with this?"

"Crystal's been living with her aunt since she got back, same as before she left."

"Wait," Sophie said tremulously. "Are you saying Bea Baskin is Crystal Holliday's aunt?"

"Well, sure. Figured you knew that. Bea practically raised the girl after her mama ran off—some folks just aren't cut out for living on an island, you know?—and of course, her daddy died when she wasn't more than twelve or thirteen maybe."

Sophie sat stone silent, glancing warily toward Carl, who appeared lost in thought.

"So, Mike, are you delivering the news in person to the whole island?"

"No, Carl," said Mike Hatton, taking a nervous swat at his knee with his hat. "Look, this isn't easy for me. I like you, you know I do. But I represent the law here too."

"So, am I under arrest?"

"Course not. We don't even know a crime's been committed. But, Carl, I know you've got a gun. And *you* know you're not supposed to, and that—"

"It's mine." The two men turned a single astonished stare on Sophie.

"Sophie," hissed Carl.

"It is, it's mine. I got it for protection," she stammered, "since I was going to be living alone. But that was silly, because I don't know the first thing about them. So I asked Carl to keep it for me so I wouldn't accidentally shoot myself or someone else."

"It's yours," Mike Hatton said dubiously. Sophie nodded. "Well, Ms. Westenra, do you have it registered?"

"No. I meant to, but ..." On an impulse, she shrugged and smiled vacuously.

Mike Hatton looked from one to the other and heaved an enormous sigh. "Well, then, Ms. *Westenra,* I think as soon as this blizzard lets up, you'd best come down to the police station and take care of that." He rose to leave and slapped his hat down onto his head.

"Yes, I'll do that, Mr. Hatton," she said, offering him her hand. "Thank you."

"Lord," he said with another sigh, "I don't know what the hell's come over this place. But," he turned back to them at the door, "I don't think anybody'd better be thinking about leaving anytime soon. Like anybody's going to," he groused, and disappeared into the storm.

CHAPTER 11

"Another game of Scrabble?" Carl slid his hands up along her arms and rubbed the back of her neck.

The blizzard had continued with only brief respites for the better part of three days. Or four. Sophie couldn't remember for certain. "Oh, no, please," she groaned. "I swear I see those tiles in my sleep. Carl," she leaned her head back against him, "I'm going out of my mind here. We might as well be in prison." She jammed her eyes shut and clapped a hand over her mouth. "I'm sorry."

"Naw, angel, it's okay. But I promise you this isn't jail, or we wouldn't be doing what we're doing most of the night," he laughed. "In fact, we wouldn't be together at all."

"Oh, you're right. I'm sorry. It's just … this is getting to me. I'm glad you're here, I am. But I just feel as though I'm holding my breath and waiting for something else to happen."

"Cabin fever, honey. Tell you what. Looks like it's not doing much more than piddling around right now, so we're gonna get bundled up and go for a walk."

"Oh, could we?" she asked hopefully.

"Well, of course! Do us all good to get out a little, especially Crow. He's a big dog, needs to get out. And he's been used to walking the whole island with Joe."

"I feel so guilty about Joe, Carl."

"Cut it out, Sophie. You're not responsible for what happened. Now, go get dressed, and let's get outta here for awhile. In fact, it might be a good idea to go to my place for a couple days even, look at four different walls for a change. But we can decide later. Go on now."

She turned to race up the stairs, but ran back long enough to throw her arms around his neck and kiss him. "I won't be a minute, I promise!" she beamed.

They picked their way with large, clumsy steps as best they could through the drifts, Carl gripping Sophie's arm to keep her from tumbling into an icy mound. But despite his best efforts, she slipped and came down hard on her back, pulling him down laughing with her. When they reached the road, it proved—thanks to the exertions of Carl and Sam Coombs and a number of others who had pitched in to help—clear and level by comparison, and Crow shook himself free of the snow that had caked on his underside and bounded across and down toward the frozen shoreline. Carl and Sophie scrambled after him, calling to him to make certain he did not wander onto the brittle ice, as they stood on the bank above the rocks. The gusts swirled in from the north and west, tossing handfuls of wet snow into Sophie's startled face and slapping her cheeks cold and pink.

"All right?" Carl asked through numb lips. It felt good to be out, and invigorating, and she bobbed her head happily and placed a woolen-clad hand over his mouth before stretching up to kiss him. "Hey, I've got an idea. Can you make it to the square?"

"Yes, but what for?"

"Because it's not bad enough for Dickie's to be closed. Why don't we see if we can't get some lunch, what do you say?"

"Could we?" she grinned through chattering teeth.

"Let's go see." He whistled for Crow and slung an arm around Sophie, and they trudged off toward town.

The neons glowed out at them from the windows of the bar, and they smiled at each other gratefully. "I'm not sure I could have made it back if they'd been closed," mumbled Sophie, as Carl opened the door.

"Well, I'll be damned," called Dickie Schwab from behind the bar. "What the hell you doing here, Carl, you and …"

"Sophie. Thought we'd take the air and see if we could get lunch. Or you outta food?"

"Carl!" A man in heavy plaid wool looked over the arm that held his beer.

"Josh? What the hell you doing here?" laughed Carl, striding over to shake his hand. "Sophie honey, this mutt is Josh Dugan, the ferry captain." Sophie and the "mutt" exchanged pleasantries, before Carl repeated his question.

"Supplies, what else? Flew in with Rabbit. There was a little bit of a lull, so we figured we'd nip in. We're hoping there's another one so's we can nip back out. But I can tell ya for a certainty Dickie's got burgers, 'cause I brought 'em."

"Yep, got burgers if you want them," Dickie concurred. "Course they're frozen."

"Well, of course they're frozen, ya ass!" hollered Josh Dugan. "So thaw 'em out, don't be keepin' the lady waitin'!"

"Coming up. Beer while you're waiting?"

"Yeah, thanks," Carl shivered, and Dickie Schwab settled two bubbling pilsners before them on the bar before plowing through the swinging doors to the kitchen.

Josh gave Carl a meaning glance, then shouted, "Bring me a burger too!" He nodded toward a table and grabbed his coat off the stool next to him. "Let's eat over there."

When they'd settled at a table across the room, with Crow curled up next to Sophie's chair, Josh Dugan leaned in toward Carl. "I was gonna come looking for you. What the hell's goin' on around here anyway? You can't believe the shit I'm hearin'. Pardon my French," he said in Sophie's direction. "And I guess this must be the little lady got whacked with a book. One reason I never read—sumbitches are heavy. But, hell, Carl! People gettin' whacked and dyin'. And now I hear ya got one disappeared, and," he lowered his voice, "I guess it's just about the last one you need disappearin'."

"Jee-sus," groaned Carl. "If I ever wanna run for President, I'll just announce it here. Whole world will know me by the next day."

"I don't get it. Two by five, nobody comin' or goin' for four days—and Rabbit checked that out at the airport too—and nobody can *find* her? Sounds pretty bad, if ya ask me. My bet she's under the ice. And we both know it happens, but man, the timing sucks." He sat back in his chair as Dickie arrived and began to unload a tray in front of them.

"I figured you wanted the platters, but I had to give you applesauce instead of coleslaw, 'cause I got no fresh cabbage and neither does Nila."

"This looks wonderful," smiled Sophie.

"Well, enjoy," said Dickie Schwab and retreated back behind the bar.

"But what you need to know," Josh resumed more quietly, "is we had a passenger on the flight over. Detective from the mainland. Guess somebody figured there's too much goin' on over here, and Mike Hatton needed some help." Sophie and Carl looked at one another surreptitiously. "Just watch your back, man. And you need any help, you let me know. If I can't get over here, then you can bet your ass nobody else can either. Matter of fact, this crap's supposed to ease up tomorrow or the next day, and when it does, I'll be making a run on the boat."

"Yeah, thanks, Josh," muttered Carl.

Josh Dugan bit off a third of the burger on his plate, and before he'd swallowed it, bellowed, "Sumbitch *still* can't cook! Ya hear me, Dickie? Ya can't cook for shit!" He pushed the plate aside and got up, dropping a pile of crinkled bills on the table. "Call me," he whispered, and was gone.

"It's impossible," cried Sophie, a large tear spilling down over her cheek. "We can't even go somewhere for a quiet lunch. I was so looking forward to this."

"Now, honey, you just sit here and enjoy your lunch. Look at Crow, he doesn't give a good goddamn, and neither should you."

"But a detective?"

"So what? You have to look at it from a larger perspective, Sophie. A lot of unusual things have happened on this pile in the last week. And it's like I told you, Mike Hatton's a good guy, but he normally doesn't have to be much more than a traffic cop."

"Unusual things, Carl?" she asked in disbelief. "At least one murder—"

"Maybe."

"—an assault on me, somebody breaking into your house, and now Crystal's disappearance."

"Look, angel, neither of us has done a thing we need to worry about the law finding out about. Come on now," he cajoled, wiping at the tear on her face.

"That's beside the point, Carl," she hissed. "Do *you* think she's alive? And if she *isn't*, then who ..."

He swallowed. "I don't know, Sophie. But let's eat, huh?" He cast an eye toward the bar. "We'll talk about this later."

"Oh, I want to get away from here. I want us to go away from here."

"We will, honey. Now stop worrying and eat. You know, you're a wonderful cook," he smiled, "but I've been craving a burger."

She took his cue and a deep breath, and smiled in turn. "I'm hungry."

Bundled up against the wind afterward, they watched Crow trot before them contentedly, most of Sophie's burger in his belly, as they skirted the edge of the park and walked along the road toward the cottage.

"It's getting colder," she said, pulling her hood closer around her face.

"Sun's going down," answered Carl, and pulled her nearer.

"You must think I'm incredibly stupid."

"Now, why would you say a thing like that?"

"Oh, Carl," she said, turning to look up into his face, "I was so sure. I was convinced that Crystal was behind all of this. And now ... Well, it's one of two things. If there's no way she could have gotten off the island, then she's still here somewhere—either alive or not. If she's alive, then she must have disappeared deliberately, don't you think? She must be in hiding."

"But why, Sophie? I know what you're gonna say—that she was behind things and figured maybe we suspected her and would have gone to the police with what we had. But what did we have? And why *then*? Why wait till after the Halloween party?"

"Well, for one thing, she saw us talking to Mike Hatton at the party. And for another, she may have thought we had a lot more incentive after that debacle with her brother accusing one or both of us of committing murder."

He gave his head a skeptical tilt. "I don't know, angel. What would she have to gain?"

"Time. Carl, time to get off the island if she was responsible for what's been happening. But you don't think so, do you? You think she's dead. 'Under the ice,' as Josh put it?"

"I don't know, Sophie," he replied somberly. "But I hope not. I know you don't have any particular reason to like her—"

"I certainly wouldn't want her dead! And especially not because of *Peter*. Oh, no, Carl, if I hated her and Peter were still alive, I'd push her into his arms, believe me! But if she's dead, there are only three possibilities: accident, suicide—or murder."

"Oh, hold on, angel! You're getting way ahead of things here."

"How do you figure, Carl?" she asked breathlessly. "Mike Hatton has already asked us nicely not to leave the island. It seems to me our future hangs on what's happened to Crystal Holliday."

"Now, honey, that *is* a little melodramatic, don't you think?"

They had reached the stone-bound yard of the cottage, although the wall was so nearly buried as to look like no more than a haphazard ruin. "Is it?" she asked warily and nodded toward the drive, where two heads were visible above the seat backs of Mike Hatton's official vehicle.

Crow had trotted ahead, and greeted Mike as he stepped down from the driver's seat. From the passenger side emerged a square man with hair receding from his forehead and graying at his temples. He wore street clothes and a jacket that Sophie deemed insufficient for the conditions, and for a moment she felt sorry for him. He must be terribly cold. Then she saw the unrelenting line of his mouth and the cynicism in his narrow eyes, and she reached over to grip Carl's hand.

"Carl." Mike Hatton strode forward to meet them. "Sophie." If she had been put off by his former distant and starched manner of addressing her as "Ms. Westenra," she found herself ill at ease with his sudden informality now. "This is Detective Kandinsky. He's come over from Bayview to give us a hand here. He'd like to talk to you about ... well, what's been going on here on the island."

Sophie continued up the front walk. "Won't you come in out of the cold, please?" she offered with neutral politeness. "I'm just going to make a fresh pot of coffee," she added, as they all followed her into the house.

"This is not a social call, Mrs. *Skala*," said Detective Ed Kandinsky.

Sophie stopped and turned a gracious smile on him. "I didn't suppose it was, Mr. Kandinsky. But we've just walked back from town in the bitter cold, and we *would* like some coffee."

She returned to the living room with a full tray and set a cup before each of them. Detective Kandinsky could drink it or not.

"So, what's this about, Mike?" asked Carl, as Sophie sat down next to him on the sofa.

Mike Hatton cleared his throat and slapped at his leg with his hat. "Preliminary report on Joe Wisdom, Carl. There's no indication," he said sheepishly, "that he fell down the stairs. In fact, I'm afraid it looks like—"

"Homicide," supplied Ed Kandinsky, "and it seems, Mrs. Skala, that you were the last one to see him alive."

"Well, now that can't be, can it, Detective?"

"Oh, why is that, Mrs. Skala?" He clearly, to Sophie's thinking, derived some satisfaction from addressing her by her correct name. It made little difference, however, since she had already shared with Carl the most potentially damaging parts of her story.

"Because whoever killed him would have been the last one to see him alive. And he was very much alive when I left his house, Mr. Kandinsky. But then, he *would* have been. I had just recently met him, and I certainly had no reason to kill him, if that's what you're suggesting. Besides, I was myself attacked a short while later, as I'm sure Mr. Hatton has informed you."

"By a mysterious intruder, Mrs. Skala."

"So it would seem, Mr. Kandinsky."

"And I don't suppose you can think of anyone who would want to harm you or Mr. Wisdom."

"It sounds as though you're assuming a single assailant, Mr. Kandinsky. But, no, I can't think of anyone."

"You know, Mrs. Skala, I confess I'm a little surprised that you seem ... shall we say, unmoved, by my use of your real name."

"Let me save you some time, Detective. I chose to use an assumed name when I came here in order to avoid any further publicity with regard to the circumstances of my late husband's death. I just wanted to start over somewhere and live quietly. Believe it or not."

"Oh, I do believe it, Mrs. Skala. Why," he said, leaning toward her earnestly, "as much of a stretch as I find it, I even believe you didn't know that the woman your husband was having an affair with was right on this island—Crystal Holliday. The very same Crystal Holliday who has now vanished—poof!—into thin air."

"You're right, I didn't know."

"Extraordinary series of coincidences—you, your late husband, Ms. Holliday and Mr. Jacobsen here. And all of these *incidents* occurring since your arrival. Extraordinary."

"It is that, Mr. Kandinsky—and *just* that. I had no reason to want Mr. Wisdom dead. He was a charming man and very kind to me. And correct me if I'm wrong, but right now there is no indication whatever that any harm has befallen Ms. Holliday. That leaves only the question of my own injuries, for which I can scarcely be held accountable. More coffee, Detective?"

Mike Hatton sprang up from his preferred perch on the arm of one of Sophie's chairs as Detective Ed Kandinsky rose stiffly. "Mrs. Skala," he said, zipping his jacket—which really was inadequate—"we're going to find Ms. Holliday, you know."

"I certainly hope so, and unharmed, Mr. Kandinsky. In the meantime, I suppose you would rather we wouldn't plan any extended vacations, am I right?"

An acid smile spread out over Detective Kandinsky's face. "You know, Mrs. Skala, technically, I can't prevent *you* from going anywhere. But I imagine I could pull a few strings to make sure Mr. Jacobsen doesn't leave."

"But why should you want to, Detective, if you think I'm the one somehow responsible?"

Detective Kandinsky cast a leisurely glance from Sophie to Carl and back, and his upper lip curled derisively. "Evening, folks. And you two stay warm."

CHAPTER 12

"You're gonna have to go without me, Sophie."

"Oh, Carl," she groaned. "I wanted you to come. Now I don't know what to do."

"You go is what you do."

"But this is all so wrong, and so unfair."

"Look, angel, it's probably better this way. Be better for me to stay here with Crow anyway. Suppose the weather turned bad unexpectedly—wouldn't be unheard of—and we couldn't get back. This way, if there's the *slightest* chance that the trip back would be dangerous, you'll stay there until it's safe. You understand?"

She gave a reluctant nod. "I do want to see her."

Reney had been so importunate when she'd called the previous night. "Please, Sophie. I've missed you so much. I've been keeping an eye on this miserable weather, just waiting for a break so I could come see you. I even called the ferry line to make sure they'd be running and that it would be safe for you." And Sophie had tentatively agreed to make the trip to the mainland, provided the weather did not take another turn for the worse.

She *did* want to see Reney. So much had happened that she needed to share with the special confidante her sister had always been. And Reney had been on a fundraising junket to New York, so they had a good deal of catching up to do, most of which Sophie preferred not to do on the phone. All she would say to Reney's repeated plea of "Sophie, come home" was "I can't until this mess is cleared up and Carl can come with me."

Carl hugged her to him and kissed her forehead. "It'll do you good to get away for awhile. And you'll have a better time gossiping, just the two of you, than you would with me tagging along. You take your car. That way you can keep the engine running and the heat on the whole way, and Josh'll get you there all right. He knows that boat, and he knows the lake. And he knows I'm holding him personally responsible for your safety. So you'll be fine. Now, let's go." He zipped her into her heavy parka and pushed her toward the door.

As he hustled her along, she said over her shoulder, "When I get back, can we do what you suggested and go out to the cabin for awhile?"

"Sure, angel. I'll get some things together to take along while you're gone. Now, hurry up. Josh'll be champing at the bit, and he'll have my ass if you're late."

Josh Dugan was waiting on the dock when they arrived, and even before Carl had closed the car door, he was shouting, "'Bout damn time, too! I got a schedule! Next time, play hidey ho on your own time, ya bum." He came to stand next to Carl, scratching his nose and indicating with a subtle jerk of his thumb Mike Hatton's SUV parked at the top of the ramp down to the dock. "Bastards," he muttered under his breath.

Carl heaved a dejected sigh as a stocky man in a plaid wool hat with ear flaps slouched up the gangplank and disappeared into the big cabin. "Look, Josh, take care of Sophie, huh?"

"Shee-ut. I'll get her there and back all right, man. *You* take care of her," he leered, and ambled over to direct Sophie up the vehicle ramp.

Carl followed him over to say good-bye. He leaned in the open window and kissed her. "Don't come back, Sophie."

"Never say that to me again," she said, running a hand gently along his cheek. "I'll see you in a few hours." She pulled the car onto the open deck of the ferry and got out, waving to him as the boat pulled away from the dock. When she saw him turn back up the incline for the short walk back to the cottage, she retreated to the warmth of the car. The lake was relatively calm now, but the air above it was bitter as ever.

They reached the mainland a full hour before she was to meet Reney, so she decided to use the time and the car to her advantage, and made a whirlwind trip through the nearest supermarket. Like a deprived dieter, she loaded the cart not only with many pounds of meat and fresh produce that included everything from leeks to pineapple, but also chips, cookies and anything else she could imagine eating with Carl. She shoved a case of beer for him onto the rack underneath, unable to remember when she had derived so much enjoyment from so mundane a task. She pushed aside the uncomfortable notion that she had escaped incarceration, but could not evade the irony that the refuge she had sought on the island had now become the thing from which she fled.

By the time she had loaded her considerable purchases into the car and found a parking place in front of the restaurant, Reney was waiting for her just inside the door. She hurried in and embraced her sister. "Oh, it is so very good to see you!" She grabbed Reney's hand and pulled her along to a booth tucked into a quiet corner. Sinking down onto the bench opposite and unzipping her parka, she took a hard look at her younger sister. "You look tired, Reney."

"So do you, Cissybeans."

"*What*?" Sophie burst into laughter. "My lord, I haven't heard that in a thousand years, I swear! I remember when we were little, and you always called me that. Do you know I can actually *see* us, in shorts and those little tops that tied at the shoulders, remember? Squatting down in the grass looking for four-leaf clovers, and you saying, 'Can I have yours if you find one, Cissybeans?'"

"And you tried pulling off some of the leaves and putting two together so I wouldn't be disappointed."

"Never really worked, did it?" Sophie smiled sadly.

"No," answered Reney, placing a hand over her sister's, "but you tried. Just as you always tried to look out for me. It was hard, I know."

"For us both, Reney."

"It was worse for you, and we both know it. Aunt Ida and Uncle Jack?" she said angrily. "They were always harder on you. *Everybody* was."

Somewhere in the background, Sophie heard Reney say "Two coffees, please," as the waitress set water and menus on the table. But the words were vague and nearly lost to the thwack of the leather belt across her bottom and legs, and her own small voice, hoarse with her cries. *Please! It was an accident! I didn't mean to do it!*

"Cissybeans?"

She straightened up in her seat and took a deep breath. "It's all right," she smiled across at Reney. "It was over a long time ago."

"It will never be over for me," Reney replied heavily.

Sophie sniffed and brushed at her cheek. "It *has* to be, honey. Look, we've survived."

"Have we, Sophie? Look at you. Look what's happening to you right now. We keep revisiting the same nightmare, only the characters and the details change," she lamented.

"Reney," pleaded Sophie.

"Sophie, don't go back. Don't go back to the island. *Please.*"

"I have to. If I didn't, how long do you suppose it would be before somebody saw that as an admission of guilt for *something* and came looking for me? And besides," she glanced up shyly to meet her sister's eyes, "there's Carl."

"Ohhh," moaned Reney. "You're in love with him, aren't you?" She scanned the ceiling hopelessly.

"Reney, please. Yes. He's so very kind to me. He's made me see that there are good men, gentle men, capable of caring, and that maybe I'm worthy of someone's kindness and affection."

"Oh, gawd," Reney prayed into her folded hands. "It frightens me, Sophie. It frightens me so much. It's bad! It's a bad configuration, you must see that!"

Sophie squeezed her hand, a pained smile hovering around her mouth. "We thought *Peter* and I were a *good* configuration. Oh, be happy for me, please."

Reney shook her head and closed her eyes resignedly. "You know I've never wanted anything else for you, darling Cissybeans."

They spent the rest of the too brief visit with their heads together, quietly rehashing all that had been going on and how best to respond to it. "And what about you, Sophie? Do *you* think she's alive?" whispered Reney.

Sophie gave her head a cursory shake. "No, but I don't know where she is either."

"Under the ice? Was that it, what he said? How long do you suppose ..." Reney trailed off and bit the corner of her lip.

"As frigid as it is?" sighed Sophie. "I don't know."

"Let's not talk about it any more now. Let's talk about things we're going to do when all this nonsense is over and we have all kinds of time to spend together. What about Thanksgiving?" Reney asked eagerly.

Sophie smiled over at her gently, at the childlike excitement that was so typically Reney. "I don't know, honey. Maybe this will all be cleared up by then, and we can have a real holiday together."

"God, how I hope so," Reney answered, picking up the bill and her coat. "Oh, I don't want to leave you here. But I have to pick up the kids."

"I'll be fine. Don't worry about me. And I'll see you again soon, I promise."

They paid the bill, and Sophie walked Reney out to her car. "What will you do while you're waiting for the ferry to leave, though?"

Sophie chuckled. "You know, shopping on the island leaves something to be desired, especially just now. So I may just snoop around some of the stores here. In fact, I may even buy myself something terribly frivolous," she said with a flick of her hand.

"Why don't you give Carl a thrill and buy some sexy lingerie? Ooh la la!" giggled Reney.

"Oh, sure! Except around here, that would be crotchless longjohns." Sophie pulled a wry face, and they both burst into laughter and fell together in a hug. She put her fingers to her lips and blew a kiss as Reney pulled away from the curb, then stood there on the sidewalk, feeling as desolate as the flat, gray landscape around her. For a fleeting moment, she thought how easy it would be to jump into her own car and follow her sister. They could have Thanksgiving, and Christmas, and then spring would come.

And then she saw Peter again, lying there, still, his hands unmoving, no longer capable of hurting her. But the hands began to move, slowly, gently, and they belonged to Carl, and skimmed over her flesh like a breeze sweet and warm and welcome. She exhaled and headed for the department store on the corner.

She was waiting at the dock when Josh Dugan arrived, and waved and smiled as he motioned her up the ramp. "Well, that's it then," he said as a pair of heavy boots disappeared up the metal steps, "two over, two back. We're gonna get hit again, sure as shit. But don't you worry, I'll get ya back okay. Figure I owe Carl that much," he laughed, and bounded up the steps to the cabin.

The sky was a solid wall of dirty gray, and the wind had begun to whip up the water into thick rolls by the time they reached the island. She drove up the incline, passing the man in the plaid hat, who bent his face down into the front of his coat to avoid the icy blasts. She should have offered him a ride, would have, but she was surprised and a little disappointed not to see Carl waiting for her in his truck. But at least there was no sign of Mike Hatton's vehicle either.

She found them both when she pulled into the driveway of the cottage. She tugged at the front of her coat absently and got out of the car, grabbing several bags of groceries because they were there and needed to be put away. Carl met her at the door, grim-faced, and relieved her of most of the bags.

"Gentlemen," she nodded coldly, and continued down the hall to the kitchen with the rest, her steps dogged by a clearly unruffled Detective Kandinsky. "I hope you won't mind if I put my groceries away while we talk."

"Not a bit, Mrs. Skala. I trust you had a pleasant visit with your sister."

"I did, thank you, Mr. Kandinsky," she replied evenly. She supposed it really was no surprise that he should know how she had spent her afternoon, and it hardly mattered, since even a sanctimonious gumshoe wouldn't be able to find anything incriminating in that.

"Well, good. I'm glad to hear it," he said condescendingly. "And glad you decided to come back."

"Why wouldn't I have come back? This is where I live. This is where … my *things* are," she smiled, as Carl set the rest of the bags on the counter and hovered near her watchfully. "So, what can we do for you and Officer Hatton?"

"Just following up, Mrs. Skala. Seems Mr. Wisdom was in fact the victim of homicide, and of course, there's still not a trace of Ms. Holliday. Not one trace, can you believe it? And of course, the longer she's missing … Well, naturally, I wouldn't want to speculate."

"Naturally. Well, it's very good of you and Mr. Hatton to come around to warn us."

"Warn you, Mrs. Skala? Why, I don't think we've—"

"Warn us that there may be a murderer on the island, Mr. Kandinsky. Naturally."

"You know, Mrs. Skala, you've got a little bit of an attitude."

"All right, look," growled Carl, "we've answered your questions. If you don't like the answers—"

"I don't, *Mr.* Jacobsen. I don't like them one bit. And I'll tell you why. There are just too many coincidences here, and I don't believe in coincidence. One person's been murdered, another one's missing, and both since Mrs. Skala came here to 'get away from it all' and just happened to hook up with you."

"Well, now you may or may not believe in coincidence, but that's what you've got here, like it or not!"

"Cool down, Carl," admonished Mike Hatton.

"Well, excuse me, *Carl*," continued Ed Kandinsky, "if my sense of logic is just the least little bit offended, my sense of trust just the least bit strained. Because what we've got here on this one little bitty island is one murder, one very suspicious disappearance—and two killers."

"All right, that's enough!" Carl lunged at Ed Kandinsky, but before Sophie could do more than grasp at his arm, Mike Hatton had launched himself between them.

"Carl!" he shouted, gripping Carl by the shoulders. "Cool it! Come on!"

Carl flung him loose and leaned back against the counter, trembling with fury.

"Nah, let him go, Mike," Ed Kandinsky jeered. "Go on, Carl. Hit me. Go on," he taunted. "What have you got, six months left on your probation? Hit me, and we'll be a whole lot closer to clearing up this mess."

Sophie threw herself in front of Carl and put her hands on his chest. "Let it go," she begged.

"Right in character," sneered Detective Kandinsky. "Carl the hothead—that's just how you killed Gary Coffey, isn't it?—and little Sophie Skala, cool as a cucumber. No crimes of passion there, huh, Sophie?"

"You bastard!" shouted Carl, and plunged forward. But Sophie clung to him, whispering feverishly, stroking his face and pleading. He swallowed hard and ran a hand over her hair. Then glaring over at Detective Kandinsky, he said menacingly, "You leave her alone. Everybody knows about what I did, and how. I *did* what I was convicted of, and I served my time for it. But Sophie was cleared in her husband's death."

"She wasn't cleared. She just wasn't indicted. There's a difference. Of course, there's no statute of limitation on murder either. But, no, I'm not talking about Dr. Peter Skala here."

Sophie turned and stared unflinching into his eyes. "Mr. Kandinsky, I don't care whether you believe me or not, but the fact is, I didn't kill Joe Wisdom, and I don't know where Crystal Holliday is. Now, unless you have some sort of warrant, I'd like you to leave."

He shrugged, and resuming his complacent smile, retraced his steps through the hall to the front door, where he stopped. "Mrs. Skala," he said, his head twisting toward her deliberately, "we're going to solve these cases, because they're all just one case. And when we do, I'm going to prove that you're up to your eyeballs in this. But I wasn't talking about Joe Wisdom or Crystal Holliday."

Sophie stiffened, and her breath caught as she became suddenly and sickeningly aware of his plan. Divide and conquer. He had, he thought, only to plant a seed of mistrust in one or the other of them, and he had calculated correctly that there was nothing he could tell her to turn her from Carl.

"But I wonder, Mrs. Skala, if you've told your boyfriend here how when you were eleven years old, you set fire to the house and killed your parents. Accident, you told the investigators. You and your kid sister managed to get out, but your parents ... well."

"Go away." Her voice was impossibly soft and clear. "Go away, you evil man."

CHAPTER 13

She could just hear over the sound of her own muffled sobs the bedroom door creak open on slow hinges, and then Crow's wet nose was jammed against her equally wet cheek. As she reached out blindly to hug him, she felt the edge of the mattress dip under Carl's weight and his hand firm, but gentle down the length of her back and over her hip. "Hey," he said quietly, "it doesn't matter."

She pulled herself up on one elbow and smeared at her nose. "What do you mean it doesn't matter?"

"I mean, you don't have to tell me anything."

"I don't understand you," she sniffed. "I should have told you before ... before things went as far as they did between us. Instead, I just let it go on, like some fresh, intoxicating, uncomplicated love affair, but it was a lie," she blubbered, "because I'm damaged."

"What the hell are you talking about?" He grabbed her by the shoulders and pulled her upright. "*Damaged*?" he laughed. "You've been sleeping with an ex-con, for chrissakes. Baby doll, we're *all* damaged, all crippled in some way or other. Look at *me*. *Look* at me," he repeated, nudging her chin up with his hand. "I killed a man. No, I didn't mean to. But it wasn't an accident in the way it's an accident if somebody darts out from between parked cars and you hit 'em. I killed a guy in a drunken rage, and I have to live with that every day of my life. And you've been living with it too, and that's the point. You know exactly what I am and what I've done, and you're here anyway."

"I know you now, I know how you treat me. I didn't know that other man that you were."

"Exactly. Whatever happened before, especially when you were a little girl, makes no difference to how I see you now. So we're not gonna talk about this any more."

She slid her arms around his back and rested her head against his chest. "No, I want to tell you." Her lip trembled and she looked up at him hesitantly. "It was an accident. Nobody meant … I mean, I found some candles, and I thought it would be nice to light them when the house was all dark. Kind of a pretend game, you know?" she asked hopefully. "And then I thought it would be nice if they smelled good, the way some of them did that I'd seen at the store. But these were plain, and they didn't smell like anything. So I crept into my parents' room very quietly to get just a little of my mother's drug store perfume." *Emeraude. It was a scent even the memory of which made her physically ill to this day.* "I thought I would just spray the tiniest bit on the candles—she wouldn't miss just the littlest bit, and then the candles would smell wonderful like the ones in the store." *The flames were so big, and they were everywhere. They were so tall, and as they crept up and up, they left behind them tatters of fabric that looked like the wind was blowing them. The rest was smoke, and when she gasped, the smoke got inside her lungs and choked her. She grabbed Reney by the arm, dragging her along the hallway …*

"Aw, Sophie honey. You didn't know."

"No, I … I didn't know. Didn't realize, and then everything was on fire. I guess I panicked. And I ran, and all I could think to do was to drag Reney outside. I had to wake her, you see," she said earnestly. "But our parents never came out."

Carl held her tight and petted her. "You were just a little girl. You couldn't know. And that was a long time ago. You made a mistake, angel. We both did. But we're here now, with a chance. Let's not waste it on things we can't change."

She nodded and swiped at her eyes. "Okay," she smiled uncertainly.

"That's better. Now we need to get the groceries put away. I'm pretty sure I saw a case of beer and about a dozen bags of chips. So I think we should get some supper and then pack up Crow and enough goodies to last till the end of time and head out to the cabin. Get a nice fire going, listen to some music, maybe reprise that first time, what do you think?" he whispered, nibbling at her lip.

"Ohhh." She clutched at him, her expression a blend of desperation and gratitude. "No, *now*. I will now."

"Listen to me," he said, pulling her off his neck. "There's no rush, honey. You don't have to do that to keep me around. I'm not going anywhere."

"But I …" she stammered.

"I know." Taking a deep breath, he untangled himself from her embrace and stood up. "Now, that might be one of the stupidest things I've ever done. So let's get moving before I change my mind. Come on," he said, slapping her bottom, "Crow's hungry."

He fed Crow, while Sophie sought to demonstrate her affection alternatively by preparing a dinner of succulent steaks, twice-baked potatoes, fresh tossed salad and a fragrant, crusty baguette. She emptied a bottle of beer into a tall glass and placed it before him, then sat down across from him.

"I don't know when I've eaten this well, angel, or been pampered like this," he smiled. "So, what did you and Reney talk about?"

"Oh, I don't know. The past, the present, the future."

"All in a couple hours, huh?"

"Yeah," she shrugged. "The past was not very good, the future is uncertain. That leaves the present."

"That's the best place to live anyway. And, hell, the future will take care of itself. Guess you had a pretty bad time as a kid, though."

"Yes," she said wistfully. "Our parents weren't very happy, I suppose. All I really remember is their anger, whether it was directed at each other or us. I was grateful for Reney, she was all I had. Even more so after ... Well. We were sent to live with my mother's sister and her husband. They didn't like me very much, I'm afraid, and never even pretended to forgive me for what had happened." She poked idly at her potato.

"They hurt you," he said, reaching across the table to take her hand. "And where are they now?"

She shook her head. "Where they were? Dead? I don't know. The day I finished high school, I took Reney and got a job and a cheap place to live, and I haven't seen them since. It was tough, but we scraped by. Reney worked part time, too, until she finished school. Eventually, we both managed to get through college," she flashed a diffident smile, "and we tried to put the past behind us and have real lives like normal people.

"Reney got married before I did. It didn't last, but she's got two great kids. And of course," she stared over at the bottle of balsamic vinegar she'd forgotten to put back in the cupboard, "you already know about my marriage."

"Don't regret it, Sophie," he said gently. "Don't miss him."

"Oh, I don't. In a way, I wish I'd never met him. But then I'd probably never have met you." She rose to clear the table, and let out a groan. "Oh, no. It's snowing again. If it keeps up like this, we'll be buried by spring." They looked at one another as the import of what she had said sank in. "Or perhaps that was an unfortunate choice of words."

"Sophie, it'll be all right. This will be cleared up."

"The snow or the murder? Oh, I suppose it will. But it's a strain just the same. We go on as though it's perfectly ordinary for people to get conked or killed, or to disappear, and all while we're stranded in a blizzard and the electricity is going out. It's crazy."

"What else can we do?"

"I don't know, but it keeps me on edge, all of it. I mean, how strange was that Halloween party? A man who was supposedly a friend and neighbor of all these people is murdered, and the lot of them—other than Mar Holliday—acting as though everything was normal."

"What should they have done? In the first place, Mike Hatton was treating it as an accident. Yeah, it was too bad, but life goes on."

"You're right. I suppose I'm being silly. But it just leaves a bad taste in my mouth." She waved it away. "Never mind. Let's get things cleaned up here and get out to the cabin and just enjoy being together."

He looked toward the window, where a continuous spatter of icy flakes clicked against the glass, and pursed his lips. "Maybe that's not such a good idea after all. If it's starting up again, I'll probably have to go back out. And I don't wanna leave you alone out there."

"Nothing is going to happen to me. Come on, Carl. *Please.* You know, I was clocked *here,* a quarter mile from the center of town, not at your place. Besides, has anything else peculiar happened since Crystal disappeared? No. The more I think about it, the more convinced I am that she's behind this, and she *is* in hiding."

"*So*-phie."

"Think about it. Bea reports her missing, and then Mr. Hot Shot Detective shows up from the mainland. Cause and effect? Or did Crystal anticipate that there would be a more serious investigation than Mike Hatton could conduct and decide it might be a convenient time to disappear? Don't forget, Bea Baskin reported her missing, and Bea Baskin is her aunt. Who's to say Bea's not covering for her, hm? For that matter, who's to say she hasn't escaped to the mainland already?"

"How?" he asked skeptically.

"On the ferry? Maybe she was in disguise."

"Honey, that's fantastic. Come on."

"Well, why not? As a matter of fact," she wagged a finger in emphasis, "there was a man on the ferry coming back today. I didn't pay much attention to him and don't know who he was. And our friendly officers of the law," she said distastefully, "have been too busy trying to catch us committing some crime to notice anyone else either. Maybe nobody noticed *her* getting *on*."

"I don't know," he said, shaking his head. "Sounds pretty far-fetched to me."

"Well, of course it's far-fetched. *Murder* is far-fetched."

They shouldn't have started at the thumping behind them, but Sophie gasped, and Carl sprang up and pulled the door open slowly. "Bea," he said flatly, and stepped aside. "Looks like you didn't pick the best time to come out."

"Hullo, Carl," she said, wiping her feet. "Doesn't seem like there *is* a best time lately. Evening, Sophie," she added, pushing back her hood.

"Bea, what brings you out in this?" Sophie felt a guilty flush wash over her, as though she'd just been caught gossiping, which she supposed she had. "We were just finishing up dinner. Would you like some coffee?"

"If it's no trouble," replied Bea Baskin, plunking down into the chair Carl had vacated. "Haven't had much chance to talk to you lately." Her gaze swept casually over Carl. "That business at the party ... and all," she waved vaguely.

"Think I'll take Crow out," Carl said behind gritted teeth. He piled into his coat, called the dog and slammed the door behind them.

"Figured you'd be wondering," continued Bea, "why I never said anything about Crystal."

"No," Sophie replied too quickly. "Well, yes. But then I realized you wouldn't have had any reason to."

"That's just it. Didn't see the point right off. Shoot, if I'da told you who all on the island is related to who all else, it would only have confused you, since you didn't know any of 'em anyway. And then when you and"—she jerked her head toward the door—"Carl started keeping company, I figured if I told you, you'd think I was trying to make a point, and there wasn't one. At least not the one you woulda thought."

"And yet," Sophie said pointedly, "you felt you should say something now, I assume because of my relationship with Carl."

"None of my business who's with who else. Course," she shrugged, "I wouldn't have predicted it, as you might say."

"Well," smiled Sophie, "if it's any consolation, neither would I. But—"

"Well, there you are. That's all I meant. Just an odd business, as people see it. You show up, get involved with the one man around here with a serious past, and odd things start to happen."

"I didn't kill Joe Wisdom, if that's what you mean, and I don't know anything about where Crystal is. And neither does Carl. He was with me the night she disappeared."

"Aw, I know that. Naw, that's not what I was getting at all. But I do believe there's such a thing as *fateful* combinations."

Configurations. That was the word Reney had used. But, "I'm sorry, I don't think I follow you," she said.

The older woman leaned forward earnestly. "It's like some foods. They're each good on their own, but then if you try putting them together, they make you sick—chocolate syrup on catfish, say. Goes for people too."

One of Sophie's brows crept up as she considered not only the peculiarity of the analogy, but Bea's audacity in offering it, and particularly in view of the circumstances. "I see," she said with a tart smile, "Carl and I make people sick, is that it?"

"Aw, now, Sophie, I didn't mean it that way. You think I'm an old busybody, I know, but—"

Sophie squirmed slightly as she recalled having used just that term to describe Bea. "You mean well, I'm sure. And I appreciate that." She meant it to be the last word, and turned her thoughts to leaving for the cabin with Carl as quickly as possible.

"I don't want you to think that I bear you some ill will, or Carl either, on account of you two getting together, because I don't. But it's like I started to say. It's not so much the people as what they carry inside of them. Sometimes it's those *things* that kinda mingle like flavors, only the flavor you end up with is something different altogether and not always good. And sometimes those things trigger other things, you see?"

"No, I don't think I do," Sophie answered coolly.

"Well, you take Crystal, for instance. I loved her like my own, did the best I could for her, and she was not a bad girl, in spite of what you mighta heard. But she was troubled, like there was something inside *her* that seemed to push her toward the wrong men. Like the things they carried inside of them called out to the wrong things in her. It was like that with her and Carl. And of course all that did was make things worse for her. It was bad for her, that business with Carl and Gary Coffey."

The chill remained in Sophie's voice as she replied, "For everyone, I'm sure."

"Oh, wasn't easy for anybody. Least of all for Carl. I know that. But what you maybe don't know is that Crystal got herself into another *situation* awhile later, and something similar happened. Another man she was involved with wound up dead."

Sophie held her breath, listening intently for any suggestion of blame, any hint of a trap. But it seemed to her prudent, given the island grapevine, to admit to some knowledge of local scandal. "I'd heard she was involved in another unfortunate relationship."

"That's my point. What happened was no more than I would have expected. Combinations," sighed Bea, taking a final slurp at her coffee and setting down the mug. She hauled herself up out of the chair and prepared to leave. "Anyway, that's what I wanted to tell you."

Sophie stared at her blankly, not at all sure what "that" was. "Are you suggesting that Joe's death and Crystal's disappearance have something to do with bad combinations?" she gaped.

Bea shrugged once more. "One thing leads to another. That's how I see it anyway. Well, I'm off."

"Wait. What about Crystal? What do you think has happened to her?" Sophie asked quietly.

Bea pulled her hood up close around her face. "Gonna be another cold one. Ah, well, I don't think sad little Crystal will feel it."

Sophie felt a chill crawl up the back of her neck. "You think she's dead."

Bea sighed heavily. Her reply was spare. "Most likely. Probably under the ice, poor little thing," she said, shambling out the door.

Crow shot past her, tongue lolling, shaking free of the considerable snow he'd accumulated. Carl followed a moment later, his lips blue, stamping to try to get warm. "If she'd had any more dirt to dish, I'da been the next casualty," he groused. Then he looked at Sophie, sagging pale and thoughtful against the table. "What's wrong, Sophie?" He peeled off his gloves and chucked them on the counter. "What did she say?"

"I'm not sure." Sophie stirred and grabbed the coffee pot. "Here, sit down and drink some hot coffee." She set a cup in front of him and plopped down. "She thinks Crystal's dead."

"*What?*" Coffee sloshed out of the cup and formed a small puddle on the table.

"I don't know what, Carl. She talked about Crystal and you and me—and Peter. Oh, not by name, not specifically, and I don't think she knows Peter was my husband. But I think she was suggesting that all these relationships, all the connections—'bad combinations,' she called them—have something to do with what's happened."

"I never heard such horseshit," he said in disgust.

"Well, if you put some esoteric spin on it, yes, but if you look at it in terms of cause and effect—"

"What cause and effect? It's horseshit, Sophie."

"Maybe not," she suggested hopefully. "I think she was trying to say that Crystal was vulnerable to begin with, and the shock of Gary Coffey's death and your imprisonment affected her mentally. And that when Peter was murdered, it was so like what had happened to her before—being deprived of a lover that way—that it unhinged her completely. You see what that means, don't you, Carl?"

"I see what you *think* it means. But how do you—or *Bea*—get from there to Crystal being dead?"

"'Under the ice,' she said," replied Sophie, her eyes clear and unblinking as she looked into his, "and suggested it was suicide."

"Oh, for God's sake, Sophie," he laughed. "What are you talking about? First murder, and now suicide? Come on! What's next, human sacrifice and cannibalism?"

"It's not funny, Carl. Don't you see? If Crystal was mentally unstable, not only could she have committed the crimes, but she could just as easily have been remorseful or fearful of being caught, and killed herself. It takes everything into account. It makes perfect sense."

"Yeah, a little too perfect. Hell, Bea doesn't know squat," he growled, "so I guess she's gonna make it up as she goes along, fireside tales to scare the kiddies."

Sophie sank back against the chair and turned a glum look on Crow. "You don't want to believe it, do you? Any of it."

"Sophie honey, I know what you're trying to do. But this theory of yours is not gonna get anybody off the hook, and frankly, it pisses me off that Bea Baskin would come over here with all this mumbo-jumbo and upset you." He reached across the table and took her hand. "It's too easy. And I think we both know life's not that neat."

"Things like that happen all the time! The news is full of such stories, and you know it!"

He placed his forehead in his hand and squeezed his temples. "Sophie," he said wearily, "all I *know* is if we don't get off this freakin' island soon, we're both gonna go off the deep end."

CHAPTER 14

"Damn good thing we can't go very far." The windshield wipers flapped back and forth furiously, and the truck crept along as Carl leaned forward in search of the road. "Probably have to plow my way up my own drive."

"Do you know what I'm going to get next time I can get over to the mainland?" Preoccupied with her own distress, she hadn't realized how near the edge Carl teetered, and was determined now to provide him with some diversion.

"A new address?"

"Oh, funny man. No, Carl, I'm going to get a sled."

He took his eyes off the road just long enough to look at her as though she had already lost her mind. "A *what*?"

"A sled. You know, like the old Flexible Flyers? At least then maybe we could have some fun in all this hideous weather, instead of just trying to avoid it, which we can't do anyway."

"Lord, Sophie," he laughed. "All right, I tell ya what. You get it and I'll pull you up the hill. And then Mike Hatton'll have us both declared incompetent, and that'll solve all our problems." The truck slowed to a crawl as they approached the cabin. "Yep, have to plow it. I'll clear enough of a path to get you and Crow and the stuff inside, and finish up later."

"Brrr, it's cold," she shivered, as he worked the key in the lock and pushed open the door. "You were right. It *is* colder here. Sometimes I think I'll never be really warm again ever."

"I'll turn up the heat and get a fire going," he replied, nudging her inside and fumbling for a light switch. "Just put your things down and come over by the fireplace. I'll bring in the rest of the stuff, and we can put it away when you get warmed up."

While he worked at the tinder with cold fingers, she judged that it would be better to keep moving and began to put away the perishables. Meanwhile, Crow began to investigate his new surroundings, his big nose snuffling along the length of the lower edge of the double doors to the back porch.

Sophie glanced over at him and called to Carl. "I guess it was one of those panes you had to replace?"

"Yep, one by the handle, naturally," he frowned.

"At least they're small, though. Could have been much worse."

"Oh, yeah. If the panes had been bigger, it would have been a bigger pain."

"Oh," she clucked. "Still unsettling, though. You're sure nothing was missing?"

"Not that I could tell, unless it was part of a loaf of bread I thought I had. But I could have been wrong about that. No, I really think it was just somebody caught out in that first blizzard and trying to get in someplace to keep from freezing to death."

"But then why wouldn't whoever it was just have told you?"

"Sophie, would you tell somebody you broke into their house, no matter how innocently?"

"Yes, I would," she insisted. "And I'd want to pay for the damage."

"Uh huh. And suppose someone less honest than you saw you do it and came in afterwards and robbed the place?"

"Well, nobody would find the things in my possession. And I *certainly* wouldn't have been able to *fence* them."

He shook his head and gestured his surrender, as Crow came panting down the stairs, trotting anxiously from one to the other of them and whining. Sophie dug through the bags until she found a box of large dog biscuits and handed him one, which he took gingerly and then promptly deposited on the floor next to Carl, before he resumed pacing.

"Hey, buddy," Carl said quietly, calling him over and offering the biscuit once more.

"You don't think he's going stir-crazy too, do you?" sighed Sophie.

"No, I think the poor thing's just confused. Joe's house was home to him, and Joe never went anywhere without him. Then all of a sudden, Joe's not around, and he's living with us at the cottage. And now we bring him here. Probably doesn't know *where* the hell he belongs. Do you, buddy?" He caught the big head in his hands and stroked it gently. "He'll be okay." He stood up and poked at the fire, then wandered over to help Sophie. "How about you? You warmed up yet?" he asked, slipping his arms around her waist.

"No," she smiled and snuggled back against him, "but you could help with that. Or did you want a snack first?"

"Oh yeah, Sophie, given a choice, I'd much rather drink beer and eat corn chips than roll around under the blankets with you," he answered with a wry smile.

"Well?" She puckered her lips up at him.

"Well," he said with a cursory kiss, "with my luck, Sam Coombs would call, and it would turn into a quickie. And that *would* be a damn shame."

"Well," she sighed, "I know I'm going to regret this, but why don't you call him? Then at least we'll know."

"That assumes we want to. But you're right." Just as he reached for the phone, it rang, and with a knowing look, he picked it up.

One corner of her mouth twisted upward. She could tell from Carl's end of the conversation who had called and what Sam wanted. "Ohh," she whined, as he replaced the receiver, "look at it, Carl. It's a blizzard! You can't go out now, it wouldn't be safe. Who in the world is going to be crazy enough to need the roads cleared right now anyway?"

"Nobody. Honey, right now, we're stranded," he said grimly. "There's no telling when a boat'll be able to get over here. So we're gonna have to try to get the airport cleared and keep it cleared. When this does stop, they're gonna have to be able to get planes in." He pulled on his parka and fished his gloves out of the pockets.

"How bad is it going to get?"

"I really don't know. But when I get back, we should probably sit down and make some contingency plans, just some common sense things."

"Like what?" she asked warily.

"Like staying in bed most of the time to save fuel," he grinned.

"Oh, you!" She leaned back against the counter heavily. "I can't believe this. I was just over on the mainland a few hours ago. Now you're telling me we're marooned on this island. Again. With Kojak, no less."

"Never mind, angel. We'll be okay. Now, I've gotta get going. Why don't you go take a hot bath? Make you feel better."

She ran a hand along his arm. "With you out in that? I don't think so."

"I'll be back as soon as I can." He kissed her cheek. "Keep the doors locked and Crow by you. I still don't like leaving you here."

"Don't worry about me. Just be careful." She huddled shivering against the doorframe as the truck melted away into the blizzard, and continued to stand there after it had disappeared, watching the snow drift in smoky tatters and settle into flawless mounds inside the porch. She had not felt so entirely alone or forlorn since she had stood gazing down at Peter, *so still on the hearth, and not another living soul on earth ...*

She locked the door behind her as she'd been instructed, and running an absent hand along Crow's shoulders, rummaged through a bag of her personal belongings until she found the copy of Joe Wisdom's book that she had borrowed from the library. She wondered in passing how it was to be returned and whether an overdue fine could be assessed if there was no librarian and the library was closed. With a dispirited sigh, she pulled a shawl out of another bag, and wrapping it close around her, curled up on the sofa before the fire and opened the book. Poor, kindly Joe Wisdom would never write his book about shipwrecks now, or any of the other books he might have had inside him, and what she held now was a legacy.

The snow gusted up hard and wet against the glass doors, and she tried to force herself to concentrate on the table of contents and not on what she imagined Carl must be facing out in this storm. But she found herself in the odd, but familiar position of reading over and over again the same words that meant nothing, and focusing instead on the empathy she felt with Crow as he shifted restlessly and whimpered next to her.

She abandoned the contents and turned directly to the first chapter of what appeared to be a continuation of an earlier and broader history of the island. This one, she quickly established, was to be a more detailed account of the families that had settled the island, and as she skimmed over page after page, she was surprised by how many of the names seemed familiar, and by how long some of the current residents' families had been here.

The DeKalbs had arrived in 1811, and within three generations, had established large and successful vineyards, and fifty years later, their first winery—just in time for Prohibition. But far from being ruined by this development, they had prospered—largely, it was now generally acknowledged—by having been fortunately located for the illegal traffic in spirits through Canadian waters.

Nor, it seemed, was tragedy a stranger to the island. A fair number of unfortunate events seemed to have been the result of efforts to get to and from the island, and would probably, Sophie realized, have comprised a part of the book Joe Wisdom had been working on at the time of his death. On more than one occasion, people had drowned while crossing the ice in one direction or the other. She was astonished to learn that a regular solution to the isolation the residents currently faced had been to haul small boats across the frozen surface of the lake between areas of open water—with the unsurprising consequence that the frozen parts were not always so frozen as they appeared. In the 1850s, one Asa Wembley had been lost in just such a tragic accident, leaving a young widow who soon found solace in marriage to a trapper named Nehemiah McKay, a happy event, as it turned out, for Patch McKay some century and half later.

In fact, it seemed that the fortunes of many of the island families had for generations been tied inextricably to the lake and their peculiar situation in it. A certain Jack Coombs, for instance, had gone down along with his small crew when the boat he captained, the Island Lady, was sunk during the Civil War, although Sophie, hard pressed to imagine the Confederates so far afield, was forced to conclude that this had been an unlucky coincidence.

She looked up from the book as Crow began once more to pace fretfully before the glass doors, a narrow ridge of hair standing up along his back. She took a deep, fearful breath, and untangling herself, rose slowly and leaned sideways to peer out into the night. Nothing was immediately visible against the gauze and swirl, no imprints in the windswept snow on the porch, and nothing at all beyond its tiny border, unless it was a brief motion in her periphery that vanished around the corner of the house. She exhaled and looked at the clock above the stove. She had been reading for more than two hours.

"What's taking so long?" she asked, patting Crow's head as he stood next to her, then setting a pot of coffee to brew. On a nervous impulse, she decided to bake a pie with the Rome Beauty apples she had bought earlier, primarily because she could see in her mind's eye Carl dragging in cold and exhausted and her settling him comfortably in front of the fire with freshly baked pie. She swept through the kitchen like a cyclone, unwrapping the packaged crust, peeling and slicing and mixing the apples with the cinnamon-sugar blend that had seemed so convenient, and only when it was successfully in the oven, crawling back onto the sofa with coffee and book.

As she continued to read, it became clear to her that then, as now, not all the tragedies that had befallen the islanders were directly attributable to conditions on the island or the elements impacting it, but were rather by-products of the circumstances in which people found themselves. Such perhaps was the case with Honora Alday.

It began, Joe Wisdom had written, *in the winter of 1842, the first on the island for Honora Alday, the eighteen year-old bride of Reminder Alday, himself twice-wid-*

owed and the father of grown sons, the youngest of whom would play a significant part in the events that followed.

Miss Honora Pettigrew, while not from a family of especial prominence, had nevertheless enjoyed a certain social freedom in her native Newville, as well as a considerable popularity among the young men of the area, on one of whom she had settled her affections and her matrimonial intentions.

But her father thought otherwise and determined to marry her instead to Mr. Reminder Alday, who, being of more mature years and possessed of a not inconsiderable farmstead on the largest of the lake islands, was thought by Mr. Pettigrew to be the better match.

And so, to her vast sorrow, Honora Pettigrew was married and transported to her new home, where she saw her prospects for happiness dwindle to an area five miles by two. Amidst the bleakness of her life, there was but one small joy, which was the time she was able to spend with Reminder Alday's youngest son, Marcus.

As so often happens, these two fell in love, and in due course, Honora found herself with child by Marcus and urged him to take her away from the island. There were so many places, she assured him, where they could live openly as man and wife, and no one the wiser. But instead of simply fleeing with her unannounced, Marcus elected to place all before his father in the hopes that Reminder Alday would grant Honora a divorce which would allow her to marry Marcus and thus legitimize their unborn child.

But he had misjudged his father's reason and his mood, and upon hearing his son's news, the enraged Reminder split his son's skull with a poleax, and this within the view of the pregnant Honora, who was therewith restricted to the confines of the cabin to await the birth of her bastard child.

That winter proved to be particularly brutal, as though Nature had decided to act in concert with the wronged Reminder Alday, so that Honora was forced to spend untold days at a time under the malevolent eye of her estranged husband. The strain of bowing beneath his hatred, as well as the burden of her advancing pregnancy soon began to work upon her mind, until her reason was irreversibly compromised. Her madness was complete when, following her travail and the delivery of a daughter, Reminder Alday took the child from her, placing it inside his coat and slamming the cabin door shut behind him. When he returned, the baby was nowhere to be seen.

Certain that her husband had murdered her infant or left it to perish in the blizzard, Honora waited until he slept and then slaughtered him with that selfsame poleax with which her lover had been dispatched. Then she wandered, barefoot and distracted, out onto the ice, never to be seen alive again.

She went to her watery grave not knowing that her child had been given to be raised and nurtured by Reminder Alday's eldest son Josiah, whose descendents still reside on the island.

Sophie shivered in spite of her proximity to the fire. Whether because of the disquiet of the night outside or her own loneliness and fear, for Carl and herself, the story disturbed her. There were features of it that resonated vaguely in her consciousness; besides the archetypal themes of dangerous love and murder, or even madness, there was something more immediate ... *Alday.* Of course. There was every probability that the descendents of Josiah Alday would have altered their surname in the hopes that the scandal would be forgotten by successive generations of islanders. So the blood of poor, mad Honora Alday might well run to this day in the veins of Mar and Crystal Holliday. Was it *that* knowledge that had somehow cost Joe Wisdom his life?

She gasped. The pie! She ran to the oven, and grabbing a dishtowel, wrestled it to the counter. It was perfectly browned, and she looked at the clock in confusion, unable to believe that it had not been hours since she had put it in to bake. She must have been more tired than she'd realized, and stressed, waiting, waiting interminably for Carl to return. And still the snow came, thick and dull and relentless, and it occurred to her incongruously that Dante had been right to put Satan way down in the center of hell, immobilized *in ice.*

She placed her forehead on the heel of one hand. Perhaps Carl had been right, and a hot bath would do her a world of good. She could think there, or not.

She snatched up her bag and headed toward the stairs. But before she had reached the third step, Crow began to bark, a hoarse and insistent ar-ar-ar, rhythmic and unrelenting. Back and forth, back and forth across the wooden floor he plunged, his front paws rising and landing separately in a motion that reminded Sophie of a circus horse.

"No, Crow! I'm just going to take a bath. I'll let you out as soon as I finish, I promise," she called down to him. It made no appreciable difference to either of them. Crow continued to bark, and Sophie continued up the stairs.

The first scream caught in her throat and propelled her backward down the stairs to land in a bruised and painful heap at the bottom. She cried out in agony as she attempted to push herself up, one clearly injured ankle having buckled under her.

The front door flung open, precipitating a second manic shriek, as, crablike, she tried to scuttle backward away from Carl. She continued to scream indiscriminately against the background of Crow's unabated barking.

"God in heaven, Sophie!" Carl rushed toward her, dropping to his knees and grasping her by the shoulders. "What the hell's going *on*?" But she was silent, her eyes wide and glazed, teeth chattering, as she stared from him toward the loft. "All right, you stay here," he croaked. He bounded up the stairs, Crow at his heels, then groped blindly at the wall to keep himself from sprawling backward as he saw her. Crystal Holliday lay in her icy bath, her face blotchy and pale, staring up at him through unseeing eyes.

CHAPTER 15

He hurtled down the stairs and stumbled to the floor next to Sophie. "Sophie honey," he gasped, "are you all right? Sophie!" He shook her, and her head bobbled rapidly up and down. "Come on," he said, dragging her up. She cried out and dropped back to the floor.

"My ankle," she moaned.

"Jesus! I'll call the paramedics," he said, scrabbling on all fours toward the phone.

She lunged forward and clawed at him. "No!"

"What do you *mean*, no? You're hurt!" He reached for the phone, but she clung to him, white-knuckled as she yanked at his shirt.

"Carl, there's a dead body in your bathtub! And if that's not bad enough, it's Crystal Holliday's dead body!"

He paused for a moment, his face bleak and ashy. "So be it." He attempted the phone once more, but she threw herself backward and tightened her grip. "Sophie!"

"No no no! Listen, listen, Carl! It's only sprained!"

"You don't know that." He eyed her, and shaking himself loose, carefully peeled off her sock and began to palpate her foot and ankle. She clamped her eyes and lips shut tight, and said nothing. "I can't feel anything broken, but that doesn't mean there are no fractures. You need help, damn it!"

"And I'll get it. I promise. But let's just sit a minute and catch our breath, please. Carl, please!"

He thumped a palm against his forehead. "At least let me wrap it. I've got a bandage"—he glanced with dread toward the loft—"up there."

"Oh, lord," she moaned. "You should keep things like that down here."

"I will from now on," he mumbled, and dragged up the stairs, trying hard not to look too closely at Crystal as he edged around the tub to reach the cabinet. He grabbed the bandage and stared down at her. She didn't look good, puffy and bluish, her fine hair drifting out from her head like algae, and there were darker blotches on her neck. "Oh, shit," he groaned, and bounded back down the stairs.

He lifted Sophie onto the sofa and began to wrap her foot and ankle as carefully as he could so as not to hurt her. She in turn tried not to whimper. He finished and sat back on his haunches. "Sophie, I might as well call the paramedics—no, now listen to me," he said over her protests. "I might as well, since I'm gonna have to call Mike Hatton."

"Are you crazy!" she shouted, jerking upright and snatching at him.

"Sophie! As you've pointed out, there's a dead body in my bathtub, and what's more, it looks like she was strangled and pushed under the water."

"Oh, dear lord!" gasped Sophie. "Murder then."

"Afraid so," he answered morosely. "And, Sophie honey, there's no way outta this for me. You wanna talk about perfect. If I didn't do it, I should have. But I'll cut a deal with Kandinsky. Full confession, Joe Wisdom too, if he leaves you out of it."

"What!" she shrieked, flinging herself forward and clutching at his shirt collar. "That is never going to happen!"

He pulled back in surprise and glowered over at her. "It damned well *is*—"

"—never going to happen! You try it, and you'll see how fast two can play that game. And believe you me, Kandinsky would rather have me! Be quite a feather in his cap. Why, maybe he could even figure out a way to pin Peter's murder on me." She lay back panting.

"Hell, Sophie, do you realize how serious this is?"

She turned on him a look of blank incredulity. "Crystal Holliday, whom I was certain was responsible for murder, assault, and breaking and entering, is lying in your bathtub, herself the victim of foul play. In addition, we've been here for several hours—a fact which does not bear thinking about too scrupulously—with the heat turned up. Yes, Carl, I know how serious it is. Now, what *we* have to do," she said, grasping his hand, "is decide what to do about it."

"There's *only* one thing to do about it. We have to call Mike. There's no other choice."

"Of course there are other choices. Carl, *think*, will you? What do you suppose is going to happen if they come in and find her here, like that?"

"Maybe it won't be so bad. We didn't kill her, either of us. The evidence—"

"Evidence? Do you think for one minute that Kandinsky will look any further than us, that he won't make sure the 'evidence' supports the simplest solution?"

"And what motive would either of us have to kill Crystal, much less Joe Wisdom?"

"She broke in and confronted you—about Gary what's-his-name, about me, about *you*. There was a struggle."

"And I strangled her and shoved her in the bathtub. And filled the tub."

"All right then! She confronted *me*—she wanted you back, she knew about Peter and me, she forgot to stamp the due date in my library book! Oh, what *difference* does it make?" she shouted in frustration.

"So *you* strangled her and shoved her in the bathtub—and filled the tub."

"Well, it seems to me *somebody* did just that."

"Sophie, you're talking about trying to cover up a murder we didn't commit. You don't think *that's* gonna look suspicious? Honey," he said wearily, "the only thing to do is play this one straight."

She sighed and leaned forward, her fingertips trailing over his cheek. "Carl, I'm not trying to cover up a murder. That would be wrong. I know that. And if it were just Mike Hatton, that might be different. But Kandinsky? If you call them now, then one or both of us will be going out of here in handcuffs. Probably both. And then what happens to us, and to Crow?" The Lab thumped his tail against the floor and whined at the mention of his name. "All I'm asking for is a little time," she pleaded.

He reached up and took her hand. "Time for what, angel? The longer we wait, the worse it's gonna be."

"Ohhh," she shook her head and dropped her face into her hands, "I don't see how."

"Look, we can't sit here and do nothing, with … well, *her* upstairs."

She pulled her face up through her hands and stared at him. "You're right," she said, hauling herself up clumsily and hobbling toward the kitchen.

"Where do you think you're going?" He snatched her up around the waist.

"Pots. Bucket? We have to collect snow—it's the one thing of which there's no shortage—and put her on ice while we think."

"Jee-sus, Sophie! She's not a halibut." He plopped her back down on the sofa.

"Look, we'd be doing them a favor, preserving forensic evidence. And it wouldn't hurt us either."

"We're not 'putting her on ice,' Sophie! In the first place, that's something I'd expect Kandinsky to say."

She ignored the comparison with its implicit insult. "All we'd have to do is drain the tub and then sort of pack her in snow. More like *under* the ice."

"Woman, do you *hear* yourself? We are *not*—" He stopped abruptly as he saw her face go suddenly placid, a distant look in her eyes the only indication of cognition.

Sophie had heard herself. "'Under the ice,' Bea said. Why would she say that, Carl?"

"What?" His face registered confusion. "Probably for dramatic effect, if I know Bea. Josh said the same thing. Why, what difference does it make, with her …" He jerked a thumb toward the loft.

"No, no, wait. When Josh said it, he meant an accident. But when Bea said it, she meant suicide, that Crystal had deliberately walked out onto the ice. Clearly, Bea wanted me to think that Crystal was unbalanced and capable of killing herself." She considered. "Although it seems to me if Crystal *had* wanted to kill herself, there are umpteen ways she could have done it, about the least likely of which I would think would be walking out onto the ice in the hope of drowning. Like Honora Alday," she said thoughtfully.

"*Who*?"

She waved a vague hand, and her brow furrowed. "There's something wrong here."

"Sophie, for God's sake! There's a body in my bathtub, and I didn't put it there. You're damned right there's something wrong here. Now, I'm gonna call Mike Hatton, and what happens happens."

"Carl," she chewed at her lip as he lifted the handset, "what if she didn't mean the ice on the lake at all? What if she meant …" She nodded toward the loft, and her eyes went wide. "Wouldn't that mean *Bea* killed her?"

"What possible reason could Bea have to kill her own niece?" muttered Carl, and began to dial.

"No, the question is who *else* would have a motive—other than us."

Carl slammed the phone down. "What, you think Bea killed her own niece to frame *us*? Sophie, that doesn't make any sense! If she had a problem with *us*, it would be on Crystal's behalf. Now, what kinda sense would it make for her to kill Crystal to frame us in order to get back at us for Crystal?"

"I realize it doesn't seem to make much sense," conceded Sophie.

"Doesn't seem to—" Carl spluttered helplessly. "It's pretzel logic."

"All right, then who else had a motive?" she repeated.

"I don't know, but we already know that neither of us did."

"No, we've decided that neither of us *did* it, and therefore, we don't need to consider motive. But what do you really *know*?"

"What are you saying?"

"Exactly what Kandinsky will say. I learned from Joe Wisdom that it was Crystal having an affair with my late, lamented husband, so they both had to go, Joe because he knew too much, and Crystal for revenge. Simple."

"Uh huh, and you hit yourself in the back of the head."

"No, I *told* you I was hit in the back of the head. Remember, I wouldn't allow you to call the paramedics. Did you feel a contusion on the back of my head, or did you just see the bump on the front?"

"Okay. Okay," he said, his head bobbing in agitation, "so you killed Crystal. Why bring her here? Why put her in my bathtub and incriminate me?"

"I didn't bring her here. She was here already—your mysterious intruder."

"And why would she come here?"

"I don't know, Carl. Waiting for you? That's what I thought anyway, when I found her here. So I killed her, but I couldn't dispose of the body right away, so I put her 'under the ice.'"

"And then begged me to bring you out here."

"To help me with the body, of course. Lovers have been known to do stranger things, no?"

"Wait," he smiled smugly, "you couldn't have killed her on Halloween. You were with me all night."

"In the first place, who knows that for sure except you and me? You could lie."

"But you asked me what I *know*."

"And do you know how long she's been up there? Maybe I didn't kill her on Halloween. But that doesn't mean she wasn't here then. Didn't you say you were missing a loaf of bread?"

"Ha! Got you, angel. I discovered the break-in the same day Joe was killed, *before* Halloween when Crystal disappeared. And I replaced the broken glass, remember?"

"And what makes you think someone couldn't have gotten in again? Jimmied the lock?"

"In the first place," he said, walking over and yanking at one of the door handles, "these locks aren't that easy to—" The door swung open to admit a blast of snow borne in on a frigid wind.

The blood drained from Sophie's face, and she clutched the arm of the sofa as she recalled Crow, sniffing along the bottom of the door, the hair bristling on his back.

"What is it, honey?"

"While you were gone," she stammered, "I think there was someone out there."

This time she did not demur when Carl picked up the phone and dialed. It was not only Kandinsky, she realized, with whom they were stranded. There had now been two murders committed on the island, and she was no longer so naive as to assume the killer had finished his grisly work.

"Mike? It's Carl. Look, I guess you better come out to my place. We've got … some trouble. Yeah, and you'd better get an ambulance out too. We've"—he took a deep breath—"we've found Crystal." He hung up the phone and, sinking down next to Sophie, reached down to pet Crow. "Well. Now I guess we wait."

She looped her arm through his and leaned her head against him. "I think you should call Josh Dugan."

"*Josh*? What for?"

She shrugged. "He said to call him if you needed help."

He huffed and smiled. "Angel, Josh is a lot of things—nobody's better on the lake and nobody knows it better—but a lawyer he ain't."

"He said if he couldn't get across, nobody could."

"And nobody *can*, honey."

"I wonder." *They'd done it more than a century earlier, after all …*

He turned and frowned down at her. "Wait a minute, what are you hatching now? What difference does it make if he can get here or not?"

"Just seems like a handy person to have around in a pinch."

"Maybe too handy sometimes. Sails close to the wind."

"That's what I meant."

"I hope you're not suggesting we run."

"No," she said innocently. He shot her a warning look. "Well, it was just a thought," she sighed.

He slipped his arms around her and nestled her against him. "Not exactly the evening we had planned, is it?"

"I can't believe I'm saying this, but I wish they'd hurry," she shivered. "It's horrible to just sit here waiting, and it makes my skin crawl to think of her up there."

"I know," he replied soberly. "I feel … bad. I mean …"

"Oh, I know it must be dreadful for you. I'm sorry," she said, reaching up to kiss his cheek.

"I never wished her any harm, Sophie. I want you to know that."

"I know that. And neither did I. Not her, and certainly not poor Joe Wisdom. But somebody did. If not us and not Bea, then who, Carl?"

"I have no idea who, Sophie, because I don't know the *why*. And maybe you'll think it's strange coming from me, but I can't really think of a good reason to kill somebody."

"None at all?"

He thought for a moment, then gave a helpless shrug. "Gotta be another way." He scowled and reached behind him to pull something out of the sofa cushion. It was Joe Wisdom's book. "What was that you were trying to tell me earlier?"

"What?"

"Some name?"

"Oh," she said, taking the book from him, "Honora Alday, you mean. Joe recounts the story in here, what he would have called another of the regular acts of human drama," she smiled sadly. "A true story, apparently, involving illicit love and madness and murder. And suicide. It seems this girl was more or less forced to marry a much older man she didn't love. He brought her to the island, where she got involved with his youngest son and became pregnant. When her husband found out, he killed his own son with an ax. After that, Honora—that was her name—was virtually his prisoner, winter being what it is here. When she gave birth to her child, her husband took it from her. Now it seems he gave it to another son and his wife to raise. But Honora, believing he'd killed the child, waited for him to go to sleep and then killed him with the same ax he'd used to kill his own son. And then, the story goes, she wandered out onto the ice and drowned."

"You're joking."

"Wait till you hear the punchline. Joe said the descendants of the Aldays still live on the island. Now, he didn't say so specifically, but I think that at some point the Aldays changed their name in the hopes of escaping the scandal of their forebears."

Carl's brow furrowed, and he gave her a skeptical look. "Not the Hollidays?"

"That's what *I* think."

They saw the approach of the flashing red lights through the front windows. "Huh," he said, "colorful little place, isn't it?"

CHAPTER 16

"Appears to be just a sprain, ma'am," said firefighter and paramedic Luke Garvey, "but you should have it X-rayed as soon as you get a chance. In the meantime, it'd be best to stay off it as much as possible."

"Thank you," smiled Sophie, "I'm sure it will be fine." Her smile faded as Garvey's partner backed down the stairs at one end of a gurney. Mike Hatton carried the other end, with Detective Ed Kandinsky bringing up the rear of the procession.

"I'll take it, Mike," said Luke Garvey, rising and packing up his gear. "I'm finished here."

Sophie pulled the shawl tight around her, and exchanging a fleeting glance with Carl, stared into the dying fire as the gurney with Crystal Holliday's mortal remains was removed to the ambulance.

"So," said Detective Kandinsky, strolling casually around the kitchen before plopping down in a chair across from Sophie and Carl, "you drove over here in a blizzard because you wanted a change of scenery, and you found the missing woman dead in your bathtub and called us. But first, Mrs. Skala, you took the time to bake a pie, is that right?"

"As I told you, Detective, I was here alone while Carl was working at the airport, and I only went upstairs just as he was returning. I didn't know she was there," she said somberly. "If you think I could have sat here calmly, much less baked a pie, knowing there was a dead body upstairs, you're very much mistaken."

"Oh, that's right. You were so shocked that you fell down the stairs and sprained your ankle. You're certainly accident-prone, aren't you?"

"Am I, Mr. Kandinsky? You may recall that my earlier injury was hardly an accident."

"Well, let me rephrase that then. I guess you just attract bad luck, to yourself and to people around you."

"All right!" Carl sprang forward, but Sophie grabbed at his arm and shook her head. "He's got no right to talk to you that way. It's beyond the scope of his *investigation*," he snapped.

"In fact," continued Kandinsky with exaggerated sincerity, "it's almost uncanny how often people that the two of you have dealings with wind up dead."

"That could be said of everyone, now couldn't it, Mr. Kandinsky?" smiled Sophie. "Including you. In fact, I would guess that you come into contact with more dead people than most of us."

"But the difference, Mrs. Skala," he returned a smug smile, "is that the dead people I come in contact with are generally dead *before* I come across them."

"How fortunate," murmured Sophie, "for them."

"Look, we're not getting anywhere this way," interceded Mike Hatton, standing between the others, his fingers working at the edge of his hat. "Two of our neighbors are dead, people I knew, and we need to get to the bottom of this. Now Carl, are you sure neither of you have been here since before the Halloween party?"

"Yeah, I'm sure, Mike. I told you, the back door was unlocked. I don't know if it was Crystal who broke in before or ... somebody else. Just like I don't know if she was already here when the killer came in," he said, running an anxious hand through his hair. "None of it makes any sense."

"Not the way you tell it, it sure doesn't," said Ed Kandinsky. "Especially since it seems the two of you are the only ones who had issues, shall we say, with the dead woman."

"Come on, Ed," appealed Mike Hatton. "We don't know that."

"*Issues*?" seethed Carl. "Neither one of us had any reason to want Crystal dead. I moved on a long time ago, and Sophie—"

"Ah, yes, Mrs. Skala, whose dead husband just happened to have cheated on her with the murdered woman. Astonishing coincidence."

"A coincidence, yes, Detective. But not so very astonishing when you consider that my late husband and I visited the island with some frequency. And this is, by all accounts, where he met Crystal Holliday. Likewise, my having been a frequent visitor is precisely the reason I decided to come here. But if you want to know whether I knew when I came here that she had had an affair with my husband, much less that she was living here, the answer is no."

"Oh, naturally. It was karma."

"I prefer to think that neither one of us had any reason to stay where we were."

"Well, now I can understand why Ms. Holliday would come back here. After all, this was her home. But you? You have money, you could have gone anywhere—Paris, Cancun, Australia. But you chose to come here."

"I wanted to be somewhere quiet."

"Seems to me you certainly did misjudge that then, didn't you?"

"So it would seem."

"Of course, it's not that you brought the excitement with you, is it, Mrs. Skala?"

"No, I brought mostly garbanzos and macaroni and cheese with me, Mr. Kandinsky."

Kandinsky's eyes narrowed and his mouth went hard and sour. "All right, I think we've played footsies about long enough. Fact is, you two," he wagged a finger between Carl and Sophie, "got a big problem here. Let me spell it out for you. Carl's involvement with Ms. Holliday bought him five years, and Dr. Skala's affair with her—well, he's dead, isn't he?"

"Any connection between my husband's affair and his death is pure speculation on your part, Detective," Sophie said calmly.

"And all of it adds up to a motive for murder, Mrs. Skala, one of the oldest motives of all—revenge. The two of you made the perfect team."

"Mm," nodded Sophie, "Bonnie and Clyde."

"Oh, you can laugh now, Mrs. Skala. But I wonder how funny you'll find it when you're charged with murder—finally."

"Well, Mr. Kandinsky, I see you've decided that my meeting Carl was no accident, and that we hatched this nefarious plan to avenge ourselves on Crystal Holliday for past grievances. But I am curious about a couple of things. If we had planned to kill her, and here—I'll give you that much—why would we call you? Wouldn't it have made more sense for us to dispose of the body? Seems to me it wouldn't have been difficult at all. For instance, Carl could simply have put her in the back of the truck and dropped her over a bank while he was out clearing the roads. And he surely could have done it before now, couldn't he?"

"That's not so difficult, Mrs. Skala. Try this scenario: one of you killed her, and the other got squeamish. And I don't think it would take much to figure out which was which, especially since it was Carl that called us."

"Mr. Kandinsky, not that it's any of your business, but if I were going to kill every woman with whom my late husband had an affair, I would be one of the most prolific serial killers in history. I assure you, by the time Ms. Holliday came along, revenge would have been the last thing on my mind. Which brings me to my other question. Whether I had a personal grudge against Crystal or not, what *possible* motive could I have had for killing Joe Wisdom, whom I'd just met? Or are you saying the two murders are unrelated?"

He gave her a cagey smile. "I'm not saying anything. I'm asking the questions, remember?"

"Of course," Sophie resumed her smile. "But I wonder if you're asking the right ones, or more to the point, the right *people*."

Doubt flickered across Ed Kandinsky's face, before the corners of his mouth were pulled up into what would have been a smile had his eyes been involved. "Now, don't you worry, Mrs. Skala. I'm doing my job, and I'll see the killers brought to justice."

"Well I wouldn't want to keep you from it, Detective. Is there something else we can do for you?"

"You know, if we were anywhere else, I'd arrest you on suspicion of murder. But under the circumstances, I doubt you're much of a flight risk, either of you. But when traffic resumes, that may very well change. In any case, I would suggest you not try to leave the island."

"We hadn't planned to. Now, if you've finished for the time being, it's been rather a traumatic night, and I think we'd like to get some sleep."

"Sleep all you want, only you won't be sleeping here."

"I beg your pardon?"

"This is a crime scene, Mrs. Skala, so I'm afraid you'll have to go back where you came from."

"I see." Sophie clambered awkwardly up off the sofa and began to gather the few personal items she had unpacked.

"And you won't be able to take anything with you. It's all potential evidence."

"Mr. Kandinsky, you can arrest me if you like, but I am not leaving without my belongings. Even you're not such a fool as to suggest that I might have brought with me this evening something with which Crystal was killed a week ago."

Detective Kandinsky eyed her coldly, before relieving her of the bag she had picked up. "All right, but we'll have to check the contents first," he said, tipping it upside down over the sofa.

"Oh, for heaven's sake!" fumed Sophie.

"That's unnecessary, and you know it!" shouted Carl. "Mike," he entreated, "come on, this is your jurisdiction."

"Carl, it'd be easier to just cooperate. He's got a right. This is a murder investigation. If you wanna file a complaint, you can do that."

"Aw," Carl waved a hand in disgust, as Ed Kandinsky finished poking through Sophie's toiletries and began to go through her clothing, "what's the point?" He changed his mind a moment later.

Sophie let out a little gasp of protest as Ed Kandinsky smirked and held up a lacy black teddy with the hang tags still attached. "Yeah, I'd say this little item might be some incentive for a certain kind of man to become involved in murder."

"I'll keep that in mind, Mr. Kandinsky," Sophie replied airily.

Carl's face went black with rage, and he snatched the garment out of Kandinsky's hands. "That's just about enough!" he shouted, then cleared his throat and handed it to Sophie with studied indifference.

"I wanted to surprise you," she flushed.

"Oh, you did that all right, angel," he mumbled.

Sophie gathered up her things and returned them to the bag. "Now, if you're *quite* finished, Mr. Kandinsky, I'll pack up the food and we'll be on our way."

"You can't take the food," Kandinsky said casually.

Sophie and Carl stared at one another and then at Kandinsky in disbelief. "Why is that, Detective?" she gibed. "You planning to dust it for prints?"

"We're taking the food." Carl's jaw went rigid as he stood up and prepared to stare down Kandinsky, who, ludicrously encased in an oversized parka he had clearly borrowed from Mike Hatton, seemed now shrunken and gnome-like. "In case nobody's told you, we're stranded for the moment, and if you think we're leaving food here, you've got another thing coming. But don't worry," he added, striding over to the kitchen and removing things from the refrigerator into bags, "we'll only take what we brought with us."

"You start taking it out," Sophie said softly, "and I'll finish packing up the rest."

He nodded and grabbed up several bags, stopping to empty Crow's water bowl and tuck it under his arm. He halted in front of Mike Hatton. "When can I have my house back, Mike?"

Mike Hatton stared down at the floor uncomfortably. "Shouldn't be long, Carl. We'll get done as quick as possible, I promise. I'll call or stop by tomorrow, huh?" He glanced up at Carl in embarrassment. "Here, I'll give you a hand," he said as an afterthought.

Sophie saved the pie until last, trying to decide how best to transport it. She supposed somewhat sourly she would have to hold it on her lap and hope Crow didn't take too keen an interest in it.

As if he'd read her thoughts, Kandinsky waved toward the counter. "Oh, and uh, leave the pie."

"Leave the *pie*?" she glared over at him.

"Yeah, you didn't bring it with you."

"And that makes it evidence, Detective?"

"Maybe," he grinned.

Sophie picked up the pie with intentional ceremony and presented it to him with a saccharine smile. "With my compliments, Mr. Kandinsky. Come on, Crow," she said, and dragging on her coat, hobbled out the door Carl held open for her. "I can't believe," she gulped against the bitter blast of snow, as Carl lifted her into the truck, "that odious little man would make us come back out in this. I hope he chokes on that pie!"

"Probably just another little dig to keep the pressure on us," he scowled, as the truck lurched up onto what he supposed was the road. "Although why he thinks he's gonna get anywhere being an obnoxious son of a bitch is beyond me."

"It's obvious he's trying to get a rise, and," she sighed, "you do seem to play right into his hands on that."

"Aw, I know," he growled, "but he really frosts my ass when he goes after you."

"I know," she replied, stroking his arm, "but that's exactly what he wants to do. And we can't let him get to us, Carl. Since he's convinced we're guilty, he's not looking anywhere else, and that means we have to."

He gave her a troubled glance. "Sophie, what do we know about it? We're not detectives."

"Neither is he much. Otherwise, he'd realize that these killings *wouldn't* be in character for either of us. They're too deliberate," she said quietly, and turned to look out the window. They were silent for what seemed like an eternity, the wipers squeaking rhythmically against random blasts of wind that shook the truck and shrieked in their ears. "None of it makes any sense," she fretted. "It should be us."

"Sophie honey, you need to stop thinking about all this for now. In fact, I don't see how you *can* think about it any more. What with all that's happened, and then finding *her* like that," he looked across at her in appeal, "I'm exhausted."

"I'm sorry, Carl. You're right, of course. We're not going to solve anything tonight. It's just that so many strange things have happened in so short a time, I hardly know if I'm coming or going. I'm trying so hard to make sense of it all."

"I know that, angel," he said, cranking the wheel and forcing the truck up the driveway to the cottage. "But what we need is a good night's sleep, maybe a hot bath to relax first."

"That would be almost more than I could hope for. And maybe it's a good thing Kandinsky threw us out at that. I'm not sure when, if ever, I'll be able to get into your bathtub again. Lord," she sighed, as he helped her down out of the truck and up the steps to the back door. "But I'm still not thrilled about having to drag all this stuff back in and put it all away again." Crow leaped down from the truck and hovered around her legs as she felt in her purse for the keys.

"It won't take more than a few minutes," Carl replied, absently twisting the knob and pushing open the door.

The wind whipped at the fur trim on her hood, and the snow began to cling to her in clumps as she stood rooted to the small porch, her eyes large and glassy. She shook her head helplessly, but he first put a finger to his lips to silence her, then pointed to indicate that she should stay where she was.

He slipped inside, looking around cautiously as his eyes adjusted to the near darkness. The kitchen was empty and silent, the only illumination the reflection of moonlight off the snow that stole in through the windows, the only sounds the roar of the wind and the clanging of the windchime out back. He pulled Sophie inside and motioned for Crow to sit next to her. She pointed toward the light switch for which he was obviously searching, but when he flipped it up, nothing happened.

Just as he was about to backtrack to the generator, a long crack of light appeared at the front of the hall, and the front door caught in the wind and burst open. Carl sprang unthinking up through the hall, Sophie at his heels. Crow bounded past them, but in his haste, Carl collided with the animal and fell forward onto all fours, Sophie crying out and grabbing at him as he scrambled to his feet and pulled the pistol from his coat pocket. He hesitated in the doorway just long enough for her, peering past him, to see a dark, hunched form plunging heavily through the drifts and the swirl, a muted flash of red bobbing up and down before the figure was swallowed up by the storm.

"No!" she begged, hanging on him, as he struggled to free himself and give pursuit. "No," she whimpered, and slithered to the floor, sobbing with exhaustion and despair. He looked down at her wearily, slammed and locked the door, and slumped down next to her on the hall floor.

CHAPTER 17

"I know, angel. I'm tired too." Carl grabbed a pillow off the chair and placed it under Sophie's ankle as she lay on the sofa. "But I have to call Mike. How would it look if we waited till morning and then told him we saw the intruder running away, but were too tired to call? With any luck, he'll wait till morning to come over and make out the report."

"When is it going to end?" she sniffled.

"Aw, I don't know. But for right now, we worry about right now. I'll make that call, and then you'll have a bath and get a good night's sleep. Things won't look so hopeless in the morning," he said, smoothing a hand along her cheek.

She reached up and squeezed his hand. "Thank you, Carl. If it weren't for you, I think I'd have lost my mind by now."

"Naw, if it weren't for me, you'd probably be snug at your sister's place eating popcorn and watching chick movies," he smiled, and picked up the phone. By the time he had given Mike Hatton a brief account of this latest trespass and agreed to meet with him in the morning, he found Sophie sound asleep. He considered for a moment carrying her up to bed, but gathered up a couple of quilts instead, and tucking one around her gently, rechecked the doors to make certain they were locked, and snuggled down into a chair with another one.

He jerked upright as he felt a hand on his shoulder. "What's wrong?" he asked groggily.

"Nothing," smiled Sophie. "You didn't look very comfortable, and I was afraid you'd have a stiff neck. You shouldn't have slept in the chair."

"I'm all right." He looked around at the gray light that filtered through the window and told him it was morning. "What time is it?"

"About nine."

"Hell," he said, pushing away the quilt, "Mike'll be here any minute. I need to make some coffee and take Crow out."

"Crow has been out and had his breakfast, and the coffee's made. I'll get you some."

"Whoa, whoa. You're not supposed to be on that foot," he said, grabbing her arm as she turned toward the kitchen.

"It's all right. Really. And I promise I haven't done anything very quickly, and I don't plan to start. So why don't you go get cleaned up, and by the time you come back down, I should have made it to the kitchen and back, hm? Oh, and Carl," she called after him as he started up the stairs, "I'm sorry for the hysterics last night."

"Don't be silly, Sophie. Talk about a nightmare. I still can't get my head around it." He shook his head and hurried upstairs.

Sophie had hobbled halfway to the kitchen when the knock came at the front door. She turned and hobbled in the other direction, pulling open the door and standing aside to admit Mike Hatton. "Good morning, Mr. Hatton. Come in, please," she motioned toward the living room. "Should we expect anyone else?"

"If you mean Detective Kandinsky—"

"I do."

"Well, I dropped him off at Carl's place. He wanted to take another look around in daylight and make some calls to the mainland."

"Wonderful. And I'm sure they'll be on Carl's phone bill. Just as sure as I am that he's having apple pie for breakfast. Well," she shrugged, "Carl will be down in a minute. Perhaps you'd like some coffee?"

"Thank you, ma'am." She stepped down awkwardly on her injured foot. "If it's not too much trouble."

"Not at all. Please sit down." From the kitchen, she heard Carl on the stairs and the murmured greetings and then his echoed steps along the narrow hall as he arrived to help her with the coffee.

"Now, what did I tell you about that ankle?"

"Here." She handed him two mugs, then picked up her own and the creamer and followed him back down the hall. "Please, won't you sit over here, Mr. Hatton?" With a gracious sweep of the hand, she indicated the chair nearest the sofa and hoped he would remove himself from the arm of the other.

He did, although he squirmed down into the seat with such apparent discomfort that Sophie was almost sorry she'd suggested it. "So," he sighed, taking a swig of coffee and trying to look official, "you say somebody broke in here and ran out the front door when you came in the back. I don't suppose you'd know who it was."

"Naw, Mike. Even if it was somebody we know, there's no way we could have made out who it was in that storm." Carl rose anxiously and walked over to look out the window. "This is so damn frustrating. It's not bad enough that there's no rhyme or reason that I can see for any of it. But then this friggin' weather makes it almost impossible to find anybody or anything." His lip curled into a cynical smile as he nodded toward the yard. "I mean, look at it. Just piddling random flakes now. But no way could anybody have found prints or anything else in that mess last night. And that's just when this guy decides to strike."

"Exactly. So they seem to be crimes of opportunity. But that doesn't make a lick of sense. Even if ya really stretch and say Joe's death and the assault on Ms. Skala were bungled robberies, there's no way to make sense of what happened to poor Crystal." He slapped at his leg with the battered, but blameless hat.

"Bea Baskin would call it uncanny," Sophie said quietly.

"Huh? What's Bea Baskin got to do with this?" Mike leaned forward in the chair, his hat still for the moment. "Well, I mean I know what she has to do with *Crystal.* But what's she got to do with the break-ins? You know something?"

"No, I don't know anything," sighed Sophie, "other than the fact that Carl and I aren't responsible for any of these ... *events.* You must know that, Mr. Hatton. Mike. At least of Carl. You know him, you know he didn't kill Joe Wisdom or Crystal. And neither did I, whatever you and Detective Kandinsky may think."

"That's just it, Ms.—well, what is it, Westenra or Skala?—I don't know what to think. I'd hate to believe either one of you had a hand in this business, but there are more coincidences about it all than I'm comfortable with too, if ya wanna know. And while I'm not wild about the way Kandinsky works, I guess somebody's gotta ask the unpleasant questions, and I'd just as soon it wasn't me."

"And we've answered your questions. But nobody seems to want to answer *mine.* You say you don't like all the coincidences, but if you don't believe that these break-ins are tied in with the murders, then you have one *more* coincidence to explain. You must see that. And if they *are* all connected, then how could we possibly have killed either of the victims? This is the second time that someone has broken in here."

"And, Ms. Skala, I'm treating this as a legitimate incident. That's why I'm here."

"What exactly does *that* mean, Mr. Hatton?" she asked testily.

He put up a calming hand. "Now, all I meant was that you two are the only ones who know anything about this."

"Well, of course we're the only ones who know about it! We're the only ones who were here. And it *happened*, Mr. Hatton. Someone was in this house when we got back."

"All right, all right. Now, is anything missing?"

Carl looked over in surprise. "Tell ya the truth, Mike, we were so beat last night we didn't think to look. Sophie?"

She gave him a bewildered glance. "I have no idea."

"Well, then I wonder if you'd mind taking a look.," said Mike Hatton, setting his cup on the table and struggling up out of the chair. He gave his belt a cursory jerk and hooked his thumbs into it.

"Not at all," replied Sophie, uncrossing her legs and setting down her own cup. Her slow gaze swept the living room. Her books leaned at the same angles in the bookcase, just as she'd propped them when she'd unpacked. A thin veil of dust lay undisturbed on the mantel and the desk on the far wall, and her laptop and papers lay on top of it in the identical disarray in which she had left them. "There doesn't appear to be anything out of place here. I'll check the kitchen."

"Here, at least lean on me," insisted Carl, sliding an arm around her waist and helping her down the hall.

She scanned the kitchen, but waved splayed fingers in token of helplessness. "I don't see anything, I'm sorry."

"Could you check the cupboards, please?" suggested Mike Hatton.

"The cupboards? All right, although I can't think what would be in my cupboards worth stealing." She pulled open two of the doors, then clutched at the edge of the counter, her brow furrowed in confusion.

"What is it, honey? What's wrong?"

"Cans," she replied, yanking open another and then another cupboard door.

"Cans, Ms. Skala?" Mike Hatton's pen hovered over a small notepad.

"Cans," repeated Sophie. "I arranged all the canned food in neat little rows, Mr. Hatton, so I'd know what I had. And the cupboards were pretty well packed to the rafters, as you can well imagine. But now everything is moved around willy-nilly, and there are cans missing." On an impulse, she jerked open a drawer. "And," she said, pulling out a can opener, "there's one of these gone. I had a spare just in case. I don't even know why. It was a cheap one, not as good as this."

"Sophie, what are you saying?" frowned Carl. "Somebody broke in here in the middle of a blizzard to steal your fruit cocktail?" The three of them searched each other's faces for enlightenment. "But why?"

"Somebody was hungry," said Mike Hatton. Whether it was a redundant observation or a prelude to another, unspoken thought mattered little, as each was involved in his own ruminations. "Could you check upstairs please, ma'am, see if there's anything else missing?" She nodded, and he offered her a hand and assisted her slowly up the stairs, followed by Carl and Crow.

Sophie poked in drawers and closets, checked her dresser and jewelry box, and shook her head. "I don't see anything missing. So," she added, turning to Carl, "I guess someone *did* break in to steal my fruit cocktail. If only that were all there was to it, he'd be welcome to it." She hobbled out of the bedroom and started back down the stairs. "Could we continue this discussion downstairs? I'd like to sit for awhile, if I may."

"I told you," groused Carl, positioning a pillow behind her back and swinging her foot up onto the sofa.

"What about you, Carl?" Mike Hatton lowered himself back into the chair. "Did you find anything missing from your place?"

"Besides part of a loaf of bread? No. And like I told you, I'm not positive about that."

"Still, that could be important."

"How? The longer this goes on, the less sense any of it makes."

"At least it's a common thread, somebody breaking in to steal food." He glanced up to see Sophie and Carl gazing at him with anticipation. "Well, it's something anyway."

"Is there anybody you know of hard up, Mike? When you think of it, it's a pretty desperate thing to do, to wander around on foot in these blizzards to break in just to steal food."

"Yep, it is. And if it wasn't for all the rest of it, I'd almost feel bad for the guy, ya know? But to answer your question, I don't know of anybody that bad off around here. Folks pretty much check on one another, and I can't imagine anybody being allowed to go hungry. But then, I'm not the best one to ask. Somebody like Bea'd know. Not much goes on around here that she doesn't know about."

"I was thinking that very thing, Mr. Hatton. You might want to ask her."

Mike Hatton perked up as he descried a solid lead that he could follow, and which moreover, had not originated with Ed Kandinsky. "I'll do that, Ms. Skala."

"There's something else, Mr. Hatton. Have there been any other break-ins on the island?"

"What? No, ma'am, none reported anyhow."

"But quite a few of the houses are just summer homes, aren't they? No one occupies them in the winter?"

"Yeah, that's true enough. Oh, I see what you're getting at. Maybe somebody's broke into some of them, as well. But then, if you don't mind me asking, why break in Carl's place and here, twice, and risk getting caught?"

"Maybe there's no food in the empty houses? Or maybe it's someone who's targeted us specifically."

"Okay, but then I don't guess they'd bother with the empty houses, would they? So I guess we don't have to worry about them."

"You might want to check them anyway, Mr. Hatton." He frowned in puzzlement. "There might be other reasons to break in somewhere. Carl may have been right when he suggested that whoever broke into his place was trying to get in out of the storm. Perhaps it wasn't a case of the killer finding Crystal there, but *her* finding *him*."

"I suppose so," he said doubtfully. "But then that still leaves a lot of questions unanswered, doesn't it?"

"Such as what Crystal was doing at Carl's house at all? Those questions are unanswered anyway."

"For the time being, I guess. But at least I have a couple leads now." He rose and jammed the notepad into his pocket. Then with an absent swipe of his hat, he announced, "Well, I'm gonna go get started on this. You think of anything else, you let me know."

"We will, Mike, and thanks." Carl saw him out the door and returned to the living room, where he pulled a chair nearer to Sophie. "So?" he asked, reaching for her hand.

"So somebody seems to know something about our movements, don't they?" she said soberly.

"That'd be my guess, yep.

"And it's beginning to look as though I *did* get whacked in the head because I interrupted a burglary. It's unbelievable."

"And that's why you were hit with the book. It was already here and handy, which tells me whoever it was didn't bring a weapon with him because he didn't expect to be interrupted that first time. After that, he obviously knew I was staying here and my house was empty, and broke in there. And that we'd gone back out there. What he didn't know was that Kandinsky had kicked us out, so he wasn't expecting us to show up here again last night. And *that* would suggest that he didn't know about Crystal."

"God, Carl," she said, putting a palm up to her forehead, "doesn't that mean we're talking about two different things, two different people entirely? I mean, if whoever was in here last night knew about Crystal, then he must have known we wouldn't be staying there."

"Unless he thought we'd be in jail by now."

"But you don't murder somebody and frame someone else so you'll be free to break into their house and steal food. It just doesn't make any sense. I was so sure all these incidents were connected, and what's more, connected to *me*. Now ..."

"I know it. But it's like Mike said, if you try to look at them all in terms of robberies, you might include Joe at a stretch. But that still leaves Crystal."

"Exactly. What happened to her doesn't seem to fit the pattern, much less the motive. Oh," she shivered, clutching his hand, "I wish we'd thought about leaving sooner, and done it."

"And I wish you'd done what I told you and not come back."

"We've been over this," she said curtly.

"No, we haven't been over this."

"We have. I said I'm not leaving here without you, so that's all there is to say."

"Sophie, I'm worried about you, about your safety."

"Why? I don't think anyone is going to kill me for my creamed corn."

"That's not funny. Doesn't it concern you in the least that somebody is watching us?"

"Oh, of course it does, Carl. I'm sorry. I didn't mean to make light of it. I'm just ... tired. Do you think," she nodded wistfully toward the window, "that it's clear enough for planes to come today?"

He stole a solicitous glance at her, lying wan against the arm of the sofa, the dark circles under her eyes more pronounced for the general pallor that had crept over her. "I don't know, angel. One or two might be able to nip in and out, as Josh would say."

"Hm," she smiled wanly, "I think I like Josh. Do you think he'll come today? Maybe we could go down to Dickie's for lunch. Or supper. What do you think?"

"Honey," he said gently, "what I think is that you need to rest, maybe take a nap. You don't look so good."

"Thanks for that. You know," she teased, "that's not a thing you want to say to a woman who's just spent forty-eight dollars on a lace teddy."

He smirked and shook his head. "You spent forty-eight dollars on something you're only going to wear for five minutes? Now, that was extravagant," he said, leaning over to kiss her.

"Just for you," she continued to smile, and closed her eyes.

CHAPTER 18

Sophie groaned and reached for the phone on the nightstand. Her hand grasped empty air, and she leaned up on one elbow and looked around in confusion. She was on the sofa in the living room of the cottage, and her nose was stuffy and her head felt like a football. Carl was speaking to someone, and when she wriggled around to see who was there, he held out the phone to her.

"It's your sister, angel."

She pulled herself up and folded back the quilt. "Reney? I'm so glad to hear from you. Yes, I made it back all right. But you sound terrible. I don't like the sound of that cough. Are you taking something for it? Do I? Yes, I suppose I do," she sniffed. "It's no wonder, I guess, with this horrible weather. I'm so sick of it. I know, honey. I miss you too. I wish you were here, but I wish even more that *I* was *there*," she sighed into the phone. "Things just seem to be going from bad to worse. You wouldn't believe it."

She could hear Carl in the background rattling around in the kitchen drawers and cupboards, but she paid little attention, being absorbed rather with relating to Reney all that had happened in the single day since they had seen each other. "I can't believe it's been only a day. It seems like ages ago that we had lunch. I just wish this would be over, and that we could leave this stupid, stupid island. Yes, honey, the first chance I get, I promise. Now, tell me you'll get some rest and take care of that cold. Yes," she smiled, "I will too. Talk to you soon. I love you, Reney."

Carl reappeared as if on cue just as she pressed the disconnect button, and handed her a mug of her favorite green tea. "Reney's sick," she said.

"Reney's not the only one, from the sound of it. You shouldn't have been out in that storm last night, and I'd like to deck Kandinsky on that score alone, never mind that fresh baked apple pie we could have been eating and aren't."

"I'll make you another. Of course," she pouted, "it would help if he'd return my pie pan."

"Maybe he will when he returns my house," grumbled Carl. "And I don't much like the idea of him rummaging around the place by himself."

"I know," Sophie said sympathetically. "But look," she added, pointing toward the window. "The sun is trying to peek through, and if we bundle up, it won't be so cold. Let's go down to Dickie's and have a few beers and something to eat that I haven't cooked, what do you say? Please?"

"Aw, Sophie, make me feel like a heel, why don't ya?" He looked at her unhappily over his knuckles. "You know I want to, but you really need to stay here and get better. But I'll tell you what. I'm going to the market to get something for that cold, and I'll not only get whatever else you want, but I'll swing by Dickie's and bring back dinner, whatever you want on the menu."

"Ohhh," she whined, but he had already tugged on his coat and pulled the truck keys out of the pocket.

"You just lie here and watch some TV or read, and I'll be back before you know it."

"But I did so want to get out. It's so hard being cooped up, even with you and Crow for company."

"I know, angel. But ya know, it's not easy for me either. As long as you're sick, I don't get to see that little black number on you," he winked, and bent down to give her a kiss.

Her eyeballs arced up and over. "Well, when you put it *that* way. I suppose I can read some more of poor Joe's book."

"Only if it won't make you feel bad. Now, what would you like? Anything your heart desires that can be had on the island."

"That limits the possibilities considerably," she grimaced. "But surprise me. If I'm not allowed out, at least I could have a surprise, couldn't I?"

"All right, that's what I'll do then. Now, I'll make sure everything is locked up tight, and you keep Crow by you."

She nodded, then listened to the hall floor creak under his steps and to the solid thunk of wood against wood as he pulled the door to behind him and the truck engine as it rumbled awake, and then to the silence of the house around her. She was glad of Crow's warm presence next to her and reached down to scratch behind his ears. But she felt immediately and keenly the absence of human companionship and realized how foolish she'd been to think she could winter here completely alone with only her tea, her books and her thoughts. No, one paid a price for escape. She sighed, and picking up Joe's book, began to leaf through it in search of something that might catch her eye and engage her interest until Carl returned.

The Hardestys, it seemed, had been early arrivals, having sold their Revolutionary War land grant and purchased twenty acres on the island. She tried to imagine what a considerable challenge it must have been for them, and found it sad in a way that those original twenty acres, which had represented so large a purchase in human endeavor and human dreams, had shrunk to the compass of her little yard. The dreams would be forgotten, and the Hardestys' unbroken presence over the course of nearly two centuries would end with the sale of the cottage, had in fact ended already with George Hardesty's abandonment. Still, she understood the abandonment, since her own dream had been so short-lived.

The book lay open on her lap, her eyes and her mind focused elsewhere. It made her suddenly melancholy to think of Joe Wisdom, of the new friend she might have had and how different might have been her own sojourn here. She turned the book over and looked closely at his photograph on the jacket, noting once again how clear his eyes were, how unaffected his smile. He'd seemed so genial and erudite, the sort of person with whom she might have passed many a pleasant afternoon or evening in easy conversation. Instead, he was dead, and it nagged at her that she might be somehow responsible, that her coming had been like a pebble in a pond, spreading ripples of misfortune that extended even to Carl.

She slumped morosely. She supposed she did love Carl, but she supposed too that she hadn't thereby done him any great favor. Maybe that's what Reney had meant, her "bad configurations." And Bea's "bad combinations." According to which, she guessed sardonically, Carl would be the chocolate syrup, she the catfish.

Bea. To her discomfort, it occurred to her suddenly that she ought to phone Bea to offer her condolences. She eyed the phone uncertainly. Bea would know by now, of course. The whole island would know by now that Crystal was dead and the location and circumstances of her discovery, and she wondered how she would be received now and whether Bea would welcome her call. She raked her teeth over her upper lip and reached for the phone and the directory. It was the proper thing to do.

She took a deep breath and dialed. The call was answered on the second ring. She panicked. What name should she give? "Bea? This is Sophie." Just Sophie then. "I … well, I suppose this must seem awkward, but I just wanted to say how sorry I am." There was a momentary silence. "About Crystal," she stammered.

"Well, thank you, Sophie." A sigh drifted over the line. "It's good of you to call, seeing what a shock it must've been for you, finding the poor thing and all."

"Yes, it was—" What could she say—terrible, dreadful, ghastly, horrendous? "It was. And I … don't know what else to say."

"Nothing else *to* say. That detective poking around in people's lives and homes, and Mike Hatton bumbling around with his little pad, and what are they gonna find?"

"If you had asked me yesterday," sighed Sophie, "I'd have said someone stranded and desperate."

"How so?"

"Well, Joe's death and the attack on me, combined with the burglaries, would seem to suggest—"

"A robber? Looking for food? Backwards. Nobody's got killed over food. No, whoever's done the killings has to steal food *because* they've done the killings. Leastways, that's what it seems like to me."

"What are you saying, that you think Crystal's … that is, that all of these incidents *are* related, that the same person is responsible?"

"Why not?"

"But wouldn't that make them, if not crimes of opportunity, then certainly random? Where's the motive?"

"*Random*?" scoffed Bea. "Why, you don't believe it was an accident that Crystal was at Carl's place. And no, I don't know what she was doing there, or even if she *was* there. At least, I know she was there when she was dead, but I don't know if she got there under her own steam, as you'd say."

"Are you saying you think somebody killed her elsewhere and then put her in Carl's house? But why?"

"Why d'ya think? Make it look like you and Carl did it."

"But I was attacked too, so what kind of sense does that make?"

"Ah, but you're still alive. Somebody could argue that the two of you faked what happened to you."

"But who would want to do that, and *why*?" asked Sophie in bewilderment.

"Well, I don't know. It's like I told you before, I don't know if this is something you brought with you or something that found you here."

"*Me*? But what about Joe and Crystal?"

"You do seem to be the common thread—you or Carl."

Sophie's eyes narrowed as she remembered suddenly why she had come to the island in the first place. "I don't know," she dissembled, "what possible connection anyone could think I had with Crystal and Joe Wisdom."

"Carl then, I don't know," said Bea indifferently.

A wave of guilt swept over Sophie as she realized how insensitive she'd been in her own stubborn search for answers. "I'm sorry, Bea. It was selfish of me to bother you with all this."

"Naw, it's all right. Ya know, poor Crystal had a rough time of it, what with men trouble and losing the baby and all—"

"She lost a baby?"

"Yeah. Well, I figured you'd have heard about that. But then maybe Carl never knew. Not like he was around, and none of it was anything anybody broadcast. Anyhow, the shock of that business with him and Gary Coffey ... well, she lost it."

"I'm sorry," Sophie said quietly.

"Ah, well, the main thing is she's finally at peace, isn't she? Anyhow," said Bea by way of conclusion, "it was real thoughtful of you to call. You come on over when you're feeling better."

Wishing there were something more she could say, but feeling at the same time that she'd said too much already, Sophie reiterated her sympathy and hung up just as the truck bounced up the drive. She heard both doors slam shut and craned her neck toward the hallway to see what that might portend.

"Sophie honey," Carl shouted down the hall, "look what I found at Dickie's." He grinned around the doorframe as Josh Dugan trailed in behind him somewhat reluctantly.

Sophie forced a pleasant smile she only partially felt. She *was* glad to see Josh and was heartened by the prospect of spending an entertaining evening, the three of them and Crow. But Bea's news had taken her at unawares, her first thought having been to share it with Carl. "Josh, come in, please. This is such a treat. Make yourself comfortable, and then tell me everything that's going on in the outside world."

"Sophie," laughed Carl, "will you let the guy eat first? I was in a hurry to get back, so we got dinner to go for all of us." He began to unpack several bags on the coffee table. "I'll get some plates and stuff," he said, backtracking to the kitchen.

"So," Sophie smiled across at Josh, "I guess you flew in."

"Yes, ma'am," he replied, easing himself down into one of the chairs. "Even though most of the lake is open, there's ice along the shore pretty much everywhere now. Doesn't mean ya couldn't get a boat out in a pinch, but the cat won't be coming out again until it thaws. We have to fly in supplies now, so I'm working with Rabbit."

"Rabbit?"

"Rabbit Whalum. Been island-hopping half of forever. Twin engine Cessna. Think he's finally got the sumbitch paid off, not that I think he ever gave a damn if he did or not," he laughed. "Anyhow, I work the cargo runs with him in the winter. Early start this year, though."

"So I noticed," said Sophie. "Just my luck."

"'Bout time," hollered Josh, as Carl reappeared with a stack of plates and utensils in one hand and a glass of fizzing orange liquid in the other.

"Gonna starve, ya bum?" laughed Carl, setting down the plates. "I had to get this stuff together for Sophie's cold." He handed her the glass and poked through the containers of food.

"So, what's my surprise?" she smiled, dutifully emptying the glass and setting it on the table.

Carl smiled sheepishly. "Cheeseburger? But it's blue cheese, and I got you onion rings instead of fries."

"*Perfect*," she laughed. "I'm so hungry. Oh, but, Josh, you have time to visit awhile after, don't you?"

He blew a stream of air out one side of his mouth. "Well, now I'd like to, but I gotta catch my ride back."

"You're welcome to stay here if you'd like. Isn't he, Carl?" she asked, placing a hand on his arm. "The spare room is small, but the bed is made up and there are plenty of blankets." It felt so good to laugh and to talk of anything but misery and murder that she found herself suddenly eager to make a small party of the occasion.

"Heck yeah, Josh, you can stay if you want. Got beer, and we'll get a fire going, shoot the breeze."

"Really give the natives something to gossip about, huh?" laughed Josh. "Guess you know that's what'll happen."

Sophie waved a hand nonchalantly. "Huh! We're so used to that. Believe me, it won't make any practical difference. I'm sure most of them already think we're murderers at worst and odd at best."

"Yeah," said Josh, dropping his burger and smearing at his chin with a napkin, "I heard you had some more trouble. In fact, like I told Carl, Rabbit's flying the girl back today, *and* that pain in the ass detective." Sophie looked over in surprise. "Oh, sorry." He mistook the look.

"No, no. But does that mean Carl can have his house back?"

"Yeah, angel. I was getting to that. Mike caught up with me at Dickie's. They're done at the house, for now at least. Until Kandinsky can think of something else he might've missed that would give him an excuse to arrest one or both of us."

"But Josh said he's leaving. Isn't that what you said?" she asked, turning to their guest.

"Yes ma'am. But I expect that's just so's he can have his nose in the autopsy."

"'Fraid so," Carl said in dull agreement.

"Ohhhh," moaned Sophie.

"Sorry, angel." Carl slipped her a shame-faced glance. "That was stupid of us to be talking about all that."

"Yeah," Josh swiped a hand along his pant leg, "sorry about that, ma'am. You're eating and all."

"Please, call me Sophie. And it's not that. I was just hoping that the good detective was leaving permanently, and wishing we could have a nice, congenial evening and not have to think about any of that. Just for a little while," she said wistfully.

Carl moved from the chair and sat down next to Sophie on the couch. "Your burger okay?" he asked gently.

She smiled and nodded. "It's delicious. Thank you. I couldn't have made a better choice."

"Good. I'm gonna get us a couple beers. You want one?"

"No, thanks. I think I'll make myself some tea."

"I'll get it."

"No, honestly," she laughed, "I need to get up and move around. I haven't moved from this sofa in hours. Anyway, I feel better. Really."

"Your ankle."

"It's better too. Not bad at all. Just a slight sprain."

He looked skeptical. "I'll help you then," he said, easing her to her feet.

"Josh, Carl is determined to make me an invalid, so we'll be right back. Make yourself comfortable."

"How about I get that fire started?"

"Okay. Thank you," she smiled, hobbling toward the hall on Carl's arm.

Her smile was replaced in an instant by gaping horror, and she screamed as she heard the simultaneous backfire and the random clatter of shattering glass, and felt herself dragged down to land with a gasp against the unyielding floor.

"Son of a *bitch*!" shouted Carl, arching over to shield her, as Josh sprang out of his chair and ran crouching toward the front door, a pistol in his hand.

He jerked open the door as an engine revved and tires screeched away, but slammed it shut again and slouched heavily against the wall. He shook his head in answer to Carl's look. "Couldn't see much more than the taillights. Dark pickup, red maybe, I dunno." He frowned as Carl scrambled to his feet and pulled a hysterical Sophie up after him. "What the hell's *happened* to this freakin' place?"

"*I* have," sobbed Sophie.

CHAPTER 19

Mike Hatton slapped his hat against his thigh anxiously and fingered the little metal cylinder he'd dug out of the wall with his penknife. "Now, Ms. Skala, I understand you being upset and all, but it makes it real hard for me to take a statement with you crying like that."

"Come on, Mike," Carl appealed, holding Sophie against him, "Josh and I told you what happened. Somebody shot a hole in the damn window. Give her a break, will ya? She's attacked, Joe Wisdom gets killed, then she finds Crystal like that, and now this, never mind the break-ins. What do you expect? This seem anything like normal to you?" he asked testily.

"Course not, Carl. I know that. Nothing much normal around here at all the last few weeks. And I'm doing my best to sort it out, ya know. But every time I turn around, something else happens. I mean," he shrugged helplessly, "this is the third separate incident I've talked to you two about in less than twenty-four hours. Gettin' so I'm afraid to answer my phone. And that's why, I don't mind saying—much as I'm not crazy about the man—I'm glad to have Kandinsky working on these murders, 'cause I've about got my hands full with the rest of it!"

"Sorry I don't share your enthusiasm," snapped Carl. "Aw, look, Mike, I'm sorry." He swiped his fingers across his upper lip. "We're all on edge. Can't even sit here and eat a damn burger in peace. It's like living in some TV cop show."

"Well, I know it. And believe you me, if we were, I'd be renegotiating my durned contract too. But I'm doing the best I can, and that's why I need to know who Ms. Skala mighta seen or talked to, *something* that might suggest who'd want to hurt her and why."

"I told you. She had lunch with her sister on the mainland yesterday. You and Kandinsky were here when she got back, you know that. We had supper, Bea stopped by, we went out to my place, and you pretty much know what happened after that. Then late this afternoon I went out to pick up some dinner and ran into Josh. Sophie hasn't been out of the house today. So she hasn't talked to anybody but you, me and Josh. Oh, and her sister called earlier."

"Bea," whimpered Sophie.

"What?"

"I called Bea, just before you and Josh got back," she sniffled, smearing a hand across her nose. "To offer my condolences," she explained in response to the uniformly blank looks on their faces. "For Crystal," she sniffed, as they still did not appear to comprehend.

"So what did she say, angel?"

"Now, Carl, I'm supposed to be asking the questions here," said Mike Hatton, turning to Sophie and adjusting himself into what he considered a more official stance. "What did she say, Ms. Skala?"

"Well," Sophie replied self-consciously, "she thanked me for calling. And she said she thought that whoever is responsible for these killings was—how did she put it now?—stealing food *because* he'd killed and not the other way around, something like that. She also seemed to think Crystal was killed somewhere else and then taken to Carl's house to frame us."

"Yeah, that sounds like just the kinda thing Bea would say. Somebody's stranded and stumbling around on foot stealing food, but they somehow managed to drag Crystal's body halfway across the island, *and* without being seen." He pursed up his lips in mild disgust. "Bea needs to leave the police work to the police. And anyhow, it still doesn't tell me why anybody'd want to hurt you, Ms. Skala."

"Well, Mr. Hatton, I'm not sure it's me that somebody was after this time. Or maybe not *just* me," she said with a surreptitious glance at Carl.

"Okay, and why is that? You know something you're not saying?" Sophie stared into the cold fireplace disconsolately. "You know, you can't be withholding evidence."

"No, I don't know anything. Nothing that you don't know. I was thinking of the Halloween party. You were there, you heard Mar Holliday. If he thought we were guilty of murder *then*, what do you suppose he thinks now that Crystal has been found dead in Carl's house? I don't see how there could be much doubt," she said sulkily.

"Whew." Mike Hatton dropped heavily onto the arm of the chair. "I guess I see your point. I hadn't thought of it, and of course, I'm not saying it was him, but I suppose I better talk to him. Red truck, you said?" he asked, turning to Josh Dugan.

"Coulda been. Dark. Looked red to me."

"Whew," repeated Mike Hatton, pulling himself back up off the chair arm and jamming his hat onto his head. "Mar's got a red pickup. You think of anything else," he sighed and made his way to the door, "call me."

They watched as he crunched his heavy way to his official SUV, then Carl closed the door and turned to Sophie. "What made you think of Mar Holliday?"

She looked over at Josh, who had scrounged up a piece of plastic sheeting from a shelf in the utility closet and was busy covering the window. "I don't know," she answered vaguely. "Seemed logical. I'm going to make a pot of coffee. I think we need it."

"Well, let me give Josh a hand, and then I'll help you."

"Naw, I got it," said Josh. "You go on. Should be all right till the hardware store opens in the morning—unless we get some more gale force winds."

She smiled inwardly with relief as Carl followed her to the kitchen. "I wanted to talk to you earlier, before …" She sighed. "I don't know if this is the right time."

He frowned in apprehension. "Sophie, what is it?"

"Bea did say something else that made me think of Mar Holliday. Carl," she said unhappily, "she told me about Crystal's losing the baby."

"What baby?"

"You really don't know?" She stole a doubtful glance at him.

"Know what? *What* baby? Only thing I know about any baby is what I told you, that Crystal told me she was pregnant, but she wasn't."

"Bea says she was, and that the trauma of what happened with you and Gary Coffey caused her to miscarry."

"*What*? No, no. That's wrong. That's a lie, Sophie. What I told you about happened before that night. Now, I don't wanna get graphic—"

"No, I'd rather you wouldn't either."

"—but I know *something* about women, and I'm telling you—"

Sophie fumbled in the wrong cupboard for a coffee filter. "I don't think I want to know this."

"—if she was pregnant, I was not responsible. Sophie," he said, grasping her by the shoulders, "the worst thing about what happened is that it was already over between her and me. Do you understand? Hell, there was no point in us even being there that night. I just didn't want to see it."

"Ohhh," she plucked at his shirt absently, "you don't owe me an explanation. She just seemed to imply that ..."

"No, Sophie. Of course, I suppose if Mar believed it—"

"Even if he didn't, just the fact that Crystal was found dead in your house would convince him that he'd been right all along. That's what made me think of Mar. Maybe I should have told Mike Hatton. But I needed to talk to you first."

"Jee-sus," he groaned, "it just never stops. I feel like I'm living in a war zone."

She slid her arms around his chest. "I know, and I'm sorry. It's because of me. I can't think you'd be involved in this at all if it weren't for me. You wouldn't even *be* here. You'd be on the mainland, and maybe none of this would have happened, at least not the way it has."

"Yeah, and maybe it would be worse. I'm here because I wanted to be, *still* wanna be, as long as you're here. Woman, ya need looking after," he smiled. "Now let's have our coffee."

Josh Dugan made a last jab at the fire he'd started, and taking the cup Sophie proffered, sank down into a chair. "Don't suppose you two have thought about leaving this heap."

"I've thought of little else, believe me," answered Sophie.

"Can't," said Carl. "Kandinsky'd be on us like carp on bread crumbs."

"Uh huh, and you think it'd be any skin off his butt if whoever it was took a shot at ya didn't miss next time?"

Carl cast a sidelong glance toward Sophie. "Cut it out, Josh."

Sophie leaned her head against his shoulder. "Why?" she asked, as he slid his arm around her. "He's right, Carl. We have a right to protect ourselves, don't we?"

"And we're going to. But we couldn't leave if we wanted to. No boat."

"Hell," said Josh, "you don't need a boat. You think Rabbit'd give a fiddler's fart about what that detective might think? Say the word and he'll fly ya out."

"Josh, even if I was stupid enough to risk it, we can't involve anybody else."

"Shee-ut, man. You're not thinkin' straight. But if you're worried about Rabbit," he laughed, "then forget that. I can get a boat over here, I told ya. Like they used to do back in the old days, drag it over the ice. Risky and uncomfortable as hell, but doable."

"I read about that," Sophie said eagerly, and pulled herself upright. "In Joe's book."

"Sophie honey, we've been over this. We can't run."

"We wouldn't be running, Carl," she pleaded. "We could tell Kandinsky where we were if you like. But at least we'd be away from here!"

"Sophie, no! He'd have us arrested on the spot. You know what a sneaky son of a bitch he is. He'd just say we ran, and then got scared and tried to talk our way out of it. And Josh would be in it up to his eyeballs too."

She slumped back against the sofa. "Then what do we do, just wait—here in the war zone," she said pointedly, "until something else happens? We're not fugitives, you know. We haven't been arrested or charged with anything, and we have every right to leave the island if we want to."

"*So*phie—"

"Look," Josh interjected, palms outward in a gesture of conciliation, "I shouldn'ta said anything. I didn't know you two already talked about this. If you need my help, you only have to ask, ya know that. But there's no big rush anyhow, since nobody's going anywhere tonight. Now, it's been a pretty crazy day, and it'd probably be better to just drop this for now and get some shut-eye. So why don't you two go on up to bed. Do you a world of good. Me and the meathound'll keep our eyes and ears open down here."

"You're probably right," Carl said wearily. "So I'll get Sophie settled upstairs and then you and I'll keep an eye on things."

"No, I'll stay too," Sophie protested.

Before Carl could put words to his expression of long suffering, Josh boomed, "By God, madam, you won't either!" Sophie's eyes and mouth blossomed into perfect little circles and remained so throughout the exhortation that followed. "In the first place, I'm not used to living like this, people taking potshots at me and shit, like friggin' I-raq! Between that and the two of you hashing and rehashing, I'm dog tired. And long as you're down here, I'm stuck with a damn chair and I want the damn couch! And woman, if that's not enough, everybody sits around going on about how normal nothin' is. Well, why'nt ya take yourselves upstairs and *do* somethin' normal! Hell, do somethin' *abnormal*, I don't care! If me and the mutt hear any noises from down here, I'll let ya know. And if we hear any noises from up *there*, I won't say a damn word, I promise ya!"

Carl removed his hand from before his mouth, cleared his throat and sought to master the laughter that threatened to erupt. "I'll get you a pillow," he smirked, and pulling Sophie up off the sofa, herded her unprotesting toward the stairs.

"Good night, Mr. Dugan," she mumbled. In the privacy of the bedroom a moment later, "Well, really," she pouted.

"Aw, honey, give the man a break," chuckled Carl. "He's trying to help. And he's right," he added, running a finger across her protruding lower lip, "it *would* do us a world of good. What do you say I run that bath we didn't get last night?"

She arched a suspicious brow. "Prelude to what else we didn't get last night?"

"Why not?" he grinned.

"I have a cold," she sniffled. "You'll catch it."

He began to work the buttons of her blouse through the buttonholes deliberately. "I'll take my chances."

"Well," she considered in the face of a weakening resolve, "wouldn't it be—I don't know—*unseemly*, to be doing that with … well … downstairs."

"*Unseemly*?" Momentary puzzlement gave way to unbridled mirth. "Josh? You mean with Josh downstairs?" he howled.

"Shhh! He'll hear you!" she hissed.

But her apparent distress only served to redouble his laughter, and he pushed her backward onto the bed and began to wrestle her out of her jeans. "In the first place, angel, you sure don't act like you're doing anything nasty when you're doing it—"

"*Awww*!" she cried in outrage.

"—and as for offending Josh's sensibilities," he continued to laugh, "he hasn't got any. Hell, honey, I've seen him do things I wouldn't tell you about under torture. Now, come on," he winked, tossing aside her bra and panties, bundling her into her robe and dragging her off toward the bathroom, "bath time."

"Ahhh," he said blissfully, as he sank back into the bubbles ten minutes later, "that feels so good. Come on, honey." He stretched his arms out toward her as she stood clutching her robe around her and fretting. "Come on. Be good for you," he cajoled.

She twisted her mouth around truculently. *It was the sort of thing Peter had done, commanding her to come to him. And if she demurred, there would be the inevitable scene, and the bruises …* But this was not the same thing. Carl was not Peter. He was gentle, and careful of her. He wanted, not to control her, but *her*. And there was nothing inevitable about it, not to him, she realized again, and she let the robe slide to the floor and clambered into the tub to land on her knees between his legs. "I still don't think it's polite somehow."

"Believe me, honey, he doesn't begrudge us a little R & R," he replied, smoothing warm water up over her back and shoulders.

"That what it's called?"

"When I'm being polite," he laughed, and squeezed her bottom in both hands. "Come on now, my little muffin. Don't play hard to get. You know you want me."

"Oh, you really *are* disgusting," she huffed, as he pulled her forward to topple against him. "What, you want to do something in *here*?"

"Why not? I always planned to take up diving. Now's as good a time as any. Course, I was thinking more along the lines of the Bimini wall, but—"

"Oh, for heaven's sake! Talk about pearls before swine."

But her petulance collapsed, and she began to squeal as his hands slipped down over her bottom and disappeared beneath the bubbles. "Don't worry," he whispered against her lips, "we can do it again on dry land after."

"Promise," she breathed, nibbling at his lower lip.

"Twist my other arm."

They left behind the shattered glass and shattered lives, the ice and steel, and abandoned themselves to one another, to heat and life, somewhere out of time, so that as she lay in his arms afterwards, the blankets pulled up close around them, she did not know whether it had been one hour or many that she had been lost within him.

"What does it mean?" she asked drowsily.

"Why does it have to mean anything?" His voice came soft out of the darkness.

"Shouldn't it?"

"I want you, want to be with you, if that's what you want to know. I don't know any more than that. Is that enough?" he asked, his hand gliding over the curve of her shoulder and down along her arm.

She snuggled against him, her fingertips trailing over his flesh in lazy circles. "It's enough."

He leaned forward and kissed her forehead. "You want more."

"No," she answered noncommittally, then raised her head to prop her chin on his chest. "Or if so, maybe I want to know that it's not desperation, not just a response to feeling as though we're under siege and grasping at life."

She was near enough to see the contours of his face in the dim light reflected off the snow below, but he drew her closer. "It's not desperation, angel. Not for me. I know desperation. It's something you don't want, something you wanna shake free of."

"So you don't want to shake free of me?" she yawned.

"No," he smiled, petting her gently. "If I had it to do over again, even knowing what I know now, I'd still be right here."

"That sounds desperate," she murmured, snuggling in next to him. "But then I guess that makes me desperate, too, after all."

"Fine," he mumbled, "now go to sleep. We can be desperate again first thing in the morning."

Chapter 20

"I'll let Crow out and feed him," Carl called through the bathroom door. He buttoned his shirt and stumped down the stairs, jerking to a momentary halt halfway, as first one and then a second sneeze exploded. "What are you grinning at, ya bum?" he growled over at Josh.

"Ha!" snorted Josh. "Helluva cold you picked up there. Yep, musta been *cold* up there last night. Now, if it'd been me, I'da snuggled up to the pretty lady. But then you always were slow."

"Screw you," chuckled Carl. "Come on, Crow, let's go out and pee."

"The mutt's been out. Poor animal had his legs crossed waiting for you to tear yourself away from your honey."

"*All* right," Carl laughed good-naturedly.

"What's so funny?" sniffled Sophie, as she descended the stairs to join them.

Carl coughed self-consciously. "Just talking about the dog," he muttered. "Come on, Crow, let's get you some breakfast."

"I'll get some coffee made. Josh, please feel free to take a shower or whatever you'd like," she smiled, smearing at her nose with a tissue.

"Thank you, but I think I'd better get down to the hardware store. See about getting that window fixed."

"No, by God, sir, you won't either," she said emphatically, then smiled with self-satisfaction at his obvious surprise. "I'm going to make us all a real breakfast for a change. And then we can all go to town."

Carl met her in the hall on her way to the kitchen. "What are you talking about?" he scowled.

"I'm making a decent breakfast. I'm tired of toast."

"That's not what I meant. Where do you think you're going afterward?"

"Downtown with you and Josh."

"No, you're not. Your ankle, remember?"

"Funny you weren't worried about my ankle last night."

"You weren't on your feet last night," he leered.

"I'm going," she replied with a syrupy smile, and nudged past him into the kitchen, where she got the coffee brewing and then began to clatter around in cupboards and pull eggs and bacon and cheese and bagels out of the refrigerator.

"Now, Sophie," he appealed, dodging aside repeatedly in an unsuccessful bid to stay out of her way.

"Will you set the table please?" She began to crack eggs into a bowl, counted, considered, and emptied the carton.

He rooted around the drawers until he found the flatware. "Look, I don't think it would be a good idea—"

"Carl," she stopped whisking the eggs and turned to look at him, "I am not going to be a prisoner." She sighed and leaned against the counter. "I need to get out. I need things, I need air, and light. This place is closing in on me. It would be lovely if we could stay in bed till we can get off this island, but we can't." She walked over and put a hand on his arm. "We need to talk about all this," she pleaded. "Last night was wonderful, but we can't use that as a way to bury our heads in the sand."

"Is that what it was?"

"Oh, Carl, you know what I mean."

"Sophie, I'm doing the best I can to stay sane here, never mind trying to make sense of it and protect you."

"I know. I know. But we can't stop living. In fact, I think maybe Josh was more right than I realized when he said we should do something normal. All I'm asking right now is to go into town with you and do some shopping—on a very modest scale, I promise you."

"All right," he raised a fistful of flatware in surrender, "all right. I should probably go check my place anyway, see what shape Kandinsky left it in. You okay with that? I can make it quick, and you can wait in the truck if you'd feel better."

She turned back to the stove and pushed the eggs around in the frying pan. "No," she shook her head, "I'll come with you. Could you please check the bacon?"

"Sure." He finished setting napkins and flatware on the table and pulled a tray of bacon out of the microwave.

"Thank you, Carl," she smiled.

"No problem," he said, transferring the strips to a plate.

"Not just for helping with breakfast."

"Well, it seems I can't deny you much of anything. Next thing, I suppose you'll be asking me to marry you."

"Oh, for heaven's sake," she said, tossing a cube of cheddar at him. "I hope that wasn't your idea of a proposal."

"Could be if you play your cards right," he winked and grabbed the coffee pot.

"Jee-sus." Josh sauntered in and glanced from one to the other before pulling out a chair and flopping down at the table. "I'm gone for ten minutes, and people are gettin' married."

"Carl is so hungry he's delusional," she said, arranging food on plates and setting them on the table. Just as she was about to settle herself into the chair Carl had pulled out for her, they froze and stared at one another.

"I'll get it," he sighed, and wandered off down the hall to the front door. He returned a moment later with Mike Hatton, bedraggled hat at his side.

"Sorry to bother you so early, ma'am," he said sheepishly.

"Not at all, Mr. Hatton. You're just in time for breakfast."

"Aw, no," he objected, not very convincingly.

"Come on, sit down. Please. Whatever news you have, you can tell us and we can hear over some scrambled eggs." Not waiting for a response, she pulled another plate from the cupboard.

"Come on, Mike," urged Carl, with a slap on the shoulder.

"I don't know if I should. Official visit and all."

"Well, we won't tell anyone, promise," Sophie insisted and set the plate down before him.

They sat for several minutes in relative silence, as there were few words, but much chewing and scraping of forks on plates. Sophie poked daintily at a clump of egg and looked around the table. She was not used to breakfasting with three men, but it pleased her that they were making clean work of her culinary efforts, and she waited until their plates began to look sparse before broaching the subject of Mike Hatton's visit.

"So, Mr. Hatton, what brings you here this morning?"

"Mm, good, ma'am," he replied bashfully, jamming his napkin against his mouth, before resuming his official posture. "I talked to Mar. Was him all right."

"How do you know?" asked Sophie.

"He said so. Not much point in him denying it, since I showed him the bullet. He knows if push came to shove, we could match it up to his rifle."

"Sophie was right then," Carl said grimly. "Probably *was* me he was after."

"Well, now that's the odd thing," mused Mike. "Says it was an accident—I know, I know—that he'd had a few too many down at Dickie's. Now I confirmed that with Dickie, who said he was pretty much shit-faced. Begging your pardon, ma'am, his words, not mine. Anyway, seems he's pretty busted up about Crystal and all, more'n I would have thought. Says he thought about coming here and having words with you."

"Guess he thought a bullet through the window would be more to the point, huh?" fumed Carl.

"Well, now that's what I'm getting around to. Says he saw somebody skulking around—his words, skulking around—outside."

"And decided to shoot 'em," supplied Josh. "And missed by a mile."

"I know. But apparently he was impaired."

"And you believe him," said Sophie.

"Well, I don't quite know, ma'am, but you got some tracks out front there—unless any of you were out there."

"*What*?"

"So were you, any of you?"

"No." Carl frowned. "Josh and I came in the back door."

Sophie set her fork down and leaned forward intently. "And when you questioned Mar about this person he saw skulking around, what did he say he saw exactly?"

"Well, he said he couldn't see much but kind of a dark bulk, except for what looked like some kind of a red hat."

"Red plaid?" asked Sophie in disbelief.

"I don't really know. Why, is there something you know about it, Ms. Skala?"

"Sophie?" scowled Carl. "Did something happen you didn't tell me about?"

"Not exactly. In fact, I *did* tell you. About the man who came back on the ferry, remember? I didn't pay much attention to him, but I remember he wore a red plaid wool hat. You know, the kind with the ear flaps?"

"Yeah, I remember seeing him, now you mention it," Josh concurred. "Didn't pay much attention, except he walked funny, stiff, kinda like a gay trying to look straight, ya know?" he grimaced.

"I don't suppose," said Mike Hatton without much hope, "you'd know who it was."

"*I* sure as hell don't."

Sophie shook her head. "I'm sorry, no. But then I don't know that many people here."

"Well, it may take some time, but it shouldn't be all that hard to find out if it was one of the locals, though it sure doesn't sound like anybody *I* know either. Course, either way," he sighed, "I don't see how it fits in with all the rest."

"Don't you?" asked Sophie with mild exasperation. "Mr. Hatton, Carl and I didn't kill Joe or Crystal. Now, once you realize that, it begins to make a great deal of sense that all of these incidents are related, and that one person is responsible—one person that no one seems able to identify."

"Believe me, Ms. Skala, nothing would make me happier than to be able to prove that. And I'd be willing enough to believe it, but you have to understand the position I'm in. I got you two talking in one of my ears and Detective Kandinsky in the other."

"But as long as he's trying to work out how we did it, he's not looking at the alternative solution."

"Well, Ms. Skala," said Officer Hatton, rising and pushing his chair in awkwardly, "I'll do what I can, I promise ya. Right now, I have to figure out what to do with Mar."

"You didn't arrest him then," said Carl.

"Well, now I didn't quite know what to do about that. I mean, what am I supposed to charge him with? Attempted murder seems a little harsh, and probably wouldn't stick anyhow. Reckless endangerment? Malicious destruction of property? Dang it," he sighed, "what you want me to do, Carl? He'll pay for the damage, I know that. Offered to this morning. He's got a big mouth, talks big, but I honestly can't see him trying to kill somebody. Now, it's up to you if you want to press charges," he more or less concluded, and yanked the hat back onto his head. "Say the word. If not, you give me a bill for fixing the damage to the window and the hole in the wall, and I'll see he pays it."

Carl's choice was evident on his face, but he looked over at Sophie for her input. "The report is on file, Mr. Hatton, including Mar's admission?" she asked.

"Yes, ma'am, it is. And if he pulls anything else like that, I guarantee you I'll slap the cuffs on him myself so fast it'll make your head swim."

She nodded, and escorting him to the door, bade him goodbye amidst his repeated thanks for the excellent breakfast.

"If this isn't about the damnedest place," muttered Josh. "Some character shoots a hole in your house, and the investigating officer, who's also investigating *you* for a coupla murders, drops by for breakfast and asks *you* to forgive the *shooter*. Couldn't pay me to live on this dirt heap. Can't get off it soon enough. And I'll tell ya something else," he groused, getting up and moving his empty plate to the sink, "if I gotta go shopping with a woman for women things, I'm damn well gonna stop at Dickie's first and fortify myself for the ordeal."

"Oh, for heaven's sake," said Sophie, "I'm going to the market to try to get some more apples, so that if Detective Kandinsky hasn't appropriated my pie plate into evidence, I can make another pie. Of course," she added wistfully, "I *was* hoping to go to that little boutique down the block. But you two," she lifted her voice above their groans, "can go to the hardware store while I'm there."

"Maybe Josh can," Carl said lugubriously.

"What, somebody is going to shoot me in the middle of town?"

"I'm not arguing with you, Sophie. Now get your coat."

She patted Crow and checked once again to make sure the door was locked before climbing up into the truck between Carl and Josh.

"Right," grinned Josh as he jumped down from the cab moments later, "hardware store and Dickie's. You can meet me there. Oh, and I'll get some spackle for that hole in the wall." He shoved his hands into his pockets and sauntered off down the block toward the hardware store, turning a longing glance on the window of Dickie's as he passed.

Island Market and Cheese World fell silent as Sophie entered warily, a defiant Carl at her elbow. She took a deep breath and plucked a basket off the stack.

"Morning, Sophie, Carl," called Nila Celestine from behind the counter. She was less ebullient than formerly. "Heard you had some trouble."

Sophie was uncertain to which trouble she referred, but supposed it mattered little. Trouble was trouble, and it seemed unimportant whether the trouble she acknowledged matched the specific trouble to which Nila Celestine alluded.

"Yes, I'm afraid so," she said vaguely.

"We all just feel terrible, you know. Can't imagine what you must think of us here, what with all the goings-on."

Sophie looked up in surprise just in time to see Nila cast an admonitory glance toward the dairy case, where Mattie Coombs stood like a rock carving. "Well, for what it's worth," said Sophie, "I don't think the residents are responsible for most of what's happened." A pointed rumble of agreement drifted from the vicinity of the cottage cheese. "I think it's an outsider, someone who doesn't live here at all," she added quickly in an attempt to forestall further inarticulate disapproval.

"That's what Mike Hatton was saying." Nila leaned across the counter in an unconscious gesture of interest. "And Mar Holliday," she said quietly.

Not quietly enough, it seemed, as Mattie Coombs, her face like a slice of dried-out Muenster, stalked out the door.

"Don't mind Mattie," she sighed, "or the others. Truth is, Sophie, none of us much know what to make of all this. And folks around here are *insular,*" she said deliberately, as though she thought it a particularly apt word to explain things in general. "I'll admit that business with Crystal doesn't look especially good, but I prefer to hold to the notion that people are innocent until they're proven guilty."

"Thank you," said Sophie, returning a sickly smile for Nila's magnanimous one. "I'm just going to pick out some apples." She strolled off toward the mounds of home-grown fruit and began to make her selection.

As Carl stood silent and antagonistic, the bell over the door jangled, and he turned in surprise to see Josh with a bag in one hand and a paper-wrapped sheet of glass in the other. "I thought we were supposed to meet you—"

"Yep, except I ran into Rabbit. Bet you can't guess who's back."

"Awww," moaned Carl, "what, already? Thought it was too good to last."

"What's wrong?" asked Sophie, placing her basket on the counter.

"You about done here?" he asked, hauling the single bag off the counter.

"Yes," she answered cautiously. Paying Nila and thanking her, she followed Carl and Josh out to the truck. "What?"

"Kandinsky's back." He helped her up into the truck and put the apples in the back with the hardware purchases.

Josh squeezed in next to her and slammed the door shut. "You know, that goober with the rifle mighta done the two of you a favor."

"How's that?" grumbled Carl.

"Because now that idiot detective can't just get a bug up his ass to arrest either one of you just because there's nobody else available. Since the drunken shooter's on record as saying he was aiming at a possible prowler—even if he's lying through his teeth—Kandinsky'll have to tread a little more carefully."

"He's right, Carl. If nothing else, Mar has cast some doubt on Kandinsky's otherwise happy and certain conclusion that we, singly or together, are guilty."

"Yep, your only real problem is that dead girl in your bathtub."

"Is *that* all?"

"But at least this has bought us some time, Carl," urged Sophie.

"Time for what?" he asked glumly.

"Time for us to figure out who *really* killed Crystal, of course. Now, come on. Let's get out to the cabin. I have a pie to bake, and I want my pan!"

CHAPTER 21

"I don't believe it." Sophie lifted the spotless glass pie plate from the drying rack next to the kitchen sink. "He took time out from picking through your house to eat the entire pie. But he washed the plate," she added with a loopy smile.

"That's the only part that surprises me," growled Carl. "I can imagine him rooting through my underwear drawer with one hand and dropping pie crumbs in it with the other."

"Hm," she sniffed in answer, "that's just about what I would expect. That and leaving the remnants to gum up the plate and grow mold. I can't even conjure up an image of him washing it. Still," her glance swept the first floor, "it's not bad. I was afraid it would look as if a tornado came through. Maybe he's an obsessive neatnik."

"He's about anal enough," quipped Josh.

"I suppose," Sophie mused, "although if it was a control issue, I'd have expected him to make a point of leaving a mess just to thumb his nose at us."

"Well, he didn't clean out the fireplace, if that makes you feel any better," said Carl.

"What about ...?" She nodded her head vaguely toward the stairs, but he shook his in reply.

"I don't think so. It's not bad, but I'll ... disinfect it."

The three of them exchanged a distasteful glance, and Josh reprised his opinion of the island as a whole. "Helluva place. This is a great house, Carl, but, man, you couldn't *give* it to me on this rock pile fulla whackos. Speaking of which," he gestured toward the window.

"Aw, damn," groaned Carl, as both doors to Mike Hatton's SUV swung open, and Ed Kandinsky descended from the passenger side. Not waiting for the knock at the door, Carl hauled it open silently and stood aside.

"How nice to see you again, Detective," Sophie said coolly.

"It's not—"

"A social call. No, I know. So has one of the stop signs been purloined, or has there just been another murder?"

Ed Kandinsky's eyes narrowed, and his upper lip curled. "I suppose you think that's amusing, Mrs. Skala."

"No, Mr. Kandinsky, I don't think it's one bit amusing that our lives have been disrupted and our freedom curtailed, and that you feel free to harass us at will simply because you think we're easy targets. Unless of course I'm mistaken, and you're calling on everyone on the island, in which case, you'll have to forgive me if I'm a little short."

Mike Hatton shook his bowed head and glanced up at her out of the corner of his eye. "Ms. Skala, please. Now, I've just been telling Detective Kandinsky here about what happened to you folks last night, about Mar and all."

"And? Or shall I tell you what Mr. Kandinsky thinks?"

"Why don't you do that, Mrs. Skala, see how we compare."

"I would guess, Mr. Kandinsky, that you think Mar Holliday was either lying about seeing a prowler, or that he took aim at one person, but narrowly missed the two he ought to have been shooting at instead."

Ed Kandinsky's laugh was forced, and Sophie wondered whether he was capable of a genuine belly laugh, and if so, what could possibly trigger it. "That's good, Mrs. Skala. First rate. Let's just say that I don't believe that shot in the dark exonerates you. Like I said, I don't like coincidences."

"So you don't believe in the mysterious stranger then. In which case, you also wouldn't believe that both Carl's house and mine have been broken into."

"And nobody else's," he scoffed.

"That we know of," she smiled. "Have you checked all the empty summer homes?"

"Haven't gotten around to it. Been too busy with things like how exactly two residents of the island got to be corpses."

"Without any help from us, Mr. Kandinsky."

"Well, now see, that's the thing that puzzles me, Mrs. Skala. If that's true, and it's also true that you've had several break-ins, I would expect you to be a lot more concerned about being next."

"And just why do you think I'm staying with her?" snapped Carl.

A smarmy grin spread across Ed Kandinsky's face, but Josh gripped Carl's arm before he could propel himself forward. The smile settled into an icy glare. "Let me spell this out for you. Maybe we can save some time here. It's possible, if extremely unlikely, that Mr. Wisdom might have lost his balance and hit his head against the stairs accidentally. But there's not a snowball's chance in hell that Miss Holliday strangled herself and pushed herself under the water to drown—in your *full* bathtub, Carl."

"And what theory would you suggest, Mr. Kandinsky?"

"I was hoping you'd tell me, Mrs. Skala, and make this easier for everybody."

"I'm sorry to disappoint you," she replied coldly, "but since Carl and I were together at my place, I wouldn't have a clue. I was hoping that with your vast experience, you might be able to account for the full tub and the unmistakable fact that Miss Holliday was fully clothed, two particulars that would not normally go hand in hand."

The detective gave an exaggerated shrug. "An assignation gone wrong?"

Sophie's eyes betrayed her loathing. "An assignation. In Carl's house, but without Carl's presence. Because he wasn't here," she said, glaring into his eyes.

"I didn't really figure either of you would cooperate. Carl knows what it is to do time, and *you* got away with it—so far. But Mrs. Skala, I would remind you of a couple things. There's no statue of limitations on murder, and Crystal Holliday wasn't just found in this house, she was *killed* in this house. Now," he said with a nonchalant wave of the hand, "if nobody's got anything to say ..."

"Yeah, I do," said Josh. "You're an asshole."

Ed Kandinsky turned a cold eye on him. "Of course, Mr. Dugan, I guess you know if you decide to help your friends here escape, you could be charged as an accessory after the fact."

"I'm shakin' in my fuzzy bunny slippers," spat Josh.

"Ha!" Kandinsky turned to leave, a weary and abashed Mike Hatton nearly running into his back as he stopped abruptly. "If any of you change your mind and want to talk, you let me know."

Sophie did not fight the urge to fire a parting shot. "Look on the bright side, Mr. Kandinsky. It's not as though you've gone entirely empty-handed. How did you enjoy the pie?"

Ed Kandinsky turned back to her with a reptilian smile. "A little tart for my taste. But I expect you just didn't have your mind on what you were doing."

"A little tart? Took you awhile to decide, it would seem. Still, I appreciate your washing the *empty* pan."

"I'm afraid your little joke escapes me. I gave it a fair chance, took two bites. But whatever talents you may have, Mrs. Skala, pie-making is not among them."

Sophie's blank expression was mirrored in both Carl's and Josh's. "Are you telling me, Detective, that you didn't eat the entire pie and wash the plate?"

"*That* pie?" The laughter stuck in his throat, and there was a flash of uncertainty in his eyes as he discerned the apparent lack of artifice in the faces of the others. "Now what scam are you trying to pull?" he asked shrewdly.

But the others ignored him, absorbed rather in the implications of this latest discovery. "That's impossible," Carl said in answer to the question in Sophie's eyes. "How would he have gotten in?"

"How did he get in to kill Crystal? For that matter, how did *Crystal* get in?"

In response, Carl dashed over to the back door and began to examine lock, latch and glass panes. He pushed at one from the outside and scrambled to catch it as it dropped out toward the inside. Holding it up in mild astonishment, "Well, guess we know how *somebody* got in," he said. "It's been cut just large enough to wedge into the frame so it won't just fall out without being forced from the outside. So I guess we need to find out who else has bought a little square of glass since I replaced the broken one. I suggest," he gestured with the pane toward Ed Kandinsky, "that you ask down at the hardware store."

"Won't do any good," Sophie said quietly. "He wouldn't have bought it here. That would be too obvious. It's small. He'd have gotten it on one of his forays to the mainland. But surely," she appealed to Ed Kandinsky, "you must see for yourself that someone's broken in."

"How convenient. The mysterious intruder?"

"Yes, *Detective*!" she said angrily. "My God, you have Officer Hatton's report of footprints at my house—"

"Inconclusive."

"—Mar's statement about a prowler—"

"Inconclusive."

"—and now this!"

"Inconclusive!"

"And what would you consider conclusive, finding someone bent over the *body*?"

"Like Carl, you mean? Or you maybe, bent over your late husband's body, Mrs. Skala? Yeah, that would be proof enough for me."

"Guess you're out of luck then, Detective," she said icily.

"Guess you are too then, aren't you?"

"Look, Ed," intervened Mike Hatton, "this does seem to me to allow for the possibility that all this really is the work of an intruder."

"Pah! Like I said, mighty convenient that old Carl should just happen to discover the loose pane in our presence."

"The pie plate," urged Mike Hatton.

"Did it themselves. Did it *all* themselves!" he said angrily. "Real stroke of luck for them, Mar Holliday pulling that stunt and then concocting that fairy tale to cover his butt!"

"Now, wait a minute." Mike Hatton raised a conciliatory hand. "I talked to Mar, and I believe he was telling the truth. And there *is* some evidence of a stranger on the island. There might be more, only we haven't been looking for it."

Ed Kandinsky flashed a condescending smile in the direction of his provincial counterpart. "And the motive?"

"Well, I don't know. But then I don't see as how *they've* got a motive either," he gestured toward Sophie and Carl.

"Murder begets murder."

"Oh, brilliant," snarled Carl. "Convenient too. Then you don't need a motive!"

"What I meant, Carl old buddy, was that the motive for subsequent murders usually lies in the first one. And as soon as I figure that out, I'll know just what happened—and how you did it."

"No, you won't," argued Sophie. "When you find out what Crystal Holliday was doing here, *then* you'll know what happened—and who did it!"

"As usual," Mike Hatton slapped his hat against his thigh in disgust, "we're getting nowhere. Now, this is still my jurisdiction, and I've got an investigation to run. So what I'm gonna do is take a look at the prints out there, see if there's a match with the ones I photographed at Ms. Skala's place and go from there."

Ed Kandinsky gave a derisive snort. "Gonna find the Bruno Maglis, are you?"

Mike Hatton hitched up the waistband of his uniform pants. "No, sir, I'm gonna examine the evidence and hope that leads me to the perpetrator, rather than the other way around," he said significantly. "So I'm going out to the truck and get my camera and see what I find out back. And then if nobody has anything *useful* to say, I'll be on my way." He plopped his hat on his head and strode out the door.

Ed Kandinsky flung up a hand in sign of annoyance and turned to follow him out. He halted in the doorway and tossed a last threat over his shoulder. "Sooner or later, one of you is going to trip. *And I'll be there.*"

"Asshole!" shouted Josh, and heaved a sofa pillow against the back of the door. He studied the others: Sophie, vacant and subdued, Carl, troubled, concern etched in the lines around his eyes. "You two need to blow this slag heap," he grumbled.

"But since we can't," said Sophie over the edge of her hand, "what *are* we to do? Mike Hatton is trying to help, I can see that. But Kandinsky's right. Even if the prints match, what's that mean to him? He'll just say we made them, and if they don't match any of our footwear, I'm sure he'll say it's because we hid or disposed of the boots in question. I'm so tired of it," she groaned. "I just want it to be over."

"Sophie, don't do that." Carl hurried across to where she sat, her head slumped back against the sofa, and pulled her upright. "Don't let him do that to you. This isn't forever. We're gonna get out of this."

"He's right, Sophie." Josh leaned forward, arms resting on his thighs. "And I say this shit's gone about far enough. Now, you came out here to check on the place and get your pie plate, and you've done that. So we need to get back. In the first place, you got a dog to take care of. In the second place, I need to catch Rabbit and tell him to take off without me." He waved off Carl's objection. "Then we need to sit down and eat like normal people before my big intestine eats up my little one. And *then*, since our friendly neighborhood cops won't do anything, we need to make us a plan to catch this character. And we can do it. He's obviously made himself right at home here, so we'll just let him think he still can. And we'll nab him. Now let's go." He stood up and headed for the door, determined to afford them no time to argue.

Carl shrugged, stuffed Sophie into her coat, and snatching up the pie plate, hustled her out the door. "Let's go make a pie."

Crow greeted them enthusiastically as they pushed open Sophie's back door, and she took a moment to scratch behind the big ears and commend him for a good dog before tossing her coat over the back of a chair and opening the refrigerator door. "Oh," she glanced over her shoulder, "could one of you please take Crow out while I start getting together an early supper? Thank you, Josh," she smiled, as he assumed the duties of Crow-walker and herded the dog out the door. "I don't suppose you feel like peeling some apples," she blinked up coyly, as Carl rummaged in a cupboard for coffee mugs.

"It'll cost you a kiss."

"Highway robbery," she laughed, and slipped her arms around his neck for the pay-off. Then turning back to the refrigerator, she said, "I got the nicest little ham. I think that would be—well, where *is* it?"

But before the ham could become a mystery, Crow swept in, and slamming the door shut, Josh announced, "Company up front."

"What?" Carl hurried down the hall, Sophie peering after him, and opened the front door to admit a lone Mike Hatton. "Well, come on in, Mike," he said, with a sweep of the arm. "So, where's—"

"I left him back at the station. Told him a story. I wanted to handle this myself."

"What now?" asked Sophie with apparent indifference. But Mike Hatton's face was less bemused and more somber than was his wont, and she felt suddenly and genuinely fearful. "Mr. Hatton?" she asked anxiously. "What is it?"

"Can I see your gun, Carl?"

Carl snorted and motioned toward the living room. "Sure. Over there on the desk." He followed Mike across the room, Sophie scurrying up next to him, as Josh watched curiously from the doorway.

Mike Hatton shifted items on the desktop, then pulled open and fingered through drawers before turning a blank stare on the others. "Not here, Carl."

"Wait, that's where I left it." Carl hurried over and repeated the search, which yielded nothing. "Maybe it's upstairs, and I just thought it was down here."

"And maybe," sighed Mike Hatton, "this is it." He drew a plastic-bagged pistol from his coat pocket.

"So where was it?" asked Carl.

Mike bowed his head and placed a fist on his hip, then stared into Carl's eyes. His own reflected reluctance and regret. "On the seat of Mar's truck. Found it in a ditch out by the quarry, Mar in it. Shot once in the head." The only sound for a long moment was Sophie's prolonged gasp. "I'm gonna have to take you in, Carl," he said, removing the handcuffs from his belt. "I'm sorry."

Sophie screamed and lunged forward as she saw Mike Hatton snap the cuffs into place behind Carl's back. But Josh Dugan had snatched at her arms and held her fast from behind. She continued to shriek and flail against Josh, as she heard Mike Hatton in his official capacity begin to drone, "You're under arrest for suspicion of murder in the death of Marcus Holliday. Anything you say can and will be used against you ..."

"I didn't do it, Mike."

"Lord, I hope not, Carl. Let's go."

"No!" sobbed Sophie, as Mike Hatton nudged Carl through the door. "Carl!"

He flashed her a smile, then, "Josh," he said, standing obdurately until Josh nodded.

Clasping the frantic Sophie in his arms as she collapsed, "Yeah, I will, buddy," he replied.

CHAPTER 22

Josh Dugan sat on the edge of the chair across from Sophie, arms resting on solid thighs, and stared down at his hands. "Mike Hatton'll do what he can, Sophie," he said above her sobs. "He's not a bad guy. It's that friggin' Kandinsky that's the problem. I'd like to shoot that SOB myself, I swear," he growled.

Not only did his rancor have no palliative effect on Sophie, it had no effect whatever, and she continued to weep piteously, until, unnerved, he began almost to regret his promise to Carl to safeguard her. He reached across and placed a timid hand on her knee. "Now, Sophie, you want to help Carl, don't you? Then you've gotta stop that"—he swallowed distastefully—"*crying.*"

She sat up suddenly and took a graceless swipe beneath her nose. Smearing at her eyes, "Attorney," she answered.

"What? Oh, yeah, I'll take care of that. Got a couple trees I can shake."

"Can you shake them now please?" she sniffled, mouth down-turned, lashes wet with tears.

"Oh, yeah, sure," he replied, stumbling up out of the chair to find the phone. Hey, it beat the hell out of walking across hot coals, which he would also have done to stop her hysterics. "Look, Sophie, you gotta know I'm not going to let Carl go down for something he didn't do."

"I want to see him."

"Okay, I'll just call Mike Hatton too, make sure we can do that."

"Josh, they'll have to see, won't they, that it would have been to Carl's advantage to have Mar alive to testify about what he saw?" she appealed.

"Course they will. And I'll mention that to whoever I line up to represent him, okay? Now, I don't mean to sound like I don't care or anything, but I wonder if we couldn't have some supper or something," he said guiltily. "I mean, we won't do Carl any good by starving to death. Dog too," he waved toward Crow.

She nodded unhappily and wobbled up off the sofa to feed Crow. As she scooped the kibbles into his bowl, she gave a hard, frustrated sigh. Joe Wisdom, Crystal, Mar—what was the common denominator? Her? Carl? Peter? All of them—Reney's "configurations"? *Was* there even a single common denominator, or was it so many degrees of separation—Kandinsky's "murder begets murder"?

She stroked Crow's shoulders and began to sniffle anew as she thought of having to climb into her bed and try to sleep without Carl there, tonight and for who knew how many more nights. Then she thought of him having to sleep behind bars as he'd said he never would again, and she began to wail in earnest, for him, but also because she was a self-absorbed cow. And in case things were not already as bad as they could be, it had—she glanced over at the window—begun to snow again, large wet clumps that collided with a splat against the glass.

She looked up to see Josh leaning uncertainly around the doorframe. His upper lip curled, and he appeared to swallow something sour.

For his part, it was with a measure of trepidation that he approached Sophie, both her eyes and nose red and puffy, a soggy paper towel jammed above her upper lip, as she paused mid-blubber to stare at him. He was reminded of why there were two ex-Mrs. Dugans out there somewhere. "Sophie?" he said barely above a whisper. "I called in a couple favors and got a top-notch lawyer for Carl. Wes Montgomery. You know, like—never mind, but he's good."

"Oh, thank you, Josh!" she gushed happily, and searched for a dry part of the paper towel into which to blow her nose. "And when can we see Carl? Would you mind very much if we saw him first and then ate?"

"Sophie," he stammered. Women *had* to be attractive to men. Otherwise, there would be no incentive whatever to try to make the acquaintance of a damn one of them. "I'm afraid we can't see Carl right now. Now, now, don't cry! Please, don't do that." He took a deep breath and poised himself to disappear in a hurry. "You see, with the snow and all … well, they thought it would be better to transfer him to the county jail on the mainland right away, so Rabbit flew them out." He braced himself for the nuclear blast that swept across the kitchen a second later, as she began alternately to shriek and bawl. "God almighty!"

Well, he'd promised Carl, so he edged over next to her and put his arms around her, patting her back rhythmically as if he were burping a baby. "Here, here, come sit down." He pushed her before him down the hall and onto the sofa. "Now, let's look at this logically." She began to sob with renewed vigor. Yeah, he'd forgotten women don't give a shit about logic. "It's going to be easier for

Carl to meet with his lawyer this way, and that's the most important thing, now, isn't it? Right?" He bent down and peered into her face. "Listen, listen to me, Sophie. This might be the best thing for Carl. If he's over there, then he can't very well be accused of anything else that might happen on this rockpile. And, hell, he's been through worse than this. I mean, he was in prison for five years—aw, Jee-sus," he moaned, as the wailing escalated.

Crow had followed them in and now whimpered at her knee and took a consolatory swipe at her hand with his big tongue.

"There now, see?" said Josh, slipping an arm around her shoulders. "You're making the dog feel bad. Besides, you remember how we said we were going to lay a trap for this perp, huh? Remember?"

She raised a soppy face and slurped indecorously. Christ, he thought, better Carl than him. Or maybe not. Probably quieter where Carl was. "Yes," she said through her nose.

"Good. Good," he smiled with relief, as she looked like being capable of speech again. It was a start. "Now, believe me when I tell you *nothing* would make me happier than getting your man back to you just as fast as possible. So that's what we're going to work on, okay?"

She nodded and slurped, and he swiveled around and snatched a tissue out of a box on the table. "I'm sorry," she sniffed. "You want food. I have food." She sprang to her feet resolutely. "I'll get food." She tottered off toward the kitchen mindlessly, while Josh smeared a hand up his forehead and watched Sophie's receding backside in an effort to account for Carl's apparent devotion to her.

"On second thought," he muttered to Crow, "I'd better give her a hand."

He found her peering into the refrigerator in confusion. "The ham is gone," she said.

"Well, that's okay," he said soothingly. "We'll have something else."

"No, the ham is *gone*." She turned a clear eye on him. "It was here, and now it isn't."

He pressed his lips together and frowned. "So, you telling me somebody came in here and stole your ham?"

"And is probably at Carl's right now eating it."

He pushed his palm back down his forehead. "What do you think, we got some kind of magician that can just poof himself in and out of houses without anybody seeing him?"

"Mar saw him. And," she added significantly, "Mar is dead."

"That fried chicken looks good."

"I'm glad. That's what we're having." She handed him a plastic container of prepared chicken and a tub of potato salad. "Why don't you take those out to the living room. I'll get some plates and things."

The "things" included soft rolls and butter, sweet gherkins, and tropical fruit salad, and as they ate and mused, Josh thought with a certain amount of guilt that he could perhaps see what Carl found appealing about her after all. She bought good chicken.

"So?" she asked, pinching off a piece of bread.

"Excellent," he mumbled around a drumstick. "I was damn near starved."

"No, I mean what do you think about the ham and ... all the rest of it?"

"That ham bothers me, same as the pie—never mind Carl's gun. Seems to me somebody's making free with yours and Carl's food and houses both—like I said, never mind Carl's gun, that was a bad break, sure as shit—and I can't make head or tail of it. But when I talked to Mike Hatton, he promised to poke around the empty houses for any sign of B & E. I don't think he'll find any."

"Why us, Josh? It seems as though people who might be seen as a threat to us somehow end up dead. But at the same time, whoever is killing them seems to want to make us look guilty. Now, you don't kill people for the sole purpose of framing somebody else, do you? Where's the sense in it?"

"You'd be surprised, Sophie. There's people just mean enough. Say, somebody who'd rather see Carl in prison for the rest of his life than dead even. And that'd hurt you at the same time. Or somebody who'd want to kill these folks for reasons of their own and got lucky and found out you and Carl'd make real good patsies."

"But who? And the pilfering. The person appears to know more about our comings and goings than I'm comfortable with. I just don't understand it," she whined. "Somebody's watching us, *has* been watching us."

"That's why we've gotta nab whoever it is."

"But how? *Especially* since he's watching us and knows when we come and go."

"Well, I been thinking about that. So when we go out to Carl's, we'll go under cover of dark, and we won't park there. We'll leave the truck a ways down the road and cut through the wooded areas on foot. We'll keep a sharp lookout, and we'll take the dog. He'll let us know if anybody's around. Then if whoever it is isn't already in the house, we'll slip in real quiet and wait. And when we leave here, I'll make damn sure nobody sees you leaving. We're gonna make it look like you're still here"

"Okay," she said eagerly. "Let's finish up and get going then."

He grabbed her arm as she jumped up. "Whoa, hold on. We're not going tonight. No, now listen to me. For tonight, we're going to let whoever it is think they've got rid of Carl and the rest of us are dead in the water."

"But," gasped Sophie, "we can't just do nothing while Carl is locked up and Kandinsky's building a case against him. My God, Josh, Carl's got a record! Who do you think they're going to believe?"

"And that, missy, is why we've only got one shot, and we damn well better get it right the first time."

"But the snow! The snow is just the cover we need."

"No. I'd rather take my chances without than risk blundering in too soon and unprepared. Sophie," he said, taking her hand, "trust me on this." Her hand was warm and soft, and he swallowed and pushed down the unthinkable. "Carl and I go back a long way, and I owe him," he added, as much to himself as to her. "I owe him." Hell, she'd probably just start blubbering again anyhow. "So, we need to sit quiet here for the night, iron out some details and get some rest. Been a rough day. You're not up to it now."

"Oh." She sank back down onto the sofa abjectly. "You're right, I guess. Although I can't imagine sleeping."

"You will, though. In fact, you might wanna have a couple glasses of wine to make you sleepy."

"Oh, how could I sit here drinking wine, while Carl is …"

"You could because you've gotta get some sleep. We'll make our move tomorrow night. Now, you got a bottle, go and get it."

She eyed him stubbornly, but did as she'd been told and returned a moment later with a bottle and two glasses.

"Here, gimme that," he said, relieving her of the bottle and corkscrew. "'Bout the only good thing about this damn place is the winery." The cork popped, and the wine glugged purple into the glasses. "Here."

She took a gulp and fell back against the sofa. "What now?"

He got up and began poking around in the hearth to get a fire going. "Now we sit here and work out some stuff until you get drowsy. Then you're gonna take your fanny up to bed, and me and the mutt and Paco here"—he pulled a pistol out of his waistband and set it on the table—"are gonna keep an eye out for the rest of the night. Tomorrow you're gonna lay low, and I'm gonna have a talk with Mike Hatton. Now drink that down."

She took another sip and sighed, "I should call my sister."

"Well, if you do, you tell her *nothing*."

"What do you mean?" she asked testily. "Why on earth not? Do you suppose she's going to tell the killer?"

"I don't suppose anything, except that the more people that know a thing, the more likely it is that more people will find out. And before you start arguing, do you know for a fact nobody's tapped into this phone?"

"That's ridiculous! You can't just do a thing like that."

"Course you can. And I wouldn't put it past Kandinsky to have done something like that to try to catch you two up, the schmuck."

"This is unbearable," she complained, throwing her head back against the sofa.

"Yeah, well, with any luck, it'll be over soon. Now, let's go over—"

"No, please, not now. Tomorrow will be soon enough. You've outlined the plan, so just tell me what you want me to do when it's time."

"All right," he said, sitting back on his haunches, as she sat forward and placed a glum mouth in her hand.

"Why don't you tell me a story. Tell me how you and Carl met."

"Hell," he snorted, "my memory doesn't reach back that far."

"Oh, come on," she wheedled. "Make it up if you have to. But then make it good."

"Naw, I don't have to make it up." He stood up, refilled the glasses, then plopped into the chair. "Cheers." He took a gulp and dragged a hand across his mouth. "We met when we were smart-ass kids in the Navy."

"The *Navy*! He never told me that."

"Yeah, well, seems like you two don't do a whole lotta talking," he laughed.

"Very funny."

"Carl doesn't talk a lot about the past, though. Can't say I blame him. Some of the past sucks, and the rest isn't real relevant, I guess, when ya think about it. Navy was probably the best of it. We got around anyway. The Mediterranean, Japan. Course we did some stupid shit. He pulled my bacon outta the fire more than once," he chuckled.

"Like how?"

"Nuh uh," he grinned. "He'd have my ass if I told you some of that stuff. We were dumb-shit kids. He *did* talk me outta marrying a girl over there, though. Good thing, too."

"Why is that?"

"Because, if you must know, I was head over heels, or thought I was—at 19 or 20—but I think she just wanted to get away from the mamasan," he laughed. "Now ya satisfied?"

"I guess Carl went on these *junkets* with you," she said with mild disgust.

"I guess you can ask Carl about that. Anyway, didn't I come home and right away marry another one I shouldn't have. Course, that wasn't Carl's fault. It was my own head up my ass.

"Then after we got out, we worked the lake freighters for awhile."

"Like Joe Wisdom," she said sadly. Her head slumped down onto her arm.

"Yeah, like poor old Joe. Anyway, that could get pretty hairy sometimes, when a bad storm would blow up. We had a few close calls, and I expect Carl saved my life at least once, maybe more.

"During that time, I got divorced, remarried, divorced again. Carl never seemed to want to settle down. Hell, that's probably why," he hooted. "Well, not for a long time anyway. I don't know what it was with him. And then …"

"And then Crystal," she said sulkily.

He emptied his glass. "Naw. I think that was more him wishing he wanted to than actually wanting to."

"Oh, what kind of doubletalk is that?"

"I was talking about you."

She flicked a hand at him absently. "Oh, don't bullshit me, Josh, to try to make me feel better. I'm not a child."

"I didn't say you were a child. I said you're not a passing fancy with him." And that, he figured, ought to make her happy and give her something to take to bed with her, or at least guarantee him a little peace.

So he was unprepared, as he glanced over at her, to see the melancholy that crept over her features, and astonished a moment later when her lower lip protruded and began to tremble, and finally, despondent, as she burst anew into fits of weeping. "Go to bed, Sophie," he said morosely. He and Carl were square.

CHAPTER 23

"Go back to bed, Sophie. It's too early to be up."

"It's nine o'clock, besides which you're awake to tell me it's too early to be up." She had dragged downstairs, pushing up the collar of her terry robe, and padded toward the kitchen.

"Could be a long night. And the dog's been out," he'd called after her.

"It's one night, and thank you," she'd called back, emptying Crow's water bowl into the sink and refilling it. Drooping like a wrenched dandelion, she had filled his food dish and set that before him, as well, before shuffling over to the counter to get the coffee started. Armed a few minutes later with two mugs, she had shuffled back out to the living room, handed one to Josh and sunk down on the sofa to blow across the top of her own. "What?"

He'd poked at his teeth with his tongue and shrugged. "I wonder if you shouldn't just wait in the truck and let me and Mike go in," he'd said.

"What are you talking about?" She had taken a quick gulp of coffee and burned her tongue.

"Plan's changed. I decided to trust Mike Hatton and tell him what I had in mind, so he's coming along. And if I was sure you'd be safe—"

"Oh, no, Josh, no way!" she'd answered petulantly, springing forward and jabbing a forefinger into his chest in emphasis. "This concerns me too, and I won't be left behind like so much excess baggage."

He'd grimaced in such a way as to suggest that that was exactly what she was. "All right! All right, but you do exactly what I tell you. And above all, once we leave the truck, you don't say a *word*. I don't care if Godzilla comes up behind and gooses you, you don't say a word, understand?" She'd crinkled up her nose and upper lip in a—silent—sneer, and made a zipping motion across her mouth.

In ill-humored resignation, he had gone on to relate the particulars of Mike Hatton's early morning visit, of which she had been blissfully unaware. It was Mike's jurisdiction, he'd insisted, and if anybody was going to apprehend a possible murderer, it was going to be him. And since Carl had been whisked off to the mainland at the insistence of and accompanied by Ed Kandinsky, at least *he* wouldn't be underfoot.

"*Possible* murderer," Sophie had groused. "I like that. But I won't argue the good fortune of not having the good *detective* here," she'd added with obvious distaste.

In addition—Josh had ignored her—since Mike was trained in police procedure and the proper use of firearms ("Like I'm not," Josh had snorted), he would be the one to head the "operation." Josh had rolled his eyes, but conceded that another man who could handle a gun would increase their chance of success and afford a greater degree of safety. Meanwhile, he'd announced, rubbing his hands along the front of his thighs and standing up, he had agreed to reconnoiter the surrounding area for the best-concealed approach to the house. He didn't need to remind her, he'd added redundantly, that she should remain inside with the doors locked during his absence.

She had realized that he meant well and was trying to do what he thought Carl would want him to, and curbed her impatience at being treated like a fool or a child. Instead, she'd made a point of nodding and smiling, and watched Carl's truck roll down the drive and bump up into the road to disappear around the curve.

She stood at the window now, feeling more than a little forlorn, wondering how Carl was and what he was doing and whether the attorney would be able to arrange bail, and missing Reney and wishing for her company and commiseration.

There was nothing to do now but wait till evening, and she turned from the window, at loose ends, and cast about for something to occupy the time. She ought to tidy up the place, she thought, as she washed the coffee cups with greater deliberation than they deserved. With all that had happened in the—how many weeks *had* it been?—she had paid scant attention to the house and had not kept up with the chores.

She gathered a basket of laundry from the bedroom, allowing herself no more than a brief cry over one of Carl's shirts, before hauling it all downstairs to the washer.

The living room could stand straightening. Between ailments and power outages, murders and guests, life had all but retreated into the single room like a hermit crab, making it well and truly a "living room." That or—with the thefts—a public bus station.

She began to fold quilts into a neat stack and fluff cushions and dust tables. The desk was disorganized, and as she began to sort through the papers and keys and odds and ends, she came across Joe Wisdom's book and was suddenly transported back to that strange October day that had started out so pleasant. The pale sunshine and the genteel picture of the coffee tray on the table between them and Crow at Joe's elbow. And then had come his warning, ushering in with the snow what had become a nightmare existence broken only by those precious, forgetful hours spent with Carl.

She held the book now as if it were a talisman, and somehow the object that had interrupted the revolution of the spheres and brought calamity down upon them and the island. *This book, this book*, she fretted, smoothing a hand over the jacket and initiating a series of "what ifs" that became quickly maddening in the way of "what ifs," but was just as quickly reduced to the question of whether her happening upon Joe Wisdom that day had set in motion all that had followed.

"Oh, Crow," she reached down to stroke the dark, boxy head, "I'm so sorry if I've turned your life upside down."

"I don't think he minds any more than I do."

Her breath caught, and she spun around and launched herself toward the doorway with a shriek. "Oh, Carl!" she sobbed, dragging him down onto the sofa and covering him with kisses.

"Hey," he smiled and hugged her close, "if I'd known this would happen, I'd have got myself arrested a lot sooner."

"Oh, don't you dare joke about it!" she cried, her hands moving over him like hummingbirds, as if she were trying to establish beyond any doubt that he was substantial. "How?" she pleaded.

"Out on bond, angel," he replied with a kiss. "That, and one of Rabbit's 'nip ins,'" he laughed.

"Where's Josh?"

"With Mike Hatton—at a respectful distance," he whispered and, loosing himself from her embrace, stood up and held out his hand to her. A smile guileless as a May morning suffused her face and, her eyes settling into dewy softness, she clasped his hand and scampered with him up the stairs.

"You can't ever go again," she begged, her face pressed against his chest afterward. "If I thought this was the last time—"

"Shhh." He tucked a strand of hair behind her ear and kissed her forehead. "Mike knows I didn't do this, and he'll do his best to help us. Josh too. They told me what they've got planned. I'm going along. Of course," he laughed softly, "Mike won't let me carry a gun."

"Carl, don't go," she said uneasily. "Please. Let them handle it."

"Sophie, you know I can't do that. It's my life on the line, yours and mine. And we stand a better chance of catching this guy with three of us there."

"Four."

"Now, Sophie honey, it'll be safer for you to stay here," he appealed.

She shook her head obstinately. "I'm going. What if you're wrong?" she said over his objections. "How can you be so sure, any of you, that whoever is responsible will show up? I mean, since Crystal's body was discovered, isn't that the last place he'd go, for fear of being caught?"

"Maybe. But he's stranded, same as us. He's gotta go somewhere, and I'm banking on the fact that he knows I've been arrested. If nothing else, he's *gotta* know Kandinsky's not looking anywhere else.

"You know, it may turn out that Crystal really was killed because she happened to be there, surprised him maybe."

"That would still leave Mar."

"Yeah, I know. And maybe he saw more than he let on. Or maybe somebody just *thought* he did."

"Oh, yes, I *see*. Kandinsky's 'murder begets murder.' Wouldn't *that* be an irony?"

"We've gotta catch him," he said earnestly. "So, if you insist on going," he mumbled through a kiss, "we should be getting up and ready to go."

"No." It drifted in and over his ear like a breeze. "Stay. Let the rest of the world fall into a chasm, I don't care. But stay."

There was a heat behind his eyeballs and above his upper lip, and a hurt in his gut like good whiskey, and he didn't bother to resist.

Josh Dugan and Mike Hatton pretended not to notice that the sun had begun to drift toward the horizon before Carl and Sophie reappeared. They could not, however, forego a shrewd glance in Carl's direction as Sophie set about blithely preparing for the lot of them a sumptuous spaghetti dinner with the grace and precision of a garden party.

"I'm still not wild about this business," Mike Hatton finished chewing and swallowed, "of Ms. Skala coming along." It was clearly part of an ongoing debate.

Josh grunted his apparent assent and crunched down on a piece of garlic bread.

Sophie shot them both a defiant look. "I'm going. If Carl's going, I'm going."

The three of them all turned to Carl in appeal. "Yeah, I know," he said, "and I've been thinking about this. We think we know how things are gonna go down, but we don't really *know*. And I'd rather not leave her here alone."

"You could stay here with her, Carl." Josh wound pasta around his fork to form a wad. "Me and Mike can do this."

"Maybe. But I think we stand a better chance of covering the place if I go along. And I don't think she'd be in any real danger, or I wouldn't let her go. I mean, I don't think this guy's got a weapon. His usual method seems to be bashing somebody or strangling them. Yeah, he shot Mar, but with my gun, and most likely for the sole purpose of incriminating me. Otherwise, he wouldn't have left it in the truck."

Mike Hatton appeared to use the pretense of thinking to push another ball of spaghetti into his mouth. "Well, I'm still not crazy about it. But I guess once we've scouted out the place, if there's nobody there, you can take her inside. Cover both doors from inside, I suppose, and holler if you see something. Josh and I are gonna cover the back door, since we pretty much know he lets himself in that way."

"I don't suppose there's any way of knowing how long we'll have to wait," ventured Sophie, reaching for Carl's hand.

"No," replied Mike, "but not long, I wouldn't think. If we're right and this creep is squatting there, then he'll show up to sleep. Heck, he might already be there, laying low after Mar," he explained, spearing a meatball.

"Where you gonna stash two vehicles?" asked Carl.

"We're not. We're all going in mine."

"A marked car, Mike?"

"Don't worry about that. There's a little lane—well, you know the one, Carl—catty-cornered from your place, with the little clearing in the trees. It'll work in the dark. I'll cut the lights when we get close. So," he pushed himself away from his empty plate and glanced toward the window, "I guess it's show time."

The four of them looked around the table at each other and heaved a collective sigh, before piling their dishes into the sink to soak and pulling on boots, parkas and gloves. Sophie knelt down to pet Crow. It had been decided that he should not go after all.

"Now, remember, everybody," Mike said, glancing at Sophie in the rearview mirror a moment later, "once we get outta this car, we can't be talking. Not a word, not a sound, no matter what, until we nab him. That understood? Everybody?"

Sophie pursed up her mouth, and her eyes rolled upward. "Yes, Mr. Hatton. Josh has already explained to me that I mustn't cry out if I'm molested by the Creature from the Black Lagoon."

"Now, Ms. Skala, I only meant ..."

She smiled over at Carl, who shook his head and leaned across the seat to kiss her.

"And it'd be better," grumbled Mike Hatton, "if we could keep our minds on the operation. Can't be careless."

"Sorry, Mike. You're right," Carl agreed, and stole another kiss.

"Jee-sus," muttered Josh Dugan, "Popeye and Olive Oyl in the back seat."

Sophie was spared the trouble of a witty reply by their arrival at the lane, which they had approached from the north so as to avoid passing Carl's house. Mike had done as he'd said he would and extinguished the headlights, so he guided the SUV carefully into the turn-off by the light of the moon off the snow and shut off the engine.

"Be careful closing the doors." He took a deep breath. "Okay, let's go."

They climbed out as quietly as they could, closing their eyes and wincing at the click of the door latches and the crunch of crusted snow that thumped dull against their hooded ears. The sound of their own breath was magnified in their imaginations, if not in fact by the darkness, and their progress seemed to them interminably slow.

Mike put out an arm as they approached the road, which they would have to cross to reach the trees that bounded Carl's property, and which would be the point at which they would be most vulnerable to detection. They stopped and slowly scanned what was visible of the landscape, praying silently that no one was secreted beneath the trees on either side, before moving with quiet urgency across the snow-covered road and into the copse opposite. There was nothing to be done about the prints but hope they would be lost to the night and the tire tracks.

They stayed just within cover of the woods, steering directly west in a line that took them parallel to the north side of the house, their breathing becoming shallower with each step nearer their destination, Carl's grip tighter on Sophie's hand until she could barely feel it any more.

When they had finally arrived opposite the north wall, Mike raised a hand to signal a halt, and slowly removing his pistol from the holster, crept alone out of the cover of the woods. It had been decided that he should do the initial reconnaissance and then signal to the rest of them either the all clear or the presence of an intruder.

Sophie, Carl and Josh waited for what seemed an eternity, but was in fact a matter of some ten minutes, before Mike reappeared and motioned to them to approach. Sophie clamped her lips together and hardly dared to breathe, as Carl crept along the porch, crouched low and as near the front wall as he could get. When his key turned in the lock, Mike waved the others over one at a time.

Once inside, the enforced silence was even more oppressive, as they recoiled from the lightest footstep on the wood, the slightest creak of a floor board. As their eyes adjusted to the denser darkness within, and they saw no movement and no human forms but their own, they allowed themselves to breathe.

Gun drawn, Mike indicated his intention of checking the second floor loft. If it was empty, he and Josh would take up their positions outside the back door. Their eyes followed each step of his feet on the stairs, their expressions pained and anxious, until he reached the top and turned back toward them, nodding and holstering his pistol. They relaxed and exhaled as one. Sophie and Carl could each just barely discern the other's smile in the dark.

Their relief was short-lived. As they waited for Mike to reach the bottom of the stairs, a deeper shadow moved across the thick darkness that enveloped the back porch, and instinctively they froze. Sophie felt Carl tense next to her, but dared not turn her head to look at him.

As they stood rooted, in terror or anticipation, a figure put something to its mouth and in a single deft movement, pressed the object against the loose pane and pushed the pane through the frame, clutching it between thumb and forefinger and manipulating the door latch open with the other fingers. The murderer had arrived. But even as the enormity of this realization struck her, Sophie knew that the others were thinking, as she was, "So, *that's* how."

They would allow him to enter. When he had shut the door behind him, then they would grab him. As he stepped inside, he reached up and peeled something from above his upper lip. The door closed.

With terrifying speed, Carl and Josh lunged forward as one and wrestled him to the floor, Mike Hatton leaping the rest of the way down the stairs to take charge. But as the intruder cried out, Sophie gasped in disbelief. Fumbling for the nearest light switch, she spun back around and clapped her hands to her mouth in horror.

"Oh, my God!" she wailed. "Reney!"

CHAPTER 24

"Reney!" she cried again, as she saw the dark bruise forming along her sister's jaw and the blood creeping into the crevices of her injured hand before it fell away in droplets to the floor. The wool hat had been flung off, and her dark hair hung disheveled around her face. The glass pane lay in ruddy-smudged shards beside her, along with the plastic suction cup.

Sophie lurched forward and, shoving mindlessly at Josh and Carl, sank to her knees to envelope Reney in her protective embrace. "Get away!" she shouted, as Mike Hatton's 200-plus-pound bulk loomed over them.

"What the *hell?*" he exclaimed, looking blankly from the crouching figures on the floor to Josh and Carl.

"Well, don't just stand there!" she shrieked. "Someone get me a wet towel!"

Carl was nearest his kitchen area and scrambled in a drawer, snatching up a dish towel and dampening it under the faucet. He knelt beside Sophie, her face both desolate and defiant, and taking Reney's hand in his own, began to dab at the cuts.

"Sophie." It was a gentle plea.

Sophie relieved him of the towel wordlessly and, helping Reney to her feet, slumped with her onto the sofa, cradling her sister's head against her shoulder.

"You know this woman, Ms. Skala?"

"She's my sister," Sophie said simply.

"Well, is this gonna get any stranger?" Mike Hatton looked around with something like desperation, the circumstances clearly beyond the scope of his experience.

Sophie ignored him, wrapping the towel around Reney's hand, pain evident in her voice as she asked, "*Why*, Reney?"

"I wanted to protect you, Cissybeans," she smiled sadly, "the way you've always protected me."

"Oh, but darling, to kill people—"

"Oh, no!" Reney sat up in alarm. "Sophie, no. I didn't kill those people." Her dark head moved rapidly from side to side in emphasis, and Sophie leaned back and observed her with a mixture of astonishment and relief.

The three men sank onto or against whatever pieces of furniture most readily presented themselves, and Mike Hatton moaned, "Lord, I guess that'll teach me to ask stupid questions. Well, guess I better call the paramedics. But then I'm gonna get to the bottom of this," he added, hitching up his belt.

"Oh, no," argued Reney. "I'm all right. Look." She removed the bloody towel she had clutched around her hand. "See? It's almost stopped."

"Still," interjected Carl. He sprinted up the stairs and returned a moment later with antibiotic cream and gauze, and first glancing down at Sophie for consent, he squatted next to them and began to bandage Reney's hand.

"We have to get her back to the cottage." Apart from her injuries, she looked to Sophie ill and haggard, and the cold she had caught wandering the island had settled in her chest.

"Just a minute now. Nobody's going anywhere just yet."

"Didn't you hear her, Officer Hatton?" snapped Sophie. "She's innocent."

"Begging your pardon, ma'am, but so is everybody in prison. Now, now," he raised a hand in a plea for calm. "Maybe she's telling the truth and maybe she isn't. But before I can decide what to do here, I think we need to hear the whole story from the top."

"Oh, for heaven's sake!"

"No," Reney placed a reassuring hand on Sophie's arm, "it's okay. He's right."

"Well, then, for starters, how long you been here, Ms.—"

"Reney. Huh, I'm not sure. After that first day we had lunch—remember, Sophie, we went shopping?—I was so worried about you. And the more I thought about it, the more convinced I was that if I could just come over here and talk to you, I'd find the right thing to say to make you come home.

"So I arranged for Kenneth—my ex-husband," she directed at Mike Hatton—"to take the kids. I thought it would only be for a day or two at the most. I told him I had to go to New York on business, made up some cock-and-bull story, he never pays attention anyway.

"I was going to call from across the bay that day the storm came. I saw the clouds moving in and the water kicking up, and I was afraid, Sophie. So I was going to call, to make sure it was the right thing to do. But then I saw the ferry getting ready to leave, and there was no time. I had to get on board."

"That was *you* that day," said Carl. "We thought you were nuts."

"I was," Reney smiled wanly.

"But why didn't you just come to the house, darling?"

"I was going to," she said, turning back to her sister, "but I wanted to call first and let you know. And, of course, I did, from the bar. But then you were so frantic, about what that man had said to you, and your involvement with ..." She flushed. "Well. And I asked you to come home, remember? If you'd said yes, I'd have come right over and stayed until we could get away. I did ask someone where your house was, and I even came by. But by that time," she nodded toward Carl, "he'd come back, and I couldn't very well ... And by then, the storm was awful, and I was so cold."

"Reney, my God! You should have just come to me. What earthly difference would it have made *what* I said just then?" moaned Sophie.

"I don't know. *He* was there, and I had some hare-brained idea of helping you by talking to that man, the one who'd upset you. The one who knew about Peter," she said guardedly.

"You talked to Joe Wisdom that day?" Mike Hatton pulled himself up and eyed her narrowly.

"No! No," she turned toward Sophie. "I found out who he was and where he lived, and I went there."

"In that *blizzard*? Oh, Reney!"

"I thought I'd never get there. I was trying to walk against the wind. I could barely see where I was going. But I found the mailbox and dragged up to the door. I knocked, but there was no answer. I knocked harder, and the door pushed open."

"So you *were* in Joe Wisdom's house that day," said Mike Hatton.

"Reney, maybe you'd better not say any more," urged Sophie.

"No, you don't understand. I went there, yes, but I never saw him. Just the dog. And I didn't mean for that to happen, for him to slip out like that. He pushed past me and ran out into the storm, Sophie. I felt terrible."

"Wait! What are you saying?" Carl leaned forward and frowned. "Are you telling us that you were in Joe's Wisdom's house after you called Sophie that day, but before Joe was found? And *you* let Crow out?"

"But that's not possible." Sophie looked up at Mike Hatton with misgiving. "You told me that Joe was killed *before* I was attacked. I was attacked not five minutes after I spoke to Reney, and allowing for the time it would have taken her to walk there in a blizzard, according to your timetable, she *should* have found Joe Wisdom dead."

Mike Hatton rubbed a big hand over his mouth in embarrassment. "I guess I could've been wrong."

"You guess you—" gaped Sophie. "If he was killed after I was attacked, then I couldn't very well have done it, *could* I?"

"Maybe that part of it doesn't matter." Josh slouched against the back of a kitchen cupboard, a finger crooked beneath his lower lip. "Even that idiot Kandinsky finally admitted Joe's death could have been an accident."

"What I said to begin with," Mike muttered irritably.

"You're right, it doesn't matter," argued Sophie. "Either way, Reney should have found a body. And she *didn't*."

"Look," suggested Carl, standing between them in an effort to mediate. "Before we start suspecting each other of God knows what, let's hear the rest of Reney's story, huh?"

"I'm not sure what else to say. I was hungry, so I ate some food. I know it was wrong. That, and breaking in here," she appealed to Carl, "but I intended to pay for everything and make amends, just as soon as the storm ended. But, of course, it didn't end, did it?" she asked with an ironic smile. "I couldn't have gotten off the island then if I'd wanted to. And then when I found out somebody had tried to kill you, Sophie, well, I really couldn't. There was too much happening too fast in too small a place, and it all seemed connected to you." She sighed then. "I had to try to protect you if I could."

"But *how*?" asked Sophie. "How did you manage it?"

Reney glanced over at Carl contritely. "I knew Carl was staying with you, and that his place would be empty, so I came out here. It's funny," she mused aloud, "how seldom you think about things like not lighting so much as a candle at night, for fear of its being seen. Nights were pretty dreary, but," she shrugged, "I got the hang of it pretty quickly."

"I don't understand how you could have pulled it off."

"I always wanted to be an actress, you know," she said with a wry smile. "But for one thing, everybody dresses the same around here. I bought a few things, filched a few others. I'm afraid this is your shirt, Carl. Anyway, it was surprisingly easy, and surprising too how little people notice."

"Oh," said Sophie, closing her eyes as recognition dawned, "you on the ferry that day, over and back."

"I was terrified you'd recognize me when you drove past me coming from the dock. But there it is—my own sister didn't know me. The rest was easy."

"My God, you went over that day to meet me for lunch. Why didn't you stay there? Why didn't you go home?"

"You were in trouble. More than you knew then."

"What do you mean?"

"I mean, I knew what you'd find that night you came here."

"All right," interrupted Mike Hatton, "I think you'd better go over this part real slow."

"No, Reney, don't say anything more."

She grabbed Sophie's hand with her uninjured one. "I told you, I didn't kill any of these people. I would have warned you, I wanted to. But you seemed to be settled at the cottage, and I never dreamed you'd come out here that night."

"What do you know about Crystal Holliday?" pressed Mike Hatton.

"I know," she replied, looking directly into his eyes, "when she was put in the bathtub. It was the day before you found her," she said to Sophie. "I was stir-crazy, and anyway, I had to call you about lunch. I needed to see you. But by that time, that detective was poking around, and I was leery about calling from Carl's phone. So I trudged into town again." Sophie wagged a disbelieving head. "Anyway, I wanted a bath that evening. I was afraid you'd get suspicious if I showed up all grubby for lunch," she smiled.

The smile vanished. "I found her. It was awful. There she was, staring up at me, her skin so pale it was almost translucent. But not in a beautiful way. She wasn't beautiful. Her lips were blue." She shuddered. "But I had no place else to go, so I cowered down here in the kitchen that night and couldn't wait to get away the next morning."

"That *was* you I saw outside the night we found her then."

"Yes. I didn't want to come back here, but I was cold and tired. You can't imagine my shock when I saw lights on and then crept around and peeked in the window and saw you. I knew you couldn't have gone upstairs, and I prayed that you wouldn't."

"Oh, Reney, Reney," sighed Sophie.

Reney mistook her sister's meaning. "I know, and I'm sorry. I should have told you. Then certainly, but even before. And if I'd had any idea that you would come out here, I'd have broken my leg to keep you from getting back on the boat that afternoon. But I was afraid, Sophie. It was *Carl's* house."

Carl huffed and leaned against his knuckles. "You thought I killed her."

Reney sighed. "No, Carl, I couldn't think that. I couldn't bear to think that. But I knew what it would mean. It was one thing for *you* to report it, but it would have been so much worse for anyone else to. Worse for you and worse for Sophie."

Mike Hatton took a couple of impatient steps, then planted himself, one hand on the hip where his gun rested. "And just how long did you figure you'd wait to tell somebody, ma'am? I mean, don't you *know* what happens to bodies when they sit? Never mind withholding knowledge of a crime."

"Yes, of course, I knew I couldn't wait long. But I hoped I might see or hear something that would point to the person responsible so Carl and Sophie would never have to come under suspicion."

"Well, now, that's my job." Mike Hatton shook his head and took a swipe at the chair with his hat. "That was just foolish and dangerous, if you don't mind me saying so, ma'am."

"All I cared about, Officer, was protecting my sister. That's all." Reney sniffed, and a tear spilled over her lower lid. Sophie pulled her close and murmured soothingly. "They don't understand, Sophie," she cried.

"Never mind, honey. This has been a nightmare for all of us. But you're safe now. And now we have more information than we had. For one thing, we know that we have fewer pieces that all have to be made to fit a theory of one person."

"Now, hold on." Mike Hatton sliced through the air with a forefinger. "I'm far from satisfied here. Okay, we know you broke in here. But what about Sophie's place?"

Reney hung her head and stole an embarrassed glance at her sister. "It's an old lock, and I used a credit card to get in. I took your food."

Sophie blew out a little laugh. "Darling Reney, you know I'd give you my last bite gladly."

"I know, and it wouldn't be the first time either," she replied, and squeezed her sister's hand.

"Yeah, well then, I guess that still leaves a couple questions, doesn't it? Like who attacked Sophie and who stole Carl's gun?"

Reney's expression was one of blank shock. "You can't think I would ever hurt Sophie."

"All right, maybe I'll give you that one."

"What reason would she have to kill Mar Holliday?"

"Protecting you?"

Reney trained on him a certain eye. "You're right about that, Officer Hatton. I *would* kill someone to protect my sister." Sophie went rigid beside her. "But I didn't."

"Aw, come on, Mike," said Carl. "Let's not make it more complicated than it is."

"More complicated, ya say? First it was one person responsible for all the murders and break-ins. Then it was one killer and one burglar. And *now* it's one person doing some of the burglaries and all the murders, and another one doing all the rest! And we're not even gonna talk about disappearing bodies and bodies appearing when they shouldn't. Lord," he groaned, "when this is over, I'm putting in for park ranger, I swear." He slumped down into a chair and sulked over his big hands.

"Yes, I see," reflected Sophie. "Most of it isn't that difficult. The murderer tried to kill me and then broke in to steal Carl's gun in order to incriminate him in Mar's death, which would certainly suggest premeditation. But I see what you mean about the bodies. Where was Joe's body when Reney was there and should have found it? And where was Crystal for nearly a week before she wound up in Carl's tub?"

Josh Dugan pushed himself away from the cupboard and stretched his sore back. "Look, it's like Sophie said, at least we know more than we did. We can pretty much rule out the 'mysterious stranger' as the murderer and start looking closer to home, I'd say." He yawned. "So what d'ya say, Mike? We did what we came here to do, caught the intruder—and *he's* real pretty, too—but you suppose we can get outta here now and get some shut-eye?"

"Yes, please?" begged Sophie. "Reney is ill and hurt, and"—she turned to her sister—"when was the last time you ate, darling? You must be hungry."

"Yes," Reney flushed anew, "I am. I'm afraid I ate the last of the ham this morning."

"Oh," chuckled Sophie, "that should have tipped me off right there. You always wanted ham over fried chicken. That, and fruit cocktail?" She raised an inquiring brow.

"And I'm afraid," Reney giggled sheepishly, "you'll find the last can of that upstairs under Carl's bed."

Chapter 25

"Do you love my sister, Carl?"

They could hear Sophie moving around upstairs as she collected laundry and freshened the guest room. Josh had taken Crow and struck out for Dickie's in search of Rabbit, whom he'd assumed had flown in with the first light. The snow still lay in unrelenting mounds, but this morning, they sparkled under a sunlit sky, the first in many days.

Carl stared down at his coffee cup, then pressed his lips together and nodded slowly. "Yes, I expect I do."

"Good. Then you won't ever hurt her, will you?"

"That's the last thing I'd wanna do."

"Good," Reney exhaled. "I suppose you know what a bastard her husband was."

"I know enough," he said a little uneasily.

"I won't ever let anyone hurt her like that again. I blame myself—"

"Reney."

"Never again," she repeated with slow emphasis.

"You really *are* protective of your big sister, aren't you?" he smiled. "Usually it's the other way around."

"I suppose there's really no way for you to know what I owe her. It *was* the other way around, Carl. It's *always* been the other way around. Since we were little. She's always looked out for me. Oh, hell," she said in frustration, "not even just looking out for me, but taking bad things onto herself and shouldering the unthinkable to spare me. You have no idea."

"She told me about how you lost your parents and how hard things were after that."

"After that?" She smiled bitterly and gazed out the window, then turned back and eyed him curiously. "So, she told you about that, did she? Which story, I wonder?"

"What do you mean? She told me about how she was playing with candles one night and accidentally set the house on fire."

The chill in Reney's eyes sent a shiver up the back of his neck, as she replied, "That's a lie. It wasn't an accident. And she didn't do it. *I* did, and it wasn't an accident.

"Shall I tell you, Carl, what life was like for us as children? Our parents were drunks, our mother an ineffectual drunk who would have bouts of contrition and try to play the good mommy, and our father a mean drunk who was way too quick with his hands. And of course, it wasn't long at all before Daddy did more with his hands than just slap us around.

"Sophie tried to protect me then too, tried to keep me out of his sight and his thoughts by taking that on herself too. And when Mummy found out, who do you suppose she blamed? Not Daddy dear. Things got increasingly unbearable, and Sophie bore the brunt of the abuse and the hatred and the beatings.

"And then," Reney twisted up her mouth and looked at him wearily, "one night, after yet another sick and vicious *incident*, I found Sophie on her bed, crying as though she'd seen everything in the world that there was to see, and it was all bad, you know?"

She took a deep breath. "And then it was simple. When they'd drunk themselves into oblivion and passed out in their room, I went to the kitchen cupboard and got the candles and took them up and lit them, held the flames to the edges of the sheets and the window curtains. And once they'd caught, I snatched up my mother's cheap perfume and sprayed it on the flames. And the balls of fire shot up, and I was glad," she whispered icily. "I was glad.

"I just sat there. But then I heard Sophie shriek behind me, and felt her grab my arm and jerk me to my feet and drag me down the hall and out of the house. She'd missed me, you see, and come looking for me, to make sure I was all right." First one and then another large tear tumbled onto her hand.

"Reney, I ..." Carl felt as though someone was chiseling at something somewhere in his chest.

Reney straightened up and wiped at her nose. "You already know, of course, that she told everyone she'd done it, set the fire. She made me promise not to say anything by telling me that if we didn't say the same thing, the authorities would separate us. I was eight, and I believed her.

"Of course, that wasn't the end of it. I'm sure she told you the sanitized version of the aunt and uncle, probably something like they just weren't really *fond* of her." She jammed her fingers against her mouth. "You can't imagine. I hope they're in hell now. I picture them there."

"I'm sorry, Reney."

She smeared at her eye. "She's been through so much that's so terrible. And that's why as far as I'm concerned, her late and unlamented husband got much less than he deserved, and why I ..." She looked into his eyes earnestly. "You *will* make her happy, won't you? She deserves to be happy, Carl."

He reached over and patted her hand. "I'll do my best," he smiled.

She took a deep breath and hurriedly ran her ring fingers under her eyes as she heard Sophie on the stairs.

"What are you two talking about so intently with your heads together? My birthday isn't for months," she laughed.

"Well, it's like this, Sophie honey. Little sister has been grilling me." He raised a hand to silence Reney's outrage. "Seems she wants to know if my intentions toward you are honorable. And I've had to tell her they are not because—ah, ah—*because* I have matrimonial designs on you." Reney gasped beside him, while Sophie merely stared at him tentatively. "Okay," he sighed, walking over and taking Sophie's hand in his own. "I'm not sure how you're supposed to do this, but"—he dropped to one knee—"will you marry me, angel?"

Sophie sucked in a breath and put her hand up to her mouth. But before she could answer, they saw Josh Dugan slump against the doorframe dramatically.

"Jee-sus. Happens every time I leave," he moaned, as Crow trotted past him into the room. He pulled himself up and headed for the stairs, pausing to look down his nose at Carl as he passed. "But I ain't wearin' any damn monkey suit!"

"Ya bum! She hasn't answered yet. Well?" he looked up at Sophie, and once again, the world shrunk to encompass only them.

"Yes," she beamed, pulling him up and sliding her arms around his neck. "Yes."

A squeal erupted from Reney, and she raced over, hugging her sister and smiling with gratitude over her shoulder at Carl.

"I think I'm gonna puke," came Josh Dugan's congratulatory message from the stairs. "And now I suppose you're all gonna want to go down to Dickie's for dinner and celebrate over his damn greasy burgers and flat beer."

Sophie feigned disgust, but lost her focus and began to laugh. "That's a brilliant idea!"

"Thought so. In the meantime, Carl—ya schmuck—can you run out to the airport with me? Rabbit offloaded a bunch of stuff for the market, and he needs some help getting it there."

Carl frowned. "Yeah, I would, Josh, you know that. Except I wonder if it'd be safe to leave them here," he nodded toward Sophie and Reney.

"Don't see why not. It's a sunny day, there's two of 'em, don't see why anybody'd try anything now. But if it'll make you feel better, I'll leave 'em this," he said, drawing out his pistol and placing it on the desk. "Besides, this won't take long. Load it on the truck, schlep it to the market and come back." He bounded up the stairs.

"Oh, go," urged Sophie. "We'll be fine. There's no blizzard for anyone to disappear into, and nobody is going to be foolish enough to risk being seen. Not at this point. There's way too much at stake."

"All right," he agreed, as Josh reappeared. "We'll go and get back then." He grabbed his coat and gave Sophie a quick kiss.

"Come on." Josh plucked at his sleeve. "You can get back to the honeymoon later. God knows," he groused out the door, "it's been going on for a month."

As the truck crunched down the drive, Sophie turned to Reney and said, "It really hasn't been that long, you know." They laughed, and started the laundry and cleaned up the kitchen, before brewing a fresh pot of tea and retiring to the living room to catch up.

"Cissybeans, I really am happy for you. I was appalled when you first told me about him. But I like him, and what's more to the point, *you* like him. And I see now that he really does love you."

"You didn't really grill him, did you?" smiled Sophie.

"I did, yes," she laughed, then added seriously, "It was important to me to know."

She sauntered over to the desk and, setting down her cup, picked up Joe Wisdom's book. "So, this is the infamous book." She turned it over. "And this is Joe Wisdom. He looks like such a nice man, doesn't he?"

"He was," sighed Sophie. "He really was. He frightened me, of course, because he obviously knew about Peter and me. But he told me he didn't mean me any harm, and I probably should have believed him and been a bit more charitable. The odd thing is that perhaps if I hadn't been in such a hurry to get away, the killer wouldn't have had the opportunity to kill him—or try to kill me. Not then anyway."

"Well, you can't blame yourself for that. From what you've told me, he might have been a little clearer about what he was trying to tell you, instead of making it sound like a threat." She took a sip of tea and wandered over to the sofa, book in hand. "So, what do you think it's about really, Sophie? Is it about you or Peter or Carl?"

"I don't know. I've gone over it, of course, again and again. At first, I assumed it *was* about me, because the coincidences were too striking for it not to be: Peter and me, Peter and Crystal, Crystal and Carl, Carl and me. And as grating as Detective Kandinsky is, he was right about that much anyway. Coincidences generally aren't really, are they?

"And then there was Joe's warning about certain people who felt that someone else bore some of the responsibility for Crystal's misfortunes."

"But Sophie, that sounds downright hokey. And if someone hadn't tried to kill you, I'd dismiss it as a penchant for melodrama, plain and simple. As it is, I still don't believe that would be a reason to murder someone."

"Don't you, Reney?" Sophie asked significantly.

"No!" Reney answered emphatically. "It's not the same thing at all. You don't kill someone over somebody else's failed love affair, for God's sake."

"I didn't think so either," Sophie said casually. "Although stranger things have happened." She looked around as if she'd suddenly missed something. "Where's Crow?"

"Hm? Oh, he was asleep in the kitchen. You want me to get him?"

"No. No, that's fine. I'm just used to seeing him lying by the fireplace. But since we don't have a fire going ..." she smiled. "Anyway," she resumed, "all the rest aside, I keep feeling that there's something else, something I'm missing, and that that book figures into it somehow. It's as though there's something in there that I've read that ought to have meant something, told me something, but it's just beyond reach, you know?"

They both sprang up as they heard a shout behind them. "Sophie, you all right?"

"Bea!" gasped Sophie.

"There you are," smiled Bea Baskin. "I thought something happened to you. Back door standing open, and Crow running loose."

"What?"

"Yeah. Well, look," she pointed toward the front window, "there he is."

"How in the ..." As Reney stared out the window, Sophie ran to the front door and called to Crow, who bounded grinning up the front steps. "How did you get out, huh?" She shrugged and turned back to Bea, who stood watching from behind the sofa. "Carl and Josh must not have pulled the door closed all the way. Oh, Bea, this is my sister Reney."

"That right? Well, how do."

"Won't you sit down?"

"Thanks, but no. Can't stay but a minute."

"Bea, I'm sorry about Mar. But I want you to know Carl did not do it."

"No, no, course he didn't. Fact is, Mar had a big mouth. Bound to get him into trouble sooner or later." Sophie and Reney exchanged a curious glance. "I told him that more than once too. Told him people who know too much and talk too much get in trouble.

"Poor old Joe Wisdom was another one like that. Always poking into things, trying to find out things. But not only did he *talk* too much," she gurgled, "but he *wrote* too much. Course that might not have mattered if you hadn't come here, dragging your story along with you. Didn't take him long to figure that out either, did it? And I knew as soon as he did figure it out, he'd have to be talking to you about it, and that *that* would be a problem. And that's why poor old Joe had to go."

"*What*?" gasped Sophie.

"No, now don't be looking for the gun on the desk, 'cause it's not there," she gurgled again, and produced the weapon from her pocket.

"Oh, no." Sophie cast a worried look at Reney and shook her head in disbelief. "What are you doing?"

"Well, now be fair. I did try to warn you, after all, didn't I? So I'm afraid you have to go too, Sophie. And your sister, since she had to come poking around too. And don't think it makes me happy, 'cause it doesn't. Not any happier than poor Joe. But there it is."

"What do you *mean*?"

"Why, you said it yourself. Something in that book, you said, bothering you. And it would have kept bothering you till eventually you nosed around and figured it out." She shook her head in mock sadness. "Bad luck you coming here."

"I don't know what you mean. I don't know anything."

"Don't you? Well, it's like this. I don't think Mar by himself would have been a problem. He wasn't real sharp, and I could have convinced him. And I don't think Crystal would have been a problem either, if it hadn't been for you. If you just would have given your rich doctor husband a divorce and let him marry Crystal, I expect she'd have been happy as a clam living the high life in the city, and wouldn't have cared a fig what happened on this island. But, nope. He had to die still married to you, so Crystal came dragging back here. And while I wouldn't kill you just on account of that, it did make it real hard to like you, Sophie."

"I don't understand any of this."

"Well, that kinda surprises me, you being a clever writer and all. But I don't expect the particulars much matter. It's like I told you before, bad combinations. If you hadn't come here and got friendly with Joe, it would have been easy. I could have taken care of Crystal quietly, told people she'd decided to go back to the city after all, and nobody the wiser, and nobody would have been hurt.

"Instead, it was a little tricky. Had to cut a hole in the ice in the pond out back and put Crystal there for awhile. Didn't want to take her over to Carl's right away, in case he had an alibi," she grinned. "But then that fool Mar found out. So I convinced him to help me move her. And then, naturally, he had to go. Well, anyway," she said nonchalantly and motioned with the pistol, "let's go down to the basement, shall we? Quieter down there."

"But how do you expect to get away with shooting the two of us?"

"Same as the others. That detective'll find a way to pin it on Carl. And even if he doesn't," she shrugged, "nobody will be looking for me, because I wouldn't have a motive, now would I?" she smiled. "Let's go, girls."

Sophie looked over at Reney and saw again the pale, frightened little girl she had tried so hard to shield and to save, and unthinking, she lunged toward Bea Baskin. The shot seemed to echo from more than one direction, and she heard her sister cry out as Reney tumbled into her and sent her hurtling to the floor to land on all fours. As she twisted around to see Reney, she saw Bea crumple, the gun skittering from her hand across the floor. Mike Hatton hovered near the doorway with gun drawn, but he was in the wrong place, and she craned her head to the left. Ed Kandinsky stood with feet planted, his revolver clasped in his outstretched hands.

She crawled around to lift Reney's head into her lap, and cradled her gently as she watched her eyelids flutter and her blood soak through the front of her shirt. "No!" she keened. "Why, Reney? *Why*?"

"Oh, Cissybeans." It was a whispered gasp. "You know I'd do anything to keep you safe. But I need you to know," she clutched at Sophie, "I didn't kill Peter."

"I know, darling. I know. *I* did."

She scrambled aside as the paramedics wheeled in the gurney, then sprawled on the floor, witless and desolate, as they took Reney away. And then she heard from the hallway a voice say, "I guess Bea will get off the island after all." She dragged herself up to peer over the back of the sofa.

"*Joe*?" she asked incredulously, and slumped back down to face Ed Kandinsky kneeling beside Bea Baskin's prone form.

"I don't think so," he said.

Chapter 26

"I want to go with Reney," whimpered Sophie. She huddled shivering in a blanket on the sofa, head resting on Carl's shoulder.

"Shhh." He looked down at her, his mouth drawn into a tight line, and ran a gentle hand over her hair. "Reney's on her way to the hospital right across the bay. They'll look after her. She'll be all right, angel, you'll see. But they wouldn't let you in right now anyway while they're working on her. So we'll wait till Rabbit gets back, and we'll fly over in a little while. We'll call first so you can hear for yourself that she's out of the woods."

"Looked to me like it went through her shoulder," offered Ed Kandinsky. "Flesh wound is all."

Her gaze glanced off Ed Kandinsky and wandered vacantly around the collection of people in her living room. "I don't understand." She raised a limp hand toward the chair opposite, where Joe Wisdom sat eyeing her sympathetically. "I don't understand how you're not dead."

"I know, Sophie, and I'm sorry. It must have been a shock for you. And I probably should be dead. But I believe your sister's peculiar intrusion probably saved my life, just as Carl's arrival saved yours that day.

"You see, I was back in my den that afternoon after you left, researching some old documents, and I never saw who struck me in the back of the head. But by then, I had several ideas about who might want to. And that's why I had to disappear.

"When I came to, it was dark, and I was alone in the house. Crow was gone, and my heart sank. You don't know how glad I was to find he'd made his way to you." He reached down and patted the big dog that now lay contented at his feet.

"I phoned Mike. When he arrived, I told him what had happened and what I suspected, and also that I thought you might be in danger if the assailant thought I'd confided something to you.

"When Carl called Mike to report the attack on you, I knew I was right, and Mike and I began to consider what was best to be done. Now, it turned out I had a pretty nasty concussion, so when Carl called later to report to Mike that Crow had shown up here, and that you feared I'd been the victim of some misadventure, the perfect plan presented itself. Mike had urged me to go to the hospital anyway, so I allowed myself to be removed from the island as a 'corpse,' and Mike put the story about that he had indeed found me dead—with one interesting, if false, detail. He said I had been found at the bottom of the stairs. Only the assailant would know otherwise, and if he—or she—did not trip up and reveal that knowledge, at least, we thought, it would give him something to contemplate."

"You *knew,*" Carl scowled over at Mike Hatton. "You let us come under suspicion of murdering Joe, and all the time Joe was alive, and you knew it!"

"Well, now," mumbled Mike, his big head drooping in chagrin, "I'm sorry about that. But," he eyed Carl defiantly, "obviously there was never any real chance of you being arrested for a murder that hadn't been committed."

"It was my idea, Carl," said Joe. "I spent a couple days in the hospital and then remained on the mainland. Mike called me with regular reports, and I continued my own 'investigation' over there.

"When Crystal disappeared, I had some idea what was going on, but it was a nasty shock when Mike told me she'd been discovered murdered in your bathtub a week later."

"Yeah, it was a pretty nasty shock for us too," grumbled Carl, "what with"—he motioned toward Ed Kandinsky—"the detective here determined to arrest one or both of us."

"I was doing my job," said Ed Kandinsky. "And when I finally found out what the two of them had been perpetrating, I had half a mind to prosecute them for a whole laundry list of things, starting with obstruction of justice. Except by then, Mar Holliday was dead. And like I told you, I don't like coincidences, and your gun just conveniently showing up on the seat next to him really got up my nose. Like I'd fall for a stunt like that," he growled.

"That a fact?" asked Carl with some heat. "Mike arrested me and shipped me off the island just the same!"

"Well, now, Carl," said Mike Hatton, lifting a placating hand, "you must see that I had to do that. It looked for all the world like you'd had a hand in it. And

Joe," he waved vaguely, "was working on some theory that pointed to Bea. But we didn't have a shred of evidence!"

"So you were just going to let me take the fall?"

"No, Carl," Joe assured him. "When I learned Mar had been killed, I knew I'd been right. But without any clear evidence, Mike couldn't arrest Bea and make it stick. So we had to make her think she'd gotten away with it again. I was confident I'd have what I needed long before you ever went to trial. Because, you see, I knew she wouldn't stop with Mar. She wouldn't have stopped until Sophie was dead too.

"Unfortunately for Mar, his death gave me what I needed. Just as you said," he turned to Ed Kandinsky, "coincidence, the same as poor Crystal's showing up in Carl's bathtub. The idea that Carl and Sophie could be so foolish as to kill Crystal in Carl's house, and then call to report it, was ludicrous. So I knew it couldn't be them, and that they were being framed. Mar's murder clinched it.

"What's more, if it wasn't Carl or Sophie, there could be only one other person on the island who could possibly have a reason to want them dead, and that was Bea Baskin."

"Bea didn't think so," Sophie said quietly. "She said as much."

"And she would have been right, Sophie. She thought I was dead, and she realized that you hadn't learned her secret *yet*, so she believed that with you out of the way, no one would ever suspect her. Not of killing her own niece and nephew, much less her niece's unborn child."

"*What*?" asked Carl, as Mike Hatton and Ed Kandinsky leaned forward in interest.

"That may be the saddest part of all," said Joe. "I believe Crystal *was* carrying a child at some point and lost it. But I think if the truth were ever to be known, it would be that she didn't have a simple miscarriage." He shrugged. "Certain combinations of drugs administered without her knowledge, a convenient accident. Bad business," he shook his head sadly.

"But why?" pleaded Sophie. "It wasn't about me or Carl or Peter at all, was it? So then *why*?"

"It was only about you and Peter in the sense that she told you herself. She had hoped Crystal would marry her rich lover and not 'care a fig,' as she put it, about what happened on or with the island. And it was only about Carl in the sense that, as a convicted felon and Crystal's former lover, he made an outstanding suspect.

"And understand the most important part, Sophie. As long as she thought she was the only one with certain knowledge, she figured that not only would no one be looking for the right person, but they wouldn't be looking for the right *motive*, and therefore, couldn't possibly look for the right person."

"And nobody's said a damn word yet about just what that motive might be," said Josh Dugan. "And that's the only way this is gonna make any sense to me."

"Ah," nodded Joe Wisdom, "Sophie actually had some information about that."

"I didn't and don't, I promise you."

"You did, though, and I believe had you seen any reason to, you would have researched it and eventually tumbled to the answer yourself. As it was, it took you no time at all to make the connection between that tragic story of the Aldays and the Hollidays."

"It was speculation," she said disinterestedly, "pointless speculation. What possible difference could it make beyond a juicy story?"

"A motive for murder, my dear. There is only one thing on the island of any real monetary value, and that is the island itself."

"Huh? asked Josh for all of them.

"Land. Specifically, lakefront property for luxury condominiums for summer residents, of which Bea was sitting on several acres."

"What of it?" asked Sophie.

"Living here can mean kind of a hard scrabble existence, Sophie. People who have businesses that cater to the summer folks do all right most years. But it's a short season, and if the weather is not good, even they may suffer. Those not involved in the tourist angle generally must be rather innovative to survive. And I think Bea no longer wanted that kind of life. In fact, I would guess she had been wanting to leave the island even before her husband died ten years ago—in an *accident*—but hadn't the means to do it."

"Why didn't she just sell her property, if it's so valuable, and leave?"

"Ah, that's where we come to it. She couldn't. You see, it's Holliday land—or rather, *Alday* land."

"I don't understand."

"If you recall the story I recounted about the Alday family, then you'll remember that Josiah Alday took the illegitimate child of his brother and step-mother to raise. But it rankled with him. Adultery then was a much more serious matter than it is now, contravening not only civil, but divine law, as well. And while he provided for the child out of family duty, he felt he must not reward the behavior that had produced this unfortunate child.

"So when he died, having first changed the family name to Holliday, there was discovered in his will a provision by which any land held at that time by the

Alday family could be inherited free of encumbrance *only* by his own direct and legitimate descendents. The descendents of Marcus's and Honora's child were granted what we would now call a life estate. They could live on Alday land, but could not *dispose* of it. The only exception to this stipulation was that in the event there were no more direct descendents in Josiah's line, the land could pass outright to the descendents of his brother's child.

"I'm missing something," frowned Carl.

"Yes, and this is it: George Baskin was a descendent of Marcus Alday, while Crystal and Mar were descended directly from Josiah. So you see, Bea didn't own the land outright, and therefore, couldn't sell it. Only Mar and Crystal could, and then only after Bea's death, since she had a life interest. And in that case, of course, the monies would have come to them anyway."

"But surely," said Sophie, "something like could have been challenged. What possible force could a nearly two century-old document have?"

"Possibly," Joe replied. "Probably. But she couldn't have done so without Crystal and Mar finding out about the terms of the will, of which I'm certain they knew nothing. She couldn't take the chance that one or both of them would want the property themselves, and have the better claim. I think she considered Crystal in particular volatile, especially after Crystal's disappointment in her relationship with your husband. And that, of course, was the source of Bea's especial spleen against you, my dear."

"She said she wouldn't kill me for that reason, but it made it hard for her to like me," Sophie said dully. Carl pulled her closer.

"And she probably meant it. You were, like me, a potential impediment to her plan to do away with Crystal, nothing more."

"But the child? If you're right about that ..."

"Yes," Joe nodded sadly. "That tells me that Bea had been contemplating all of this for a very long time."

"How terrible," sighed Sophie. "I thought this was about things like passion and jealousy, and instead, it's turned out to be about money. All this for money."

"Yes," agreed Joe, "probably the worst motive of all. Well," he said, smoothing his hands over his trousers and rising, "it's been an exhausting day, for you most of all, my dear. And I confess I'm anxious to return to my home and familiar surroundings, with Crow. I thank you again for taking such good care of him." He bent down and kissed Sophie's cheek. "And you must promise to come see Crow and me any time you like."

She scratched Crow's muzzle and then watched as he followed Joe to the door, tail wagging and eager to be off.

"That goes for me, too," said Mike Hatton. "I'm gonna drop Joe off at home and then flop down in my recliner and thank the Almighty. But first, I promise you I will put in the necessary call to have the charges against you dropped, Carl. I hope you understand—"

Carl offered his hand. "It's okay, Mike," he smiled, and walked them to the door.

"That's my ride too," said Ed Kandinsky, lingering before Sophie.

"So, Detective, what happens now?"

He pursed his lips and scratched at the back of his neck. "Well, Mrs. Skala, I got what I came for. I came to catch a murderer, and I've done that."

"You were right, you know, about murder begetting murder."

"In this case, yeah. But it doesn't always work that way, you know," he said with a grudging smile.

"Goodbye, Mr. Kandinsky."

"Goodbye, Mrs. Skala." When he reached the door, he turned back to her. "Oh, and Mrs. Skala, when you use those baking apples in a pie, you want to use more sugar."

"I will bear that in mind, Mr. Kandinsky," she smiled.

Carl closed the door behind them, and Sophie saw the lights pan across the window as Mike Hatton backed the official SUV out of the driveway.

"Well," she said soberly.

Carl leaned over to kiss her, then picked up the phone and dialed. She heard him ask about Reney, and then only his acknowledgement of the information he received, and she waited for agonizing moments to learn Reney's fate. He replaced the handset and smiled over at her. "Reney is resting comfortably. She's expected to sleep through the night, but we can call first thing in the morning, and then you can talk to her. She's going to be just fine, angel."

Sophie closed her eyes in blessed relief.

"Heck of a gal, Reney," Josh said with something bordering on admiration. "But then, you both are. I don't know too many guys who'd take a bullet for somebody else."

"We're sisters, Josh," she said simply. "Now, you *are* staying the night, right?"

He blew out a puff of air and considered. "Long as I don't have to listen to animal noises all night. I'm bushed." She turned an expressionless gaze on him, and he pulled an innocent face and headed toward the stairs. "Think I'll take a shower."

"Well, make sure you put your head directly under the spray," laughed Carl, "and clean out your mind."

Sophie's head dropped back wearily against Carl's shoulder, and she stared somewhere beyond a spot above the mantel. "I hardly know how to feel. It's so strange not to be fearful or constantly on guard, constantly tense. We don't have to hide inside each other now, Carl. But in a way, that frightens me too."

"What do you mean, angel? Why would that frighten you?"

"Now we're free, what will we do with our freedom? Now that we don't have the fear and the shared threat of destruction to hold us together, will we be all right, do you think?"

"Are you having second thoughts?"

"About what I want? No. Oh, no," she said, her fingertips gliding along his cheek. "But I remember what you said to me that first time you came over. Do you remember? You said that as far as I was concerned, you were the last man on the island."

"Sophie honey," he chuckled, "that was wishful thinking. You can't honestly think I'm with you by default."

"Are you sure this is what you want?" she asked earnestly.

"Course I'm sure. After all, a man doesn't need but one woman with a really fine ass."

She sprang upright and gasped. "I can't believe you said that!"

He began to laugh and pulled her back to rest against his chest.. "Woman, you gotta lighten up."

"Oh, you!"

"Come on now," he said, pulling her up off the sofa. "No more questions. Let's go up to bed."

"What about Josh?" she whispered.

"What *about* him? He can put a pillow over his head. Come on, angel, let's go upstairs and exercise our freedom."

Epilogue

"Hello, Sophie," beamed Nila Celestine from behind the counter. "I heard you were back."

"Yes." She turned toward the sunlight that streamed through the door of Island Market and Cheese World. "And isn't it a beautiful day?"

"Yes, it is, and congratulations."

After the early and determined onslaught, winter had abated long enough in February to allow Sophie and Carl to slip off the island for a quiet Valentine's Day wedding, attended only by Reney, radiant with health and joy as she held Sophie's small bouquet, and Josh Dugan, who, spared a tuxedo by the informality of the ceremony, put the best spin on things and handed over the rings.

The newlyweds had spent the next two weeks at what Reney obstinately referred to as "Peter's house," sorting through the contents to determine what to keep and how to dispose of the rest. In the end, Sophie had slipped her arms around her husband's chest and, leaning against him contentedly, smiled, "Let it all go." She had turned the key over to the agent and turned her back on the house and that part of her life.

Winter had made a last petulant stand early in March, before retreating and leaving in trails behind it the cold winds that blew off the still frigid lake. But the days were almost uniformly sunny, the sky a luminous blue with bunchy clouds that had the appearance of whipped topping. And they made the most of the days, making small adjustments in their households or taking unhurried walks along the lanes or the high banks above the lake and getting to know one another. They made the most of the nights in the same way.

"So, what do you plan to do now, you and Carl? I suppose," Nila said glumly, "you'll be leaving the island. Can't say as I'd blame you."

"Actually, we don't know yet," smiled Sophie. "It's as though the whole world has opened up along with the lake. So many choices."

While it was true that they had come to no irrevocable decisions about their future, they had explored—in leisurely fashion, there was no rush now—a fair number of options. For one thing, Carl's probationary period would end within a matter of weeks, and they had determined to visit the southwest before too much longer. Sophie had never been, Carl had always wanted to go, and they felt that perhaps the desert might even lead them to a decision about the lake—and the island.

Uncertain whether their life together lay on the island now, or away from it, they had also considered making a permanent home on the mainland and spending summers here. But so far, they had not gotten even so far as to give up one or the other of their houses. The cottage was cozy and nearer the water, but she had not purchased it and didn't know now whether she would. Carl's house was roomier, if not as well situated, but would require certain modifications of design to convert it from a bachelor's cabin to a proper home for the pair of them.

She smiled as she considered how insignificant a worry it was after what they had come through to find each other.

"I don't have to tell you how glad we'd all be if you stayed. There's some people feel real foolish, I can tell you, and we all feel guilty."

"Whatever for?" asked Sophie. "You shouldn't. How could anyone possibly have known? Except Joe Wisdom maybe," she chuckled.

That was another way in which, accompanied by Carl, or alone if he was helping Josh on cargo runs, she had passed pleasant hours she had thought were lost beyond reach. She and Joe might stroll, Crow weaving between them, from the park to the library. Miss Evinrude had been cajoled back into service until a replacement could be found, and there had even been talk of forming a committee of volunteers to man the circulation desk in the interim. Sophie had agreed to take a turn if it came to that.

Other times, they might sit before the fire, at Joe's house or their own, and sip tea or sherry and exchange anecdotes. That, in fact, was how Sophie and Joe had hit upon the idea of collaborating on a book about the spectacular events that had taken place on the island that winter.

She would miss Joe Wisdom, she thought with a sigh, if her life with Carl took them elsewhere. It made her sad to think of him and Crow both growing older and eventually passing away without her even knowing.

"Ah," Nila Celestine said wistfully, "things are changing, Sophie. And to be honest with you, I don't know whether I'm sad because they're changing too fast or not fast enough. Live your whole life in a place like this, and think you know everybody and everything there is to know, then come to find out your comfy little world is just a facade."

"Bea doesn't change everything," Sophie said sympathetically.

"Changes more than you know. Why, Bob Haskell's already talking about selling out—even the chickens—and moving to the mainland. Mike Hatton making noises about going off to be a forest ranger. Pretty soon there won't be anybody left. Place'll be uninhabited except for Memorial Day to Labor Day, and no permanent residents at all," lamented Nila.

"I don't think so. People are probably a little unsettled just now, but I bet that will change with spring here. Wait and see," she smiled. "Now, I'd better get my shopping done."

Besides the things on her short list, she bought an extra pound of bacon, three, rather than two, bottles of wine and several chunks of cheese that they probably didn't need, but which she hoped Carl would eat, and juggled the bags out to her car.

Carl walked into the kitchen as she set the bags on the table and began to transfer the contents to their appointed places.

"Hey," he smiled, pulling her close to kiss her.

"Hey yourself," she smiled, then looked up at him soberly. "So, what do you think?"

"I think," he leered, "we should clear everything off the table and—" She arched an admonitory eyebrow. "But since that doesn't seem to interest you just now," he sighed. "This is it, angel." He spread his hands in a gesture of inclusion. "Nothing much here."

"You're here."

"Ah, but I'd be wherever you were, so I don't much care. But," he said in response to her obvious disappointment, "I have been thinking about it. You've seen it at its worst, Sophie. So I think you—we—should stay here for the summer. That way you'll see it at its best, and maybe you'll decide to stay, or maybe you'll decide it's not enough for you. At least you'll know."

She exhaled with relief and nodded. "All right, that's what we'll do then. Help me with dinner?"

"What are we having?"

"Chicken pot pie. I made it earlier, so I just have to pop it in the oven and make a salad, maybe some fruit and cheese for after."

"Oh, I love your pot pie!"

"I know. I think you married me for my pot pie."

"No, baby, I married you for your lingerie. Speaking of which," he grinned, squeezing her behind.

"You know, Carl, I keep forgetting how subtle you are. But," she said, sliding the pot pie into the oven and checking her watch, "I can spare an hour."

He twisted up his mouth and appeared to be contemplating something momentous. Then grabbing her by the hand and dragging her toward the stairs, "I can do it," he said.

Summer blew in quite literally one night, as hot and clear and altogether gorgeous as any Sophie could remember, made more so by the freedom with which she darted between the island and the mainland.

She saw Reney often, and if she was "Cissybeans" to her sister now, it implied a familiar joy, rather than the shared misery of a painful past, and it made her happy to think that Reney had finally thrown off that past and expunged its ghosts.

Both Reney and her children were frequent visitors that summer. Sophie would wait eagerly for them, seven year-old Eloise and ten year-old Molly, to race up the lawn into her outstretched arms and then listen attentively as they recounted their most recent adventures. And Sophie was struck, as she watched them one morning clambering along the rock wall before the cottage, watched as Eloise tumbled to the ground and Molly took her sister's hand and smoothed her hair, as Eloise smiled and scrambled to her feet, by their similarity to Reney and herself. Alike and yet not. Molly and Eloise were happy. And she realized again that, just as she and Reney had been bound together by and trapped within their nightmare childhood, so too had she and Carl been drawn together and imprisoned by fear and tragedy, by the island. But she and Reney were free now.

That evening, as Reney supervised the girls' bath and helped them get ready for bed, Sophie walked across the road and climbed down onto the broad rocks that made up the breakwall, easing herself down to sit with knees drawn up before her. She could see the faint blur and wash that marked the mainland.

Carl found her there, and lowering himself to sit behind her, wrapped his arms around her and rested his chin on her shoulder. She leaned her head to nuzzle against his face and sighed.

"You've made up your mind," he said.

"Yes. I can't stay here, Carl. I came here to hide, and I don't want to hide any more."

"Good." He kissed her cheek.

"Is it?" she asked with some surprise.

"Yep. When I was over there last week," he nodded across the water, "I went to see this great place. Big loft condo in an old warehouse they've renovated, right on the water. Now, I know there's no yard, but—"

"Why didn't you tell me?" She sat up and looked at him squarely.

"Because, angel, I was waiting for you to think things through and reach the decision you had to."

"You knew all along."

"Yeah," he said simply. "I've been in prison. We both have."

"I wonder if we aren't still," she said sadly.

"What's that supposed to mean?"

She looked long at him. "You've never asked me about Peter."

"I didn't need to."

"I lied to you."

"No, you didn't, angel," he squeezed her. "You just didn't volunteer the information—any more than I did mine."

She twisted around to face him. "You told me so I could choose. So." She took a breath. "I'd found out about Peter's latest affair, and I'd had enough. And I'd finally gotten the courage to leave, and I told him that. Naturally, there was a scene, the usual shouting, and he hit me. I fell over a table. I saw stars and things flying through the air and crashing to the floor, and I dragged myself up and put my hand on one of them. I'm not even sure what it was, some pointless decorative objet d'art of Peter's, I guess.

"I thought he would probably kill me if I didn't defend myself. So I took a swing at him with it, but he grabbed my wrist and wrenched it away from me. I knew he was going to hit me again, so I lunged backward to try to wriggle out of his grasp. And then all of a sudden, his hand slipped, and I tumbled backward and landed in a heap on the floor. I scrambled up to get away, but he didn't grab me or hit me again. I looked over in disbelief at the fireplace. He'd fallen backward too, against the bricks, and fractured his skull.

"I was afraid at first to touch him to check for a pulse, because I thought he might be pretending, to trap me," she explained. "I pulled my knees up and huddled on the floor against the sofa and watched him for any sign of movement. I don't know how long. Maybe he was still alive, maybe he wasn't. But after I'd waited for what seemed long enough, and he hadn't moved, I called the police.

"Naturally, they found my prints on the statue or whatever it was, but even though the evidence wasn't conclusive, it allowed for what really *did* happen.

That's why they failed to indict, you see. So although I didn't kill him deliberately, I *was* responsible for his death."

"Sophie honey," said Carl, grasping her gently by the shoulders, "*he* was responsible. Reney was right—he got less than he deserved. But now it's over. It's over, and we're free. Now, let's get back to the house," he smiled, and pulled her to her feet, "and visit with the family."

By the middle of August, they had transported most of their personal effects to their new home. It was spacious and airy, and even the prospect of winter there was undaunting. They looked forward to sitting before the big fireplace with the drapes open to the bay and the certainty of life and light behind and around them.

"This'll work out great, angel. You're still close enough that you and Joe can get together to work and visit."

"I'd like to have Joe here for the holidays, Carl. And Crow, of course."

He stood behind her and wrapped his arms around her as she gazed across the bay. "I think that would be great." He leaned around to kiss her cheek. "But right now, what do you say we inaugurate the new bed?"

She turned her head to give him a quick nod and smile, then paused before the expanse of glass to look out over the water from whence it jutted, gray and indistinct. The beehive. The island.

978-0-595-44737-4
0-595-44737-6

Printed in the United States
85190LV00004B/226-255/A